MW01257316

MY FAMILY'S ROLE IN THE WORLD REVOLUTION AND OTHER PROSE

Writings from an Unbound Europe

■ □ ■ □ ■

BORA ĆOSIĆ

MY FAMILY'S ROLE
IN THE WORLD
REVOLUTION AND
OTHER PROSE

Translated by Ann Clymer Bigelow

NORTHWESTERN UNIVERSITY PRESS

EVANSTON, ILLINOIS

Northwestern University Press
Evanston, Illinois 60208-4210

Works by Bora Ćosić originally published in Serbo-Croatian: *My Family's Role in the World Revolution* as *Uloga moje porodice u svetskoj revoluciji* (Belgrade: Nezavisna izdanja, 1969; Zagreb: Znanje, 1987). Copyright © 1994 by Rowohlt Verlag, Berlin. "Russians by Trade" ("Rusi u vidu zanata"), "The Romeo's Trade—A Major One" ("O velikom zanatu, švalerskom"), "Us and the Electricians" ("Mi i električari"), "Our Embroiderers" ("Naše pliserke"), "How They Fixed Our Hair" ("Kako su nas frizirali"), and "A Story about Dogcatchers" ("Šinterska") in the collection *Priče o zanatima* (*Tales about Trades*) (Belgrade: Nolit, 1980). "In Praise of Young Pilots and Others" ("U slavu mladih avijatičara i ostalih") in the 1966 (Belgrade, Nolit) edition of *Priče o zanatima*. "Diary of an *Apatrid*" as "Dnevnik apatrida" (Zagreb: Durieux, 1993); originally serialized in the Belgrade newspaper *Borba* (1992). "Hamsun's Baedeker" as "Hamsunov Baedeker," *Erasmus* 7 (1994): 64–74. "Final Conversation with Mr. Verdurin, of Rovinj" as "Završni razgovor s gospodinom Verdurinom, rovinjskim," *Erasmus* (1995): 83–91. English translation and compilation copyright © 1997 by Northwestern University Press. Published 1997. All rights reserved.

Ann Clymer Bigelow's English translation of "Russians by Trade" previously published in *Description of a Struggle: The Picador Book of Contemporary East European Prose*, ed. Michael March (London: Picador, 1994). Her English translation of "How They Fixed Our Hair" previously published in *North Dakota Quarterly* (Winter 1996): 5–9.

Printed in the United States of America

ISBN 0-8101-1367-8 (cloth)
ISBN 0-8101-1368-6 (paper)

Library of Congress Cataloging-in-Publication Data

Ćosić, Bora.
  [Uloga moje porodice u svetskoj revoluciji. English]
  My family's role in the world revolution and other prose / Bora Ćosić ; translated by Ann Clymer Bigelow.
    p. cm. — (Writings from an unbound Europe)
  ISBN 0-8101-1367-8 (cloth : alk. paper). — ISBN 0-8101-1368-6 (pbk. : alk. paper)
    1. Yugoslavia—History—1945–1980—Fiction. I. Bigelow, Ann C. II. Title. III. Series.
PG1418.C59U413 1997
891.8'2354—dc21   97-15118
                                                              CIP

The paper used in this publication meets the minimum requirements of the American National Standard for Information Sciences — Permanence of Paper for Printed Library Materials, ANSI Z39.48-1984.

■ □ ■ □ ■

CONTENTS

■ □ ■ □ ■

TRANSLATOR'S NOTE

IN HIS FICTION OF THE 1960S, BORA ĆOSIĆ OPENLY REFUSES
to make sense of the "world revolution." He is still buck-
ing official views in his antiwar essays of the 1990s.

Rather than use the standard English translation of the
foreign-language passages my author has cited, as is cus-
tomary, I have translated Ćosić's quotations from Proust,
Hamsun, et al. from the Serbo-Croatian versions he used.
These were the renditions he mulled over and drew upon
as he wrote; they were the versions he wove so thickly into
his essays.

Four native Serbo-Croatian speakers now living in the
United States have given countless hours to the interpretation of these texts. They are Dr. Mateja Matejić, emeritus
professor of Slavic languages at Ohio State University; Drs.
Bogdan Baishanski and Miroslav Ašić, professors of mathematics at OSU; and Dr. Omer Hadžiselimović, long a
professor of English at the University of Sarajevo and now
a visiting professor at Earlham College and Indiana University. I thank each of them profoundly for his inspiring
support.

Professor Dušan Puvačić of the University of London
School of Slavonic and East European Studies helped fine-
tune the English text of *My Family's Role in the World
Revolution.* My colleagues at *The Current Digest of the
Post-Soviet Press,* Ronald Branch in particular, have fielded
many a screwball query; Gordon Livermore has been generous with his computer expertise. Thanks to them as well.

ANN CLYMER BIGELOW

■ □ ■ □ ■

MY FAMILY'S ROLE IN THE WORLD REVOLUTION

I

MOM MADE A POUCH. ON IT SHE EMBROIDERED THE WORD "Newspapers." She also embroidered Dad sitting on the pot with his pants down, reading. The embroidery was in three colors—for Dad, the pants, and the newspaper. Dad looked like himself except that, probably to get even, Mom made him bald, which he really wasn't. In the pouch was newspaper cut up with a big kitchen knife. Grandpa did the cutting; he only used papers Dad had finished reading. I wrote all this up as a homework assignment called "Our Life in the John, Etc." Mom said: "What kind of a disgusting school is that, dragging everything out in the open? It's awful!" I answered her: "As if anybody asks *me!*"

Mom climbed up on the windowsill with a rag in her hand. Here she hung out over the three-story-deep hole and wiped the windows. Inside everybody was shrieking; Grandpa wanted to hold onto her legs; one of my aunts fainted. Dad asked: "Do you have to hang that way to do those?" She said: "Yes!" Mom had tomatoes cooking in a big laundry pot; this was boiling fast. Mom stood on a stool and reached over with a long wooden mixing spoon to stir it. My uncle said: "What if she falls in?" The tomatoes spurted out all over, got on the wall and scalded our fingers. Mom tried to explain: "There's no other way!" Life was full of dangers.

Mom brought home a chicken that raised a big squawk and let feathers fly all over the place. I dragged the chicken around on a string for a while, and then Mom grabbed it by the wings and cut off its head in the toilet bowl. Mom flushed the toilet; the headless chicken stood in a corner shaking and got blood on Mom's slippers. This was horrible, but fun. Mom issued the command: "Time to stretch the curtains!" The curtains were washed and still damp; Grandpa and my uncle grabbed the edges and pulled like crazy. Mom kept warning them: "It won't do me any good if you rip 'em to shreds!" Grandpa grumbled: "Like we're on shipboard!" Mom replied: "I'd be better off doing it all myself, even if I'm not strong like a man!" Mom stretched out sheets of pastry dough; they were big, they were spread over the backs of the chairs, the air trembled, and you could hear the sound of it all. Mom hung up Dad's shirts in the bathroom. The soaking wet sleeves dripped down like a rainstorm, and Grandpa asked: "Do I have to carry an umbrella to take a shit?" Mom lined up jars of pickles on the Bösendorfer-brand piano. The jars were wrapped up in shawls to cool; they made the piano sag a little in the middle. Mom spread out beans to dry on old newspapers; all this rustled, up on top of the cupboards. Mom cut up a three-month supply of noodles; she laid the noodles out on the beds to dry. Dad shouted: "How long is this state of emergency going to last?" My uncle said: "I'm gonna put up scaffolding so we can get around!" I asked: "Are we at the theater?" Mom said: "Someday you'll go looking for me and I'll be hanging in the attic!" Grandpa asked: "Why?" Mom answered: "When things get too bleak!"

Mom was eating stuffed cabbage, but a piece of cabbage got stuck in her throat. Then she started gasping and waving her arms in the air; finally she managed to swallow it. Afterward she told us: "I already had one foot in the grave—I could have died right in front of everybody!" Grandpa said: "Think of it!" She went on: "But what's that compared to the time I got shoved in the water from behind!" Later she said: "If it hadn't been for that big strapping sailor who grabbed me and asked do you really not know how to swim?" Mom was always telling some awful story from her own life or somebody else's, but she would add one that was even more horrible: "And there was that time I was falling out of the streetcar and the professor man yanked me so everything on me popped open!" My aunts said: "Lucky you!" Grandpa remarked: "Now you've hit a new low, I must say!" Mom pointed to the Young Salesclerks' calendar hanging on the wall: "It's all there in black and white!" She had recorded all Dad's sober days and the birthdays of everybody in the family, as well as the anniversary of her fall down the steps of the Ta-Ta department store. Mom claimed: "I was at death's door for eight days!" The time periods Mom used were eight days, fourteen days, and six weeks; she liked the interval of six weeks best; all this referred to the length of different ailments.

Mom got toothaches. She would wrap her head up in all sorts of cloths and howl away; we wouldn't recognize her. Grandpa heated up the iron and held it to Mom's cheek. It burned her, right through her shawl, but it didn't stop the toothaches—quite the contrary. Then Mom said: "Here, some bone's sticking out here!" Everybody felt the bump on Mom's leg, which later went away. Mom kept saying: "If I just knew the day and hour I was going to die, I wouldn't worry at all anymore!" My uncle told her: "I doubt that, seeing how scared you get of a worm in an apple!" Mom announced: "I saw a maniac in a doorway on Empress Milica Street!" Everybody stopped talking, and she added: "All he had on was a raincoat, unbuttoned, and it wasn't even raining!" Then she turned to me and screamed: "Do you have to listen to all this filth children shouldn't hear?" I said: "Yes!" Later she told everybody: "If this poor child wasn't around I'd tell you about this movie I haven't even seen!" Right away Grandpa jumped in: "I s'pose it's something smutty!" Mom said: "No it's not, except that the guy comes up to the girl with a criminal look in his eye, and she, in tears, starts unbuttoning her beautiful marquisette blouse!"

Mom went out on the stairway to give some food to a beggar, and afterward told us: "My favorites are the ones that come and say: 'My mother's dead, my father's in the hospital, and I'm berserk!'" Grandpa answered her: "That's the way it oughta be!" Mom explained: "That's right, so then I see there are people even worse off than we are, and I give them two-day-old paprikash I would have thrown in the garbage otherwise!" Then something else occurred to her: "When I think how it takes all day to fix a dumb dinner that gets gobbled down in ten minutes!" Grandpa asked: "Well, what do you want?" Mom said: "Nothing—I don't complain, since I know how many blind people and cripples and different freaks there are, while I'm as healthy as a horse, thank God!" Mom was forever bringing up stories of injustices and dreadful diseases that were raging all around us, but she would always find some way to end up on a happy note. Dad kept saying: "Mothers are sacred!" but it sounded mocking, somehow. My aunts let me read a story about a mother who gathers twigs barefoot in the forest, except later the wolves come and tear her apart.

II

Dad carried a suitcase full of little cloths marked with numbers—Roman numerals and regular ones. He would show the cloths to various people at the bar and tell them: "These are just samples—who knows where the real merchandise is!" Grandpa said: "That's what I thought!" Mom wanted to make pincushions out of some of the cloths; Dad protested: "Keep your mitts outa my business!" Dad was always going out somewhere with this suitcase, but never took a trip. Grandpa would explain: "It's just his excuse to hang around with the riffraff!" Then Dad took a coffee mug out of the suitcase and slammed it down on the floor, but the mug didn't break. Mom said: "That's spooky!" Dad explained: "It's not real glass. I can get a whole dozen if you pay first!" My uncle concluded: "Not a bad deal if some glass factory isn't missing 'em!" Grandpa protested: "Who's got time to dream up such idiotic things?" Dad also worked with cooking pots—Eterna brand and other kinds. Dad sold the pots door to door for the Kastner und Oehler Company and others. Then he started working at a hardware store, counting nails. The store also had meat grinders and Goldner Icebox chests, but all Dad counted was nails, one by one. Mom went to the store to take him a thermos of chicken soup; later she told us: "Poor devil—he's still counting!" Afterward she grabbed me by the arms and said: "We're all alone!" Dad started selling meat grinders. He would say: "Here, this way!" and stick his fingers in the hole. One lady started turning the handle; Dad shrieked and threw the machine on the floor. The lady said: "I didn't realize!" Dad came home, took off his shirt and said: "My back itches!" We could see red splotches on it; Mom immediately started wailing: "Oh no, you've been poisoned!" My uncle took a look and explained: "Somebody cheated you as far as the quality of their wine!" Dad replied: "Liquor used to be cheaper but just as good!" Dad stood in a washbasin and wanted somebody to cut his corns. Mom squatted down and started slicing the skin off with a razor blade. Dad warned: "Don't maim me!" Dad got up early, headed for the bathroom, but then bumped into a table and broke his toe. Blood spurted out of the broken toenail like out of some little faucet. Dad took a swig out of a bottle of lye, thinking it was beer. He spat out the poison and swore; it left a white spot on the parquet floor. Dad himself was fine.

Everybody knew how to repair something around the house; Dad did the most dangerous jobs. My uncle kept saying: "I'm just waiting for the day you get electrocuted!" Dad would look down from the top of the ladder and command us: "You just hand up the pliers, and leave the rest to me!" Mom would answer: "If I'd known I have to hand you everything, I'd have done it myself!" Mom found Dad's suit neatly folded in front of the bathroom door. Immediately she shrieked: "I'm sure he locked himself in and then cut his stomach open with a big knife!" Grandpa said: "We should get so lucky!" The door was unlocked; Dad was sitting in the bathtub reading the newspaper and whistling. I came in to see him. Mom screamed: "Why don't you lock the door when you're so naked with the child around?" Dad asked: "You expect me to take a bath with my clothes on?" Dad left to go sell meat grinders; the landlord came and said: "I want to check the plumbing!" but right off he tried to touch Mom's arm. She told him: "Get lost! What do you think you're doing?" The landlord replied: "So what's the big deal?" Then he turned to Grandpa and said: "'Scuse me, Pop, sir!" Mom stuck a rubber hot-water bag in her bed and said: "At least this'll keep me warm!"

Dad came home and asked: "Are you ironing again with a toothache?" Mom answered: "When you have to have this dumb white shirt for your blasted store!" Dad grabbed the iron, which was red hot, and threw it out the window into the courtyard. Then he opened a bottle of beer; the cork flew up in the air; Dad said: "Things are lookin' up!" Grandpa looked out the window and told us: "He could have killed the janitor!" Dad grabbed hold of two chairs and did a handstand. Grandpa asked him: "Why don't you join the circus?" I shouted: "Hooray for the Klutsky Circus!" My uncle explained: "They went down in the ocean!" Dad said: "Mr. Prohaska gave a lecture on freedom, and then worked out on the horizontal bar for half an hour!" Grandpa contended: "I'd give each of 'em twenty-five lashings they'd never forget!" My uncle added: "I also heard some speech of a political nature, but the speaker kept showing his bare ass and that was incomprehensible to me!" Mom concluded: "They're all great people—the creators of mankind!"

Dad's coworker was opening a rubber-goods store. The store had bathing shoes, balls, inflatable balloons, and other things. Mom wondered: "I suppose it has what you stick in a cigar so it'll explode in your face!" Grandpa fumed: "He ought to be ashamed of himself, selling those nasty things!" I got taken there early to be the first, honorary customer. They offered me an inner tube, a rubber Mickey Mouse, and Ping-Pong balls, very small ones. I chose shit—artificial, rubber shit. They wrapped it up, shook hands with me, and announced: "The store is open for business!" Later I deliberately set the thing on a rug; my aunts were aghast: "Why, that fine professor who was just here, we never would have dreamed he could do such a thing!"

My voice began to change; Grandpa looked around and asked: "Who is that talking?" Mom explained: "Wait 'til it gets done changing and he'll be singing arias!" My arms and legs and all my bones started to grow. At dinner Mom told Dad: "You've finally got to explain it all to him; I can't since I'm a woman!" My uncle chimed in: "I'd say you're too late!" I went into the john; Mom shoved Dad in behind me. She kept telling him: "Talk to him man to man!" Dad watched me pee and told me: "There's nothin' to it—it all comes naturally!" I said: "I know!"

Dad came home at dawn and headed right for the shower; this went on pretty long. Then he appeared, nicely dressed and very cheerful. Mom said: "Just drink this Russian tea now and you'll be fit as a fiddle!" Grandpa admonished Dad: "A letter ought to get written about your behavior and be mimeographed and sent out to all our relatives, even the most distant ones!" To placate us Dad said: "I was gonna buy everybody a chocolate bar, but then I saw I didn't have a cent!" Mom whispered: "My poor better half—nobody's ever on *his* side!" Dad pulled some Nestlé-brand chocolates out of his pocket, started lining them up on the table, and explained: "I won these in a raffle!" Inside them were little pictures from the life of Captain Grant and other great people. Mom let me have the pictures, but she melted all the chocolates into one and said: "This'll be for Christmas!" Dad kept buying lottery tickets that said "State Lottery" and had a picture of a naked baby in a pile of money, also just a picture. Grandpa explained: "A tax on the nincompoops!" Dad insisted: "Some day I'll win a million, and then I'll go to America!" Grandpa said: "Ha, ha, ha!" Grandpa would cite the dates Dad had been sober like they were the greatest sensation in Europe; he would repeat Dad's off-color comments, and then he let everybody know about the seventy dinars Dad owed him.

Right then Dad had a small bullet from a Flaubert pistol removed from his knee, left there in childhood. After thirty years the bullet had begun to move around; Dad's leg swelled up. Afterward he brought the bullet home in a matchbox; it was rough and very black. In the pantry among the jars of stewed plums was a jar with tonsils in it, my uncle's, but that was something else again.

III

I had an indoor rowboat. It never did have oars; actually, there were only handles; the boat didn't have a bottom; it was for building muscles. They had me sit on the movable seat and told me: "Row!" I asked: "Why?" They explained the advantages of well-developed muscles over undeveloped ones and asked me: "What do you want to be so puny for?" I answered: "I wanna be a madman!"

In the front hall was a hat rack made of a stag's antlers; coats were hanging on it. I kept wanting to know: "Where's its head?" In the dining room on glassed-in shelves lay snails, starfish, and sea urchins pulled out of various seas. Mom liked to explain: "These are from our beautiful Adriatic, where I swim way out even though a shark might eat me!" On a table stood a conch shell. On the shell was a picture of a sailboat caught in a storm—a terrifying scene of the watery elements. If you held the shell to your ear there was always some sort of rustle coming out. I wondered: "What's that sound?" Mom told me: "Be glad you don't know!"

Mom had a cup that was silver. She said: "It was for first place in the Charleston—I danced my head off winning it!" Then she explained: "In one night I wore out a beautiful pair of shoes, brand-new ones, going from one partner to another!" I told her: "Donald Duck won a trophy in a dumpling-eating contest!" My uncle bragged: "I've got a deck of cards and instead of signs like spades or clubs on them they've got pictures of actresses, and you oughta see what kind!" I asked: "Where are all those chocolates Dad brought me and Mom put 'em all in a cake we never even saw?" Mom chided me: "That's nervy—I indulge your every whim and you're still not satisfied!"

We had a piece of glass we would put in the milk pan to keep it from boiling over, and also a padlock, an American-made one that was very odd. The padlock didn't have a key; it opened with a combination; they forgot the combination; the American padlock became unusable. Grandpa asked: "How can we open the firewood shed now?" Some things we'd always had; others came from our relative Gustav Foretson in Detroit. Packages arrived with little gadgets for getting rid of static on the radio, pimple creams, and a Popeye outfit complete with a pipe—a miniature, fake one. Right away Mom and my aunts started applying the cream; I tried to put on the outfit; it was too small. Mom said: "That's all right, it's just a present!" Dad and my uncle started dividing up the cigarette paper even though the package didn't have any tobacco. Grandpa asked: "There isn't anything for me!" All of this was life, unfair as always.

My uncle said to me: "Let's go sketch balconies!" On the balconies in our neighborhood were bicycles, old chairs, fishing poles, and flowers; none of it was any good or of any use. Grandpa protested: "What's that you're doing?" I replied: "I want to know what all there is!" One of my friends had a "camera," something he'd made himself out of paper, which you'd pull on and you could see a drawing inside. I wanted to have that camera. My friend simply wouldn't give it to me; I grabbed half of it away from him, but I couldn't tell from the torn piece how the whole thing was made. Later I threw the half away. Mom told me: "If you let us pull that darned molar that's gone bad, you can have a wind-up rabbit!" I asked for the rabbit first; afterward I said: "I don't *want* my tooth pulled—it doesn't hurt at all!" I wound up the rabbit and it hopped on Grandpa from behind. Grandpa screamed: "What the devil is that?" My uncle wound up the record player that was called "His Master's Voice" and had a little trumpet on the side. Right away Mom brought out her machines from the kitchen and lined them up on the table. They all had handles and were very shiny. These machines were for grinding coffee, poppy seeds, and walnuts. Mom said: "I have everything I need!" Dad had a little machine for sharpening razor blades, also with a handle. There was a machine for making ground meat patties, a so-called Fleischmaschine, which also was good. Grandpa cautioned Dad: "Watch your fingers!" Sometimes we all cranked at once.

That was unbearable. Then we listened to famous radio stations like Zagreb, London, and Berominster. This last one was best; Radio Berominster was always telling about fires, plane crashes, and other slaughter; because of that it was marked in ink on the dial. I asked: "What are all those stupid gadgets for, like the Rex-brand vacuum jar, the curling iron, and the douche?" Right away my aunts remarked: "Goodness, it's a lovely day today, isn't it?" And it was.

IV

My uncle made a batch of chocolate candy; he put in a laxative called Darmol, which was probably German. He claimed: "They're very good—try one!" We all started clutching our tummies; my uncle insisted: "I didn't mean to, honest!" I tried to blow soap bubbles. Grandpa asked: "What am I gonna shave with now?" I made airplanes out of newspapers. Dad screamed: "I haven't even read 'em yet!" Then I made a snake with red eyes out of modeling clay. Mom took one look at it and fainted on the spot. My aunts also fainted sometimes, from powerful scenes in books, from the heat, sometimes from sheer melancholy. My uncle fainted once, by accident, when he tipped over and fell off his chair. He got a brain concussion, but later remembered everything. Dad fainted when they tried to sober him up by giving him vinegar. Grandpa was always on his feet and said angrily: "Enough of this ridiculous nonsense!" I also wanted to faint, but didn't know how.

My aunts warned us: "Watch out, there's a bat!" Right away everybody crouched down; later it turned out there wasn't any bat after all. Mom commented: "Always something to cope with—some insect, or a brazen landlord, or someone selling completely unusable cooking pots!" Grandpa asked: "What do you even open the door to those good-for-nothings for, anyhow?" My aunts answered: "What would our life consist of otherwise? All of that's so exciting!" Grandpa said: "Maybe to you it is!" Right then I hit my head on a door; blood gushed out of the broken skin right into my eye. Mom screamed: "Oh, no, you've been run over by a streetcar!" I was fiddling around with the kerosene stove; a flame darted out and burned my fingers. I stuck my hand under the wide-open water faucet; that made the whole thing swell up. My uncle took my picture to remember it by; the photograph showed my finger wrapped up in a bandage. Mom asked me: "Why aren't you a girl?" Then Mom broke a big bowl brim full of floating island; the egg whites went sliding across the parquet floor like little clouds of some sort. My uncle tried to bring his bicycle indoors and broke a pane of glass in the front door. My aunts dropped a bottle of perfume on the floor. The whole building began reeking of something horrible but expensive, with a Japanese name. Grandpa dropped a plate that had pictures of gondolas, water, people, and Venice in general. He tried to excuse himself: "That doggone thing!" Mom started wailing: "I wish I'd died!" I went out on the street in roller skates and immediately knocked down a 250-pound fat woman.

Dad had a Soko shirt loaded with buttons. I locked myself in the john, put on the shirt, and started buttoning it up. The sleeves were stiff; when I got halfway done the sleeves went straight and covered up my hands. Outside the door everybody started yelling and pounding; my uncle kicked the lock open. Dad came with scissors and cut up the shirt in little pieces. My aunts cried. Mom said: "We're beyond help!" My younger aunt got her dress cut apart another time. She suddenly got convulsions of an unknown sort; she started to feel faint and breathe heavily. In her delirium she kept mentioning the names of some nonexistent islands, and one other thing that men have. Mom tried to explain: "She just heard that somewhere!" By early evening they couldn't bend her arms; Mom took a razor blade and carefully, along the seams, she separated the whole dress into its original pieces. Dad gave a lecture in his sleep on the subject of the Soko organization; Grandpa jumped out of bed and yelled: "I'm gonna call the fire department!" My uncle woke up from his after-dinner snooze and started quizzing each one of us: "I didn't admit to anything, did I?"

The glasses in the china cupboard rattled, and the chandelier swayed. Grandpa ordered us: "To the doorjamb!" We all huddled together in the doorway until the earthquake was over. My uncle declared: "That must have been in Turkey—I'm sure they've got a slew of dead people there right now!" Our building shook a lot of other times, too, but mainly because of streetcars going by. Then my uncle climbed up on the wooden seat in the john, slipped, and broke the toilet bowl with his leg. The leg was bloody and all covered with shit; Grandpa said: "Well, if he's not gonna sit down like a man!" My uncle was oiling the Grizner-brand sewing machine; the needle went through his index finger. I was celebrating the victory of the Yugoslavia soccer club over Prague's Sparta club; I hopped up on the hot stove, even though I was barefoot. We all lay around and moaned; my uncle's finger and the soles of my feet were wrapped up in bandages. We also had bugs. Mom would run all around the kitchen with a slipper in her hand and kill them with brutal blows. Men arrived, made us leave the apartment, and said: "Take all your food and drink with you!" Then they put down poison, but the bugs came back again. Later we all had to hold onto the stovepipe and the rag wrapped around it so soot wouldn't burst into the room when the chimney was being cleaned. In a field outside town an artificial wooden tower was set on fire; the fire department got called, but when they arrived the whole thing had already burned down. They doused the soot-blackened thing, then sang an anthem or some such. Mom said: "We never get anywhere in time!" Afterward she took me for some Tutti-

Frutti-brand ice cream, which was very green. Mom warned me: "Don't eat the whole cone the man was touching with his dirty hands, dangblast him!" We also had a dressmaker who would come. She sat all day long at the sewing machine, which whirred away; Grandpa protested: "I can't hear a thing with that going!" In the evening the dressmaker let out a blouse she had just finished making for Mom; she sat down at Grandpa's desk to eat supper; afterward Mom sterilized this plate in boiling water and explained: "I don't know if she's healthy!" I got the mumps, which wasn't such a dangerous disease, but still . . . I hit one of my aunts in the eye with a spoon. The eye turned black and blue; I promised: "I'll never do it again!" They bought a new chandelier, but broke it as they were putting it up. To console herself Mom took out the meat grinder, but used it to make something totally different — cookies. Many times we went to the station to meet relatives; sometimes they arrived, but usually they didn't. Mom would explain: "They're at the spa!" or some such place we never went to. I climbed up on the windowsill and started throwing pillows down on the street. A policeman picked them all up and brought them upstairs. The policeman asked: "Mr. Ćosić, are these yours?" In the evening Dad kept looking in the window across from us; some woman was changing her clothes there. Then she turned the light off; Dad said: "Damn!" I declared: "This is what family life is!"

My uncle started disguising himself. He put on an old dress of Mom's; down inside the dress he crammed various rags — very dirty ones, then put on makeup, and sprang on us during dinner. Right away Grandpa broke a plate out of fright. Later Mom greased up her face with her American daytime and nighttime cream. I tied a black monogrammed hairnet of Dad's around my head. My aunts gave themselves homemade hairdos with little pieces of newspaper for rollers. Dad accidentally shaved off part of his mustache. Grandpa took one look at us and asked: "Who are *they?*"

V

My uncle brought home a girl who wore glasses. Right away everybody started teasing her. They asked her: "What do you like best?" The girl replied: "A nice juicy wiener!" Dad roared with laughter; I didn't know why. There was a boy, Voja Bloša. Bloša had photographs; he would show them if you paid. I said: "I need two dinars to see Voja's photographs!" Mom asked: "What are they of?" I replied: "A brother and sister, except they're naked and hairy!" Mom ordered me: "Don't you move an inch out of here!" Voja Bloša told me: "Let's go sell razor blades!" I told him: "I'd rather read *Van the Great* or some other book!" Grandpa warned me: "You'll get water on the knee from so much reading!" Mom explained: "Better than if he goes bike riding and gets hit by a moving van and gets killed!" Voja Bloša suggested: "Let's go crawl through the pipes!" Pipes lay along the street; workers were burying them in the ground and eating some sort of bacon and onions. We crawled through the pipes a long time without stopping. Mom shrieked: "What if they bury you alive in the sewer!" Afterward she said: "My poor child, going around with no-goods and people that cuss!" I announced: "I wish I knew Japanese!" Mom answered me: "And get your brain damaged!" Voja Bloša explained to me: "If we pull our eyelids back with Band-Aids, then we'll be Japanese!" We got Band-Aids out of the medicine chest; after that we stuck them over our eyes diagonally and rushed in where everybody was. My aunts shouted: "Here they are!" Mom dropped a big bowl full of plum preserves; Grandpa said: "Don't you see it's those two good-for-nothings?" Later on I borrowed a wristwatch from Boltek, a Czech, but broke it. Then his mom came and said: "It's a family keepsake, from Brno!" Grandpa asked: "What is this woman talking about?" I said: "I don't know!" There was a boy with an apparatus on his leg; the apparatus was made out of metal bars and little pieces of leather with holes in them; when he walked it creaked. Certain parts of the apparatus looked like ice skates; the boy limped a little from all this. I asked: "How come I don't have an apparatus?" Grandpa answered me: "You're out of your mind!" There was another boy; he had an artificial glass eye, also a very odd thing. A third boy had a little pump permanently hanging out of his ear. My friend Alexander Simonović had a hole in his neck; inside the hole was something like a button. He would always press that button when he talked, but all you could hear was something like: "Ks, ks!" Mom said: "These are all after-effects!" I had once fallen and hit my forehead, but I didn't get hurt. Mom said: "Your father climbed up the gymnastic equipment so many times when he was tipsy, and nothing ever happened to him!" I had one other friend; he was hunchbacked. He told me: "My mom dropped me when I was little!" I consoled him: "So did mine, except I came out of it all right!"

Rahaman Aron, David Azriel, Velimir Efri, Maurice De Mayo, Haim Buli, and his brother Uziel were friends of mine. None of them ate pork, but they all had fine names. I announced: "I want to be a Jew!" Grandpa said: "Now there's an idea!" My friends continued to come into our courtyard, where we traded various things. To get one Lineol-brand toy soldier with a leg missing, I gave away seven books from The Pink Library for Young People. Grandpa commented: "You can see they're kikes!" I explained to him: "I've already read the books, and I need the soldier for my war with Voja Bloša!" The books told everything about Pegasus, the winged horse, and about Bernard Palissier, who discovered porcelain by setting his own furniture on fire. We kept on hanging out in the courtyard, which was greasy from soot, and slippery. Ana Šilović, the knife sharpener's wife, also jumped out the window into the courtyard. She was in a housecoat, but was kind of puffy. We played chess in the courtyard; Miroslav had red chessmen, from Hungary. Later we also played in Miroslav's kitchen; it stank of urine, I mean the john. Mom asked me: "How can you sit in that stench?" I explained: "All I care about is chess!" The game my aunts adored was "Mensch, argere dich nicht," or Parcheesi; I didn't understand either one of these names. The game consisted of little wooden men running around a board made out of cardboard; we used dice to do all this. I was never able to win at this game; afterward they would kid me and say: "Off to bed, squirt!" Mom liked entering contests best of all, so she was always taking the labels off bottles or shoe-polish boxes and sending them someplace. She entered a guessing contest with "A Summer Vacation in Sušak" as first prize, but she won third prize, which was five boxes of Radion laundry soap. Then she said: "Just that is plenty enough!" Somebody banged on the door and said: "Open the door, Ma'am, your kind husband has sent me!" Mom asked: "What's my husband's name?" They read his name off the nameplate and told her. Mom said: "I'm alone in here at the moment with my frail little boy, but you're not going to fool me, you thieves!" Grandpa came back from the basement and said: "Someday somebody's gonna come and steal everything we've got while we're out for a walk!" Mom asked: "What is there to take?" We got stuck in the elevator; Mom banged with the umbrella and shouted: "There's a child in here!" I got scared one other time, by a movie where Pat and Patachon fall into boiling water. Then a professor man came and pointed at me: "Does he twitch in his sleep?" Mom replied: "Yes!" He explained: "That is due to overly frequent participation in exciting games at an overly young age!" Right away Dad tore up the Parcheesi board, into pieces.

We saw two movies with Deanna Durbin; in the first one she gets her head cut off; in the second she and a man are kissing each other in an armchair. I asked: "How can a woman with her head cut off do these things?" Mom turned to me in the dark and asked: "Aren't you asleep?" When we came out of the theater she wiped her eyes with a handkerchief and told me: "You're lucky you're a child!" I saw another movie about the life of some dog with the stupid name Krambambuli. The film was really dumb and also sad. We went to a waiting room, and Mom advised me: "You read these picture magazines you can't under-stand, be a good boy, and wait while the doctor man exam-ines Mama!" Various people asked me what my name was and if I was a good boy; this went on very long. At the shoemaker's Mom argued about some shoes and told me: "They never keep their word!" We also went to other places; Mom kept knitting some sort of sweater and telling me: "Nothing but waiting, all our lives!" These rooms all stank and a lot of people were whispering. Mom would warn me: "Don't touch anything—these are patients!" Then one of our relatives got her stomach cut open and a five-pound stone taken out. My aunts went to have a ton-sil operation but they came back home, perfectly healthy. One floor below us Anica was dying; we could constantly hear her coughing and screaming something. Mom closed the window. Later she said: "Don't anybody dare bring a stray dog or cat in here, because I can't stand that!" My aunts studied their coffee dregs and said: "An officer who's no relation to us will bring us a package or it'll be some news!" In the evening we saw the northern lights in the form of a big red cloud, and after that an air raid with sirens howling and airplanes that don't drop bombs at all.

I had a dream about all this afterward. I also dreamed my legs got tied up with a big chain, and a car that runs over me afterward. The professor man said: "You shouldn't go to the movies so much!" Grandpa said: "That's obvious!"

VI

Mom suggested: "Why don't we get our pictures taken and send them to our relatives who live abroad!" She and I went into a completely dark room; the photographer demanded: "Smile!" Mom explained: "This is for our aunt in America!" We had photographs before then, too. One was of Dad wearing a hat and carrying a cane; he looked a lot older as he walked along in front of some bank. A picture got saved of Mom making whipped cream with the famous German gadget called a Schneekasten; this was in a garden. Another important photograph was of me eating ice cream; this had been taken on some street. Mom kept saying: "Those were the days!" On some photographs of relatives I poked their eyes out with a needle. Afterward I said: "How did these holes get here?" My aunts also collected photographs of absolutely unknown people who weren't related to us. Grandpa asked: "Who are these creeps?" My aunts were aghast: "Creeps? Them?" Then they explained to us: "This is Tyrone Power, who acts in every film there is!" Mom concluded: "Really it's better if all we keep are the pictures of our kith and kin scattered all over the globe!" My uncle protested: "What's the point when we've never even met 'em?" Mom objected: "You talk that way about your own uncle who lives in Písek, Czechoslovakia, which nobody's ever heard of but it still exists?" My uncle said: "I can't help it if he does!" I knew there were various sorts of aunts in America, as well as some relatives who didn't know our language at all but just played in a firemen's band or something. Mom asked:

"I don't know who else would send you face cream for daytime and nighttime if it weren't for them!" Grandpa said: "Nobody!"

Some men down in the courtyard shouted that they were looking for scrap iron, leaky cooking pots, or anything else. Right away Grandpa objected: "We're not giving 'em anything!" Mom pressed him: "What if they fix the bathroom faucet for me?" Grandpa said: "Them?" Others arrived with guitars and started to sing. My aunts leaned out the window and tossed them slips of paper; on these they spelled out their requests regarding some song or other. My aunts wrote: "Forgetting You Is Hard!"; this was a title and they had underlined it. A singer called up to them: "You mean me?" My aunts blushed. My aunts requested some other songs, too, incomprehensible ones like "Curly," for example—a song about Russian prisoners with their hair shaved off. All this cost money. While I was at school my aunts broke into my coin bank that looked like an alarm clock and tossed all my money down to the phony singers in the courtyard. Afterward the singers came upstairs and asked for a glass of water. They drank the water and then said: "Lovely water, we're university students, do you read Marx?" Grandpa said: "Get out of here!" My aunts described all this in their diary; they cried a little as they wrote.

My aunts started getting signals of different sorts from the neighborhood. A tailor kept pointing to his heart and several other parts of himself. My uncle explained to my aunts: "He's inviting you to go downstairs!" My aunts got out a large photograph of Gary Cooper in a white suit; on the back of it they wrote: "I can't go out today!" The tailor across the way ironed a sleeve for a moment and then went on signaling. Mom worried: "Just so nobody sees us!" Grandpa declared: "It's high time they had a raid on all the sickos!" Right then a dancing instructor came to visit us and warned: "Without the slow foxtrot you're not a modern man!" Grandpa stared at him wide-eyed: "You telling *me* that?" The dancing instructor turned to my aunts and said: "No, really, you'll enjoy it!" The instructor claimed he was from Zagreb, which he wasn't at all. Another professor told us about the latest way to operate on an appendix, using hypnosis and saying: "You in warm tub, you not on operating table—you only think that!" Mom explained: "He read that in some run-of-the-mill junk novel, not in a medical book!" Mom was also visited by a Mr. Miller, who was from our country but had a German name and hair that was always very smoothed down. Mr. Miller coughed constantly but at the same time offered to take our picture, for free. Mom asked Dad: "Can we get infected from these photographs?" Mr. Miller asked: "Do you want a picture with your only son, or with your sisters?" Mom decided: "Better with my sisters!"; this was for health reasons. A man came who was selling Yale locks: "Nobody can unlock them, not even me!" My aunts trembled: "That same guy again!" Mom calmed them down: "What can he do to us when we've got a houseful of men?" My aunts started in again telling about the movie where the powerful sailor says to the girl: "Now, strip to the skin!" Then they told how he says: "Thanks, I just wanted to get a look!" All this got said in the semi-dark. Our neighbor lady, Darosava, claimed: "That leg in the ad for silk stockings, that's *my* leg—here, look!" Right away she wanted to show us how much the legs looked alike; she always left a smell of mildew and something else unfamiliar but sweet. Mom said: "Goodness me, what a bizarre world!" Dad replied: "Don't you have anything better to rack your brain over?" She said: "No, I don't—they're human beings too, every one of 'em!" Grandpa said: "You all are enough of a pain without the rest of the world to boot!" Dad added: "It's good they're slaughtering each other like animals!" Anica, who kept coughing downstairs, later died; new smells started coming up from there, something like mint candy. All this was very contagious, and exciting. Grandpa kept saying: "That's life!"

My aunts sighed. Then they said: "So many women were already famous at our age!"

Princess Marta Bibesko wrote a touching story: "Maria, Queen of the Serbs!" Mom read it and said: "I'd like to send her a thank-you letter!" There was also Boško Nanić, "a magician of national repute"; he worked with a female assistant. Grandpa objected: "I'm fed up with all these clowns!" The pilot Giovanni Giuseppe flew a gadget he called an "air ball"; afterward it fell apart. Grandpa said: "That's what he gets for being a fake!" There was also Mr. Dragutin Tafanek and Little Mara, and Mr. Bakić with his group of all Serbian gymnasts. Dad said: "They're good!" There were Alkalaj and Debicki, the famous Soko heroes. Dad claimed: "They're colleagues of mine!" General Pavlichenko, a Kuban Cossack, put on a performance for charity, after which he recounted terrifying moments in his career. My aunts begged Dad: "Have him come sing to us to the balalaika and other things!" Mr. Dragutin Hart, the state executioner, announced the hundredth hanging of his career. My uncle admitted: "I'd like to see that myself!" Philip Morton began holding his famous sales, for which he published a catalog: "Unbelievably Cheap!" Mom affirmed: "I like shopping at Morton's sales better than anyplace!" My uncle insisted: "I saw the American actor Douglas Fairbanks come through our railroad station!" Grandpa told him: "Why wouldn't you when you're always hangin' out there?" Mr. Tadija Sondermajer flew his own airplane. Dad announced: "That is my age-long, unfulfilled desire!" Mr. Ilić-Rakovački introduced a way of examining lungs using electric current. Grandpa fumed: "Everybody finds some excuse to make a pile of money!" Mr. Slavoljub Penkala invented the device of the same name* for writing with ink, and besides that he knew how to fly an airplane, also very well. Mom claimed: "I saw his

*Penkalo is the Serbo-Croatian word for fountain pen — Trans.

picture in the paper—he isn't much!" Mr. Kušaković invented toothpaste, a means of cleaning teeth that are dirty. Grandpa commented: "Why not!" Anton Dreyer began to brew beer he called "Serbian." Grandpa shouted: "See, what did I tell you!" There were the brothers Kunewalder, manufacturers of everything. There was Gourjorovski, who owned a mineral-water factory. Then there were Talvi and Mandilović, the proprietors of a newly opened salon that also was Serbian. My aunts said: "There are so many of 'em!" Grandpa remarked: "If they're Serbs, I'm a Frenchman!" Dad said: "They all belong here, though!" Mom worried: "Only how do we remember their names?" There was Mr. Šlomović, a manufacturer of shoes of various types. There was Solomon Moni Ruso, a dealer in groceries and housewares. Mom remarked: "That I like!" There were Petar Kozina, owner of a shoe factory, and Jovan Smejkal, a sausage maker. Mom insisted: "Everything of his is always fresh!" There were also the Višacki brothers, quilts for brides; Ana Csilag, cosmetics, Vienna; and both Ivan Svandtner and Josif Carillo, textiles. Dad lamented: "Some people are lucky!" My uncle chimed in: "And then there's George Weifert, the man who can do anything!" Dad agreed: "I saw him at a dinner honoring young salesclerks—he's quite a guy!" Grandpa commented: "Do tell!" My aunts' favorite was A. Rusojevna, hats. Mom disagreed: "I don't like the way she makes those things—like some kind of plate on your head!" We could also remember Mr. Bataveljić, Mr. Theodore Klefiš, custom-cut meats, and also Ana Poluško and Darinka Prizetković, without profession. Mom said: "God forbid *my* name should get spread all over the newspapers, even for the most reputable reasons!" There was also Mr. Sima Konforti, one of the nicest names I knew. Mr. Premović, electric light fixtures, Mr. Julius Majnl, coffee and tea, Mr. Jarolimek, linoleum, and finally, Mr. Šonda, chocolate, also had their signatures. Some of these I thought were abbreviations of much longer and even prettier names. All these businesses were listed on the back page of the newspapers Dad read the longest in the john, and some were written on the store signs. Grandpa went ranting around the apartment and then asked: "And *us?* What's the matter with *us?*" My uncle told him: "Tikan Pavlović, the greatest boxer of all time, lay down in front of a train with some dame!" Mom replied: "Him I don't envy, although he did used to come here for coffee, poor guy!" Dad asked: "How come everybody else figures out a way to be better off, but we never do?" Mom explained to him: "Everybody invents some machine or else they bet on the horses, or they just steal!" Grandpa concluded: "That's the easy way!" My aunts said: "All we ever wanted was to be opera singers, but what's the point when the unsurpassable mezzo-soprano Miss Olga Oljdekop already exists?"

Our neighbor lady Darosava kept explaining: "My father was a general, and I started out as a lady-in-waiting, only I got sick of it later on!" Darosava claimed she knew all the world-famous scholars, soccer players, academicians, and kings, and that she had had intimate relations of a romantic sort with them. Grandpa said: "In actual fact it was just one repairman after another!" Mom would brag: "My son goes to school with the sons of generals and salami manufacturers, and others!" And then: "All those children are dressed like little lords, and some of them come with their mouths smeared with rich people's breakfast consisting of eggs!" Grandpa concluded: "Those are decadent families that give themselves an artificial boost— with food!" Because I was in excellent health I had soup for breakfast made of browned flour with little lumps in it, which was very bland. Mom said: "In the schoolyard I have excellent conversations with those rich parents, and they all enjoy the jokes I tell, especially Mr. Popović, the salami manufacturer!" Grandpa explained: "You can make up for anything if you're healthy, you live long enough, and you have a lot of money!" Mom declared: "I don't know about that, but I can't complain, since there are examples of drunkenness and bickering and rowdiness everyplace, and yet people are still safe and sound!" Grandpa said: "Now there you've finally said something!"

We ordered calling cards that told everything about us—our names, addresses, and other information the police would need. Mom liked these cards a lot; she would flourish them in the presence of the neighbor women and say: "We're always busy!" Mom also maintained: "You've got to have friends everywhere!" Grandpa replied: "Right, as if all they had to do was wait on us!" Mom saw it differently and was always asking policemen, watchmen, and other people with armbands if she could do something forbidden, like cross the street in the wrong place, for example, or get an abnormally large piece of meat for half price. Afterward she would brag: "When there's a will, there's a way!"—even though she hadn't gotten anything.

VII

We had a coil-spring arm exerciser. I could stretch it twelve times, Dad thirty-five times, my uncle ninety times. My uncle could eat forty-five plum dumplings—before dinner, no less. My aunts knew how to do a colored-pencil drawing of Lake Bled that was like the real thing, and also a sunset, and some other things, all from memory. I had a Mainel und Herold accordion, the most famous brand in the world. I got my picture taken with the accordion, on a balcony. I performed a lot of hits and other songs on my German-made accordion; Mom always wrapped her head up in a towel dipped in vinegar; this smelled. There were other smells, excitement, and goings-on outdoors, outside our building. I kept asking Mom: "If your head aches I don't have to play any more!" She reassured me: "That's all right, it's not gonna go away anyhow!" My uncle could draw a picture with a single line. Right away Grandpa asked: "How's that?" My uncle said: "Like this!" and without lifting his hands off the paper he drew ships, flowerpots, and naked women. Dad tried to cut my aunt's profile out of black cardboard the way he'd seen them do it in some bar. His hand shook a little; my aunt ended up without any nose. I cut women models out of the magazine *Woman and the World,* ruining certain parts the same way. My uncle scolded me: "You're wreckin' the best part—the tits!" My aunts looked down on all this, and together, using their colored pencils, they did yet another rendering of their favorite subject, "Lake Bled." Grandpa took a look and said: "It's easy slappin' out hills when they all look the same!" I wanted to do a drawing assignment called "Free Choice, or Your Own Idea." Mom begged: "Let *me!*" Mom loved doing all the drawing assignments, no matter how hard they were. She drew "View from Kalemegdan," crammed with little houses and some trees, and then tiny boxes that were supposed to be cars. Finally she added a lot of people out for a stroll, but she spoiled the whole thing with a giraffe; every one of her pictures had to have some animal in it. Grandpa objected: "Let the child do his own work!" She defended herself: "Can I help it if I like to draw?" Dad warned: "If they find out his mother drew it for him, he'll flunk!" She said: "No, he won't!" and right away she offered to write a poem for my Serbian assignment. She told me: "Some day, God willing, you'll learn how to write poetry so I don't have to do it all myself!" Grandpa said of Mom: "She doesn't talk straight anymore!" A lot of things Mom said sounded like a lecture, only I never knew what about. Grandpa asked me: "Do you hear this?" I said: "Yes!" Mom was reading the story "The Misunderstanding" to my aunts. The story consisted of a lot of familiar words, but there were also some others, a little bit garbled, that nobody understood.

It told about a mixup between a woman who was taking her clothes off and a man who was giving dictation. The guy said: "Aha, you're here!"—then turned his back and started dictating something about the female body and what made it better than the male body. Meanwhile, she got undressed; afterward he turned around and said: "Ah, yes, the sculptor is one floor down, I only give dictation, but as long as you're here I'll take you to the bedroom!" Our relative Nikola had a different book; it was called *The Parts of a Woman;* it was quite grubby. Nikola worked at a shoe-repair shop; Mom said: "You can see it gets used a lot!" There were two books there, hanging from a nail; each one was on a loop made of twine. The first was the one about women, and the other was called *Tsar and Revolution.* Mom said: "Let me borrow that first one!" Later Dad said: "Let *me* see it!" She answered him: "I'm not done with it yet!" Dad said: "What do you want it for? You already know about it!" She said: "So what!" My aunts read the books *Ingeborg, Devaitis,* and *When the Heart Grows Faint*—just things that made you cry. I wanted to read the book *Karik and Valya,* from Russia, about turning big people into little ones. Mom warned me: "It'll ruin you!" My uncle had a little notebook called *How to Become a Monster in Eight Lessons.* All this was happening in the spring.

Then the comic strip *Torn between Duty and Love* started to come out, about the fearless commander of a German submarine who falls in love with the British consul's daughter. It had a lot of sinking of British ships, kissing, and other war horrors. My uncle kept springing a little book on us called *Fallen Woman,* a famous work about two people sleeping in one bed. Mom read *Hunger* by Knut Hamsun, a very instructive thing about stomach rumbling, written by a German spy who was very much disliked. Our neighbor lady Darosava marveled: "You've got so-o-o many books!" I said: "We also have a book

about Soviet aviators hidden in a stove we don't use!"
Everybody said: "That's not true at all!" My aunts knew
by heart everything they had read; they would always add
something of their own in the margin as they went along.
Grandpa noticed this and said: "Isn't there enough nonsense in those dog-eared things already?" This was mainly
because of a lack of understanding. Each person talked the
same way, but still there were some differences. The oddest foreign word was "alaon"; this was the name of the stone
Dad stopped the bleeding with when he shaved. Likewise,
I thought *Colas Breugnon* was one word and referred to a
brooch. My uncle knew how to declare his love in four
languages; he learned this out of the handbook *Love
Around the World,* with pictures. Sometimes I was amazed
we could understand each other at all. Some words were
really old, some totally new; they were all jumbled together. Stories, novels, and various other books existed about
a whole lot of things, but real life was different.

VIII

At school they had me blow up a balloon, a fairly longish
one. I brought the balloon home; right away Grandpa
screamed: "Throw that rubbish out!" Mom immediately
popped the balloon with a hot curling iron. Guests came
to stay overnight; in my bed they stuck a little girl who
was very skinny. My uncle said: "Let him learn!" Mom
said: "It's no big thing, they're still children!" The girl had
pigtails; in my sleep I pulled her hair; Mom shouted from
her bed: "Quiet down over there, you two!" Afterward
the girl left. I told Voja Bloša the whole story; he replied:
"You silly guy!" I asked: "Why?" Our neighbor lady
Eleonora from upstairs came and said: "I explain everything in great detail to my only daughter, who is just five
years old!" Mom protested: "Heavens!" I added: "They
showed *me* some picture of Russian tanks in action in a

Finnish forest!" She said: "Each to his own, you can see that!" Everybody else went speechless. Afterward my aunts kept whispering something to each other as they rummaged through their little bottles, medicines and stuff. I noticed that women always have secrets consisting of little boxes and other things; Grandpa would snort at these scenes. In one store Mom asked: "Do you have female snaps?" Afterward she took me into a dark room; they put sunglasses on me and said: "Now take your underpants off!" All this was in front of some lamp. Dad asked where we'd been, then said: "Ultraviolet treatments are good for you!" Grandpa concluded: "The level of science today is enviable, even though it's totally wrong!"

There was a school for foreign-language study, the so-called Berlitz School. Mom maintained: "It draws only the classiest people, store clerks, flute players, and poor girls about to graduate without anybody of their own!" Grandpa declared: "In other words, bums—every one of 'em!" Many secret things got said at the school, mostly about love and politics. A relative of ours found a harpist at Berlitz—a Jew; later she ran away to America with him. Grandpa said: "So, see, I was right after all!" Mom defended her: "It was fate!" There was another school, for artistic drawing—the Josić School, named after its founder. My uncle stated: "They bring a gal in off the street and draw her naked—it's great!" Mom protested: "That's not true, all they draw is a plate full of apples and oranges, which are worth their weight in gold as far as that goes!" There was also a school for little accordion players, by the fine name of Melody; the most important person at the school was Mr. Albin Fakin, a Slovene accordionist who was quite short. Grandpa asked: "Is he a dwarf?" My aunts left to go draw those apples at Mr. Josić's, my uncle tried to check out the Spanish instruction in the women's section at Berlitz, and Mom said to me: "Listen here, you're no slouch, either—you learn the accordion!" My uncle simply wouldn't admit which language he was studying at the Berlitz School, right above Jovan Smejkal's sausage store. My aunts came home from Mr. Josić's a bit nervous; it seemed the apples had in fact been exchanged for something else. I stayed in the group accordion class; we would all sit around our leader by the name of Fakin and together perform the famous Slovene nature-study anthem "In the Mountains the Sun Is Shining." Afterward we switched to rhythm exercises under the direction of Mr. Milošević, who was cross-eyed. We acted out a number called "Haymaking"; even though we were short of tools we *were* dressed in peasant clothing. Squinting one eye, Mr. Milošević tried to talk me into bringing my aunts for the number called "Harvest Victory," which was impossible to perform unless girls participated. My aunts consented; all of a sudden everybody in the family was arrayed like in the painting *Slaves from Herzegovina*. Grandpa said: "It's just what you deserve!"

My aunts decided to enroll in a "program for high school graduates," a school of a completely incomprehensible sort. Girls and boys who wanted to be office workers above all else went there. Grandpa kept asking: "What do they teach there?" My aunts would reply: "All sorts of things!" My aunts would bring home their classmates and explain: "We have a right to have colleagues, too!" The colleagues ate potato sugar and drank sour-cherry liqueur Mom had made; then they started telling various jokes and other things. The colleagues came at all hours; they were forever rustling things, whispering, and showing each other handwritten notes. The professor man from downstairs happened to come in; one of the colleagues immediately swallowed a notebook page covered with writing. Later I asked: "What do they swallow paper for?" Mom explained to me: "It's homework, you don't know anything about it!" All this really did look like some sort of school, only a totally idiotic one. One of the colleagues came on a bicycle and handed my aunts some other papers; right away I asked: "Are we gonna eat 'em?" The papers got shoved in a hole under the parquet floor; afterward that board creaked a little. Mom explained to me, proudly: "We're all going to get hanged on Terazije Square because of this!" Dad sat us down and said: "Now I'll translate this filth for you that's always coming over the radio in German dialect!" Dad listened to a song while staring at the chandelier, and said: "This is about some slut named Lili Marlene who's waiting at the gate for her lover, some corporal!" Mom said: "It's a good thing the child doesn't know German!" My aunts took me into the bathroom and explained: "The only German word you have to learn is *jawohl!*" I asked: "Why do I?" They told me: "So you can say it to a German on the street and then you're safe!" I asked what the word "sixnine" meant, but my aunts didn't know anything about that.

Finally, there was one other school, a school for fakirs. A girl in a man's coat came, took some bandages out of her bag, and said: "Now we're going to learn how to make a turban!" Then she started bandaging heads—my aunt's, Mom's, and Grandpa's. Grandpa insisted: "I don't have anything wrong!" The girl in the coat gave Grandpa a severe, soldierly look: "But no, these are really turbans!" Mom had a violet turban, with a brooch that went on her forehead; the one made of bandages was like it, but not exactly. Then my uncle tried to put his hand up the turban girl's skirt; she said: "No, you don't!" My uncle stopped.

Relatives came—five of them; among them was my cousin, who was very fat. Earlier my cousin had competed in the *Adriatic Guard* contest for the fattest child in Yugoslavia. My cousin took second place, right behind the monster-child Arpad Rozavelgyi from Subotica. My cousin was still quite big; his mom explained: "Our whole place burned down!" Mom spread out mattresses on the floor; the relatives were lying everyplace; we kept jumping over them all. Mom said: "I just don't know if I'll be able to peel potatoes for you all!" They said: "Just do what you can!" The relatives sat on the balcony and looked at the sky without moving a muscle. Grandpa told them: "Don't wear yourselves out!" Mom said: "They're safe and sound, that's the important thing!" The neighbors said: "It's like a boarding school at your place!" Grandpa barked: "So?" Dad kept coming home early; I wondered: "Why isn't Dad at the bar?" Mom replied happily: "Do you really expect the German military police to let him walk around the streets?" Dad carried around lists of signatures and amounts contributed for war orphans; in the other pocket he kept a little slip of paper with an ink-smeared five-pointed star on it; he kept asking: "Wanna give something for the guerrillas in the woods?" Mom warned him: "You want to get yourself killed?" Grandpa reassured her: "God looks out for the drunks!"

IX

They did arrest Dad, but because of the pin in his lapel. The pin had a crossed spoon, fork, and hammer on it; the pin told everything about the hardware business, before the war. They were bothered most by the hammer, a symbol of rebellion, but the spoon and fork told them the opposite; they let Dad go. They arrested other people, too, all because of little pins or things like that. My uncle informed us: "They've picked up the Baruchs—even the children!" Grandpa explained: "Well, with a name like that!"

Dad himself began getting hold of a lot of valuable things; Mom asked him: "Can you bring home the famous drug acetylcholine for a friend of mine whose nerves are shot?" Then she demanded: "Find me two kilos of lard somewhere, whatever it takes you!" Finally she said: "Bring me some of those things for Darosava; she wants to give them to a friend for his birthday!" Dad asked: "Where am I going to find her rubbers now?" I was sawing up a piece of plywood, cutting out figures of Indians; Mom whispered to Dad: "Not in front of the child!" Voja Bloša explained to me: "You put it on and afterward you don't have a baby!" I said: "I'm sure there are other inventions we don't know anything about either!" Voja Bloša replied: "I doubt it!" A young lady from the first floor had a bandage on her leg. Voja Bloša assured me: "Every woman who does those things has a bandage!" I asked: "Maybe she fell down!" Voja Bloša told me: "Like heck!" Dad brought home a fish that was still moving; right away Mom said: "This'll be for you all; as for me, I wouldn't dare because of the bones!" Grandpa warned: "Go ahead and be choosy then!" The neighbor lady Darosava brought playing cards and announced: "Now we'll find out the whole truth!" She started laying out the cards, very grubby ones, on the table; Mom said: "Here, let me get the plates out of the way first!" Darosava reported: "This cavalry captain you see here is a prisoner of war right now!" Grandpa said: "Obviously!" Mom requested: "What I want to know most is when my poor husband's going to stop drinking!" Grandpa wondered: "What good will that do you?" My uncle claimed: "There's a man who can stare at a lamp and see everything that's gonna happen!" Grandpa fumed: "Either he's lying or it's some special kind of lamp!" My uncle explained: "It all costs fifty dinars!" Afterward he added: "And then there's the guy I saw who measures your strength!" Grandpa asked: "Why?" My uncle replied: "You just hit this scale where it says to!" Grandpa told him: "If I were that idiotic!" Then my aunts told a story about a woman opera singer and a prisoner who was hidden in a well. A painter from some church was also there, and then a judge, who was fat; the singer later killed the judge with a pair of scissors. The judge sang, too; he was named Krsta Ivić, a member of an opera company; the painter was named Mario and supposedly was an Italian. Then Ilse Werner performed a song with whistling in it; she had very thin legs, but that didn't matter. This took place in a movie I didn't see; Voja Bloša gave me a word-for-word account of it. Right then I watched *Innocence Unprotected,* another movie with gentle punching in the head and love talk. There was also a woman who played the accordion, and a newsreel that showed Eleanor Roosevelt taking a bath. Dad brought home Arda-brand cigarettes then, which were Bulgarian. Grandpa announced: "I'd sooner roll crushed mulberry leaves in toilet paper!" The janitor smoked something else; it made the stairwell stink. Voja Bloša asked me: "Why don't we try it?" I answered: "My tummy hurts!" Voja Bloša said: "Everybody smokes now!" But what smoked the most was the Shell company in Čukarica, which American bombers set on fire. That was the most smoke in our whole lives, or ever.

X

Our neighbor Olgica, the police clerk's daughter, came and said: "Dad is ordering you to lend us the following things!" Olgica had a list; on the list were a meat grinder, a trough, and coffee cups, unbreakable ones. Everybody in the family hated the police clerk's lists for the purpose of demanding various parts of the household, and also the Germans, the culprits in these borrowings. Mom kept explaining: "All they do is borrow a cup of sugar and then never return it!" Everything in our life was divided up like in accounting books: into the things that were at the neighbors', and the rest, which we still had. Grandpa said: "I'd be nuts before I'd do double bookkeeping like that!" Mom asked him: "What if I forget things?" My uncle made a tandem bike. In the attic he found a bicycle, an old one, and added some more pipes to it; the bicycle suddenly

stretched out. Afterward he explained: "This is for cou-
ples in love!" but he gave it to my aunts. My aunts got on
the tandem and promptly crashed onto the pavement, in
the courtyard. My younger aunt tore her silk stocking.
Grandpa shouted: "Just go ahead and have fun!" Even so,
tandem bikes spread rapidly throughout the city; despite
the incident with the stocking, my aunts later mastered
the pedaling perfectly.

My uncle claimed: "I can make every possible thing
that exists, only in miniature!" Grandpa asked: "Who needs
it?" Mom said: "But the reverse—you can't do that!" Dad
brought home a lot of big boxes filled full of matches and
some much smaller ones that were empty. We all started
cramming the matches from the big boxes into the little
ones, exactly fifty of them in each. Grandpa admitted:
"This counting'll drive me nuts!" My uncle asked: "Can't
the guys in the monopoly do this themselves?" Dad said:
"But you want to make some dough!" Mom concluded:
"What don't we have to do just to keep body and soul
together!" Dad consoled them: "This isn't so bad, it's a
cottage industry!" Later all this fell through. Grandpa set
about punching holes in some little cards. He maintained:
"This'll be a big job that pays, even though I don't know
what it's for!" Dad kept bringing him the cards and telling
him: "Just keep punching!" Then they dragged in a pile of
green canvas and some laths; all this had to be put together by hammering, unbearable hammering! The neighbors
banged on the wall and shouted: "Stop that noise, you
animals—this isn't a mill!" Grandpa admitted: "The people are right!" My uncle suggested to my aunts: "You can
support yourselves by making signs for a photographer's
studio window!" In very nice handwriting my aunts wrote:
"What isn't in the window is in the store!" but they
refused to draw the fascist victory sign, which was also
required. My uncle said: "Then I don't know how you're
going to get by!" Dad explained: "A shoe man wants us to

put pieces of wood together to make sandal soles!" Dad brought home a bag full of wood. We put the sandals together on the old dining-room table, which was pretty valuable; the table got totally destroyed by this. My uncle hit his finger with a hammer and announced: "A shoe man—that's the last thing I ever wanted to be!" The janitor's wife asked: "Are you reporting these jobs or not?" Dad said: "None of your business!" and threw her out. From then on she said: "Good morning, sir, Mister Ćosić, sir, how are you, sir?" Mom thought of making a hat out of newspaper; Grandpa warned her: "But when it rains, then what?" In the kitchen they were mixing something in a pot; Mom told me: "Watch out, this is poison, or actually liqueur for men, who get dead drunk on it!" Grandpa said: "Don't you have anything better to do?" Mom answered him: "Me, you mean?" She told us all the things she had done that day and said: "Just counting them up is hard, much less doing them!" I refused to eat soup made of browned flour with little lumps in it. Mom warned: "You'll miss me when I'm gone and cry when no one's looking!" That was awful.

The baker came and asked: "Would you help me paste in ration coupons?" Right away Grandpa started putting in the little stamps; he did this using flour and water. I pasted in postage stamps from Jamaica, New Zealand, and similar places; my aunts went on pasting in the series Actors of My Life, beginning with Tyrone Power, who was all in smiles. My uncle studied the pasted-in coupons and declared: "It'd be easy to make these and have 'em look real!" Grandpa warned him: "The very idea!" Mom wailed: "Damned poverty!" My uncle said: "If you aren't upper crust it's nobody's fault but your own!" Grandpa protested: "There isn't any upper crust left anymore!" My uncle asked: "Then who are those dudes who go around wearing hats and carrying canes?" Grandpa replied: "Policemen, and they spy on *every*thing!" Mom said:

"How could police be elegant and all decked out like that?" I wondered: "Where do the upper-crust people live?" Mom answered me: "Better not ask—then you won't be disappointed!" I said: "That man you said was upper crust, he's an art teacher with ragged sleeves!" Mom told me gently: "You don't understand!" Mom again made a point of mentioning the bank clerk from before the war who had grabbed her by the breasts so she wouldn't fall out of the streetcar and get killed. The man who grabbed her kept changing professions in her stories; first he was a sailor, then an incoherent road-repair man; at the moment he was young, refined, and very perfumed. Mom said: "He was a gentleman from head to toe!" Dad asked: "So?" My uncle even had a book *How to Behave Like a Gentleman*, with pictures, that was underlined in many places. Grandpa protested: "How can they issue regulations about gentlemanly conduct?" My aunts said: "Surely it only has confirmed examples from all through history!" Grandpa stated: "All history has in it is slaughter and gold heists, and nothing but!" My uncle commented: "Do you see how gentlemen always have their jackets and trousers out of the same material?" I explained: "My history teacher's a gentleman, and I saw him stick his finger between the geography teacher's tits!" Mom asked me: "Haven't you gone yet to get ice cream that'll give you a sore throat?" Grandpa concluded: "All they did was steal a heap of money, and now they're dribbling it out little by little!" Mom objected: "They didn't steal anything—they're the sons of generals and industrialists!" Dad said: "As if there were that many generals!" Grandpa said: "It just gets on my nerves when somebody makes money and you don't know how they're doin' it!" Mom cited many examples of honest people who work hard to make a living, like soda-water manufacturers, for example. Right away Grandpa jumped in: "Them? They take ordinary tap water and make a pile of money on it!" My uncle corrected him:

"They have a machine that does it all and also a chemical they stick in that water!" My aunts maintained: "In movies all the greatest lovers drink club soda that fizzes all over and foams up!" Dad said: "The only way it's any good is when you squirt it in wine out of a siphon bottle and make a spritzer!" My uncle announced: "In Russia they give out club soda absolutely free!" Grandpa asked: "How do they make any money?" Mom concluded: "There will always be people who tell lies and keep body and soul together that way!" My aunts asked: "Is it true Mr. Gogić turns old fur coats inside out and makes new ones out of unusable animals?" Mom said: "If he'd just make me a muff, since I'm an old customer!" Dad commented: "That's all you need!" Mom insisted: "Don't you see winter's coming, and fast?" My uncle warned: "This winter's nothing—when the Russians come all the winters'll be like in Siberia, wait and see!" Grandpa asked: "How do you know?" My uncle went on: "In Siberia a man's nose falls off as soon as he goes out in the cold!" Grandpa said: "That's what they get—what do they go outside for?" Mom brooded: "If I just had all those designs and all that training I could make slenderizing corsets myself!" My aunts asked: "Why do that?" Mom answered herself: "But what would that leave for Madame Nina, who is an expert at creating brassieres and hernia belts?" My uncle said: "Lucky her, think what she must grope onto!" Mom went on: "What matters most to me is having fine underwear on in case I fall down on the street and they take me away!" Grandpa asked: "Who?" Mom told us: "I know for sure that a lot of those painted-up floozies with the crocodile-leather purses don't even have a slip on!" My aunts declared: "The purse is the mirror of every woman, especially from the inside!" My uncle explained: "After the war the Russians are going to go from door to door with big briefcases and pull out presents for all mankind!" Grandpa said: "If they're that foolish!" Then Dad protested: "So much talk, but there's nobody to iron me a shirt!" My uncle told us: "A laundress asked me if I'd seen the movie *Lady of the Tropical Nights,* which is great!" Mom said: "As for laundry, I could get a doctor's degree I've washed so much of it, since there's a houseful of you!" Dad asked: "Is it true that everybody in Russia goes around with their clothes unironed?" Mom wondered: "Will clothing and the human body stop getting dirty in the future?" My aunts replied: "The greatest kings of France didn't bathe at all, but just used the fragrances of different fruits!" Grandpa said: "That's why those old goats deserved to get chopped up on the guillotine like turnips!" My uncle concluded: "Man is the animal that stinks, we can't help it!" My aunts started to cry, softly. Afterward they said: "Who would think it, looking at a picture of Ronald Colman or Johnny Weissmuller swimming!" Mom said: "Grooming is the whole key!"

XI

Mom began standing in various lines; this was in front of different stores. She stood there pretty long; afterward they told her: "There's nothing left!" This kept repeating. Mom herself participated in this buying and selling. She would go in to a store owner and say: "Kind sir, would you buy this glass with a depiction of Venice on it, even though it's a bit cracked, unfortunately!" Mom dragged a lot of expensive things to this store, but some she brought back because they were of no use or no good. Even so, we later had fewer and fewer glasses with inscriptions on them, just as we ended up without that statue of the stag in the middle of a roar. This didn't help us much. A woman came and said: "All this'll be taken care of by my nephew who works on a ship, but 'til then give me fifty dinars!" Somebody else complained: "Still nothing—and I was sure I'd win the state lottery!" One woman we knew confessed: "I'd open a hat shop, but I don't know how to begin!" Grandpa asked: "So?" My uncle told us: "Darosava has a beau who comes on Tuesdays!" To me it sounded like "bull" or something like it.

There were people who tried to convince us they were related to us somehow. They were all pretty dirty. Some of them tied their coats closed with string and wire, and said: "We like working at rich people's houses best, because then we hear them fight and break expensive plates in their rage!" Grandpa added: "Not to mention the silverware that always disappears afterward!" A bearded man tried to convince us: "The last judgment is coming!" Grandpa told him: "What do you mean 'coming'?" Then some character came peddling a cure for baldness. My uncle explained to him: "I've got hair galore, but no money!" Then a very refined gentleman knocked and proposed: "Give me a thousand dinars now and I'll bring you that bacon!" Grandpa asked him: "Why *us*?" He held up a slip of paper and told us: "They wrote here I should come to your place!" He also said: "My address is such and such!" Mom agreed: "All right, then!", gave him the thousand dinars, and went to that address. There they told her: "My dear lady, you're not the first to come looking for that house—it was destroyed back in the bombing!" There was also a man who offered: "I'll get you sugar cubes, just give me some old clothes and I'll give you my name and address." Mom gave the man Dad's trousers; at that address they told her: "Nobody here deals in trousers—we've never even heard of the guy!" One woman claimed: "Here's a picture of my husband, who's going to bring a special heater from Vrnjačka Banja, only you have to pay a certain amount of money!" Mom looked at the photo and said: "Poor people—the things they've got to do!" Mom gave the whole amount; the woman took the photo and disappeared forever. Mom and my uncle went to the registration bureau to get the addresses of some people they only knew the names of. There were boxes there; for every person they knew where he was and what he was. For the ones Mom and my uncle were looking for there wasn't anything. Mom concluded: "Whoever meets me cheats me!" That was the truth.

XII

My aunts told us: "Yesterday we noticed a really weird sunset—like some sort of blood on the horizon and stuff!" My uncle claimed: "I saw 'em pull a corpse out of the Danube; who knows how long it was in there. It was at least five hundred pounds!" Voja Bloša said: "I saw a naked woman!" Mom beat her chest and sobbed: "Damned, damned war!" She used to say: "Immortal, immortal Gigli!" the same way; that referred to some singer and was different.

Dad confided to us: "I heard there are fountain pens you find on the street and when you open 'em up they explode!" Grandpa declared: "I haven't got anything to sign!" Mom ordered me: "Don't pick up anything off the ground, not even gold!" My uncle stated: "A store clerk got butchered to death in Kumodraž!" Mom hugged Dad tight and begged him: "Don't go out anywhere!" He replied: "I could give a fuck!" Some sort of circle appeared around the moon. The neighbors came and said they'd seen some Russians. Mom asked: "Ours, or real ones?" They replied: "How would *we* know?" My aunts told us in horror: "Some snatch children and make sausage out of them!" Mom moaned: "Imagine eating my own child and not even knowing it!" My uncle told us: "One famous woman partisan commissar rides around on horseback and cuts off priests' balls!" After that he also said: "I heard there's a brothel with thirteen-year-old sluts!" I thought that was some kind of store, and I asked: "When's Dad gonna open a brothel?" "Stalin—Executioner! Churchill—Gravedigger of the Serbian People!" was written on one wall, and "Those boobs!" on another. Mom sighed: "He'd be better off blind than to read all those awful things!" My friend Srba Radulović got his foot cut off by a streetcar; afterward he wore some sort of artificial wooden one stuck in a shoe. Mom warned me: "You see?" Somebody else lost his leg up to the knee from riding a bicycle. Mom said: "What do I keep telling you?" My uncle told about some madman who goes into a bar and says: "Now you're gonna see a man who's conquered everyone, even himself!" After that the man aimed a pistol at his own head and fired. Mom said: "That's nerves!" I watched a dignified gentleman in a hat get tied to a pole at the marketplace and spat on. Mom revealed the secret to me: "Poor guy—he's a speculator!" Afterward I saw another man in a hat kick a woman; the woman was wearing a fur stole; the man was saying "Phoo!" to her. We heard and saw many things, and afterward we retold it all, especially about the dreadful crimes and other improper things. We went to visit the wife of a riverboat captain when the captain was away; she was lying on an ottoman; a carnation stuck out of her ass. My uncle asked: "Where's she find these carnations now?" Voja Bloša said: "Let's go see the janitor's guts wound up on the telephone wire!" There were other parts of a human body on the wire, too, but we couldn't identify them. I went to see a perfume shop with spilled powder and some man, a pretty bloody one, in the window. Dad kept leaning out our window and saying: "Here they are again!" Grandpa asked: "What are they throwing!" Dad replied: "Prob'ly bombs!" Grandpa went on: "Not shit?" Grandpa kept insisting that the Americans, high up in their airplanes, were going to unbutton their trousers and start shitting on us, right on our heads. My aunts protested: "Them, when they have the handsomest actors in the world?" Mom put on her fur coat, even though it was summer, and announced: "I want to die like a lady!" The police clerk told us: "There's nothing up there but Negroes who don't look where they're throwing, what can I say?" I later found a pile of dinar bills in the mud; Mom said: "If we survive, we'll buy a kilo of lard with all the money!" Grandpa twisted the dial to Radio Berominster and banged on it for all he was worth, but we couldn't hear anything. Then on the stairway I stepped into the spittoon. Mom carried me in her arms and kept calling for the others to come. Afterward they washed my leg off, but still . . .

XIII

In the courtyard, on top of the chipped vases without any flowers in them, somebody had set empty American milk cans, and an empty bean can. The cans were bent up, with the lids torn off. The only good thing about them was the writing—the different letters. Lieutenant Vaculić and my uncle moved back to the opposite wall; then Vaculić started firing a burst of shots toward those cans, which said "Milk" and "Beans." Mostly he aimed at letters like *B* and *a*, because of those holes in them. After the first shots the professor from the ground floor came out and held up his arms. Vaculić told him: "Are you nuts?" The professor put his arms down, uncomprehendingly. Afterward my uncle fired some volleys, but did much worse.

Our liberators, comrades from the Twenty-First Serbian Brigade, asked: "Are there any Nazi machine gunners around here?" My uncle said: "All we have here are those people selling artificial wind-up mice!" Russian soldiers also came and asked: "Any mines—*da* or *nyet*?" Mom replied: "The only mine I have is my poor husband and that alcohol in him!" The Russians didn't believe her. My uncle asked: "How are we going to begin a new life when nobody believes anybody?" Lieutenant Vaculić said: "Just listen to the speakers from the common people, they'll explain the whole truth to you!" The speakers were all on stools and other furniture; from there they explained many useful things; everyone else was on the ground, practically kneeling. I explained to Voja Bloša: "They're the ones gonna set off the wind-up mouse!" Right away women started shrieking and saying: "O-o-o-o!" Lieutenant Vaculić screamed: "What is *this* now?" I replied: "Little tiny animals that are like real ones!" The mice salesmen saw how confused the public was; then they said: "We apologize!"

My aunts sat in the kitchen with the officers and some university students. The students knew how to imitate Hawaiian guitar playing by going "Hm-hm!" through their noses. Mom called them Hawaiians, probably since she was flustered. There were also other songs my aunts performed, pretty oddly; instead of words they went "Pa-pa-pa!" That itself was quite enough for us. Our neighbor lady Darosava, a great expert on men's bodies, various ones, said: "Now we can do anything we want!" Grandpa asked: "Only I assume stealing isn't allowed!" Mom said: "Of course not, when there's nothing to steal anyway!" Comrade Abas declared: "If nothing else, now everybody can say what they've been holding in!" Right away Voja Bloša said: "My mom has false teeth and sleeps completely naked!" It was clear my aunts had something to say, too, but they resisted. Vaculić recited an unintelligible poem about a submachine gun, a soldier's weapon that talks like a man, only stupidly. Captain Jovo Axe thought a while, then asked: "How can a live person write a book all by himself, like Comrade Lenin, for instance?" Mom replied: "My son writes poems about national heroes and the seasons on toilet paper, which is all there is, only he's real shy!" Mom started calling Dad "My comrade!" She would say: "My comrade is a bit carried away with recently occurring historical events, but he'll get over it!" Grandpa didn't know who she was talking about. Dad was vomiting in the john. My aunts sang the song: "Let all that is rotten sink into a cold grave!" Comrade Abas said approvingly: "That's right!" My comrade Kalafatović asked: "Even though my mom's a dressmaker, can I recite my poem about Comrade Kirov murdered at a railroad station?" Captain Jovo Axe said: "Who's stopping you?" My uncle told us: "Many artists are absolutely devoted to their people, but the most devoted one of all is Dragoljub Aleksić, a native of little Knjaževac!" Grandpa asked: "Is he that swindler that bites through fake chain?" Mom said: "And hangs by his teeth from under an airplane and waves our new national flag!" The officers admitted: "We're in the mood for drawing!" One of them took my aunt's hand, laid it down on paper, and started tracing around the fingers with a pencil. Mom said: "It looks real!" My aunts sketched still-unliberated areas of the country, that is to say "Bled," an island with a little church, and then using a model, like for instance Jovo Axe, our comrade. Grandpa watched the frowning captain, who stood like a statue while this drawing was going on, then asked him: "Where'd you all get these names like Hare, Crow, and Axe?" I concluded: "Useful tools and birds!" Vaculić explained: "Because they all came from the common people!" The soldiers sat next to the stove where pieces of useless furniture were burning; my aunts created unforgettable likenesses of them with eyebrow pencil, which they didn't need anymore. Someone from the neighborhood brought in a really little baby and requested: "Draw the youngest citizen of our liberated town!" The baby sounded out unintelligible words: "Gulp!" "Agoo!" "Glaif!" and so on. Jovo Axe sounded out the letters "U," "S," "S," "R"; that was majestic. My aunts scanned the syllables of a new song: "Shi," "Ra," "Ka," "Stra," "Na," "Ma," " Ya," "Ra," "Dna," "Ya."* Grandpa kept trying

*A Soviet patriotic song, "Shiroka strana moya rodnaya" ("Broad Is My Homeland"). — Trans.

MY FAMILY'S ROLE IN THE WORLD REVOLUTION

to read the American word on the little package that said "Breakfast!" Mom said: "All this has broadened our horizons!"

Afterward Vaculić's comrades fired a pistol into the air, out the window. The neighbors thought another city had been taken, and that actually was the case with my aunts, and all of us. Mom acknowledged: "We are yours!" Everyone around us was young; they put out their cigarette butts on the parquet floor. Vaculić asked: "Shall I break this cut-glass goblet from the period of bourgeois rule?" Mom sneaked another, regular one into its place. Dad said: "Break any one you want!" We said: "Right!" Vaculić got teary; Grandpa asked: "What's with him?" Mom explained: "It's art!" My uncle asserted: "Communism is joyful!" The officers sang, patted my cheek, drank brandy, and afterward vomited from the balcony. On the ground floor the same day that clerk died of tonsillitis, and this didn't fit in. Somebody shouted from down below: "Is nothing sacred?" We replied: "No!" All of us were terribly happy; this made some of us shake and stumble like when you first wake up. One real skinny comrade started giving a speech about the annihilation of mankind; suddenly dangerous foam which was all white appeared around his mouth. Grandpa asked: "He wasn't bitten by a mad dog, was he?" Afterward the comrade fell down on the pavement and started issuing orders in an unintelligible voice; my uncle sat on his chest and begged him: "Hey, man!" Mom said "Poor kids!" and stuff. The comrade later suggested: "Excuse me, now I'm fine, but next time stick my finger in a socket and give me a good jolt!" We said: "Fine!" Dad wasn't aware of himself either; he stood on one leg and put his forefinger to his temple; this was called "French thinking." Dad finished his number and announced: "There's an American powder for alcoholism, only it's very expensive!" Grandpa asked: "Haven't we had about enough?" We replied: "No!" Vaculić said: "Do you see the difference? Now there's just singing, and shooting at tin cans and stuff!" We agreed: "We see!"

XIV

Then Captain Jovo Axe pounded the table with his fist and said: "We're going to turn everything upside down now, right from the foundations!" Mom answered him: "Me, too, when I sit backward in the streetcar, everything's upside down for me afterward!" Comrade Abas explained: "What's been valid in your life up to now we've got to turn topsy-turvy, for historical reasons!" Dad corrected him: "Well, sure, when I look at you from up on the ladder when I'm fixing a short circuit, everything looks topsy-turvy to me, too!" A ruddy girl in boots announced: "But that isn't all!" Grandpa said: "Oh?" We were all sitting in the kitchen and talking; even so, it looked to me like a performance of some sort, since everybody was talking loud and pounding their chests and the wooden furniture.

Lieutenant Vaculić admitted to us: "We're going to let all the animals out of the zoo, like the elephants, lions, alligators, and stuff, to live freely with the other people!" Grandpa said: "That I'd like to see!" Mom reconciled herself: "I don't have anything against any kind of beast as long as they're tamed and they eat out of my hand!" My uncle said: "I, on the contrary, can't stand their stench and their other properties, and that's why I like going to the circus where I spit on the bears and snakes, which growl and can't do anything back!" The ruddy comrade in boots wiped her nose with the back of her hand and shouted: "We're going to fight for the brotherhood of people, animals, and the rest of humanity through persuasion alone!" My aunts announced: "We're prepared to sleep thirty members of a liberation brigade!" Right away Grandpa interjected: "Go ahead, if you don't want to get any sleep!" They went on: "But we can't take monkeys, on account of our innate feminine fear and since we've got a child in the house!" Mom admitted: "And I'll go mad if it comes to such consequences!" Comrade Abas reassured them: "On the contrary, we're gonna turn the madmen into human beings, too, and not throw them into chains and cold water like in the prewar period!" Grandpa said: "You know best!" Comrade Abas confirmed: "Of course we do!"

Captain Jovo Axe, in a very happy mood, announced: "We're going to call your attention to a way to flush the toilet with one flick of the hand, like this, that you'll hardly notice!" Grandpa was amazed: "Look at that, would you!" Jovo Axe explained to me: "I'll teach you how to write with your right hand and use your left one to help scratch behind your ear, or take care of a few other needs!" I replied: "Fine!" Jovo Axe watched Grandpa chopping up old furniture and announced to us: "And after that, I'll teach you how to sleep in a real bed like you've never even heard of before!" Comrade Abas started coughing, which meant we needed to talk about other things, but Jovo Axe went on: "My job is just to make sure you don't guzzle water when you're hot, and to keep the covers over you at night!" Grandpa agreed: "Oh, that's fine, then!" I noticed all of us were drunk, although I didn't know what on. At the end Lieutenant Vaculić said: "We are capable of turning nature itself in our direction, be it flowers, rivers, or lakes, although the seas are much harder!"

Then Comrade Jovo Axe informed us of the following: "In regard to prosperity, it's all determined in advance, except that everything has to go a lot slower than we thought!" Grandpa asked: "What do you mean?" Jovo Axe presented the fact of the slow growth of the tallest tree being the surest. On this Grandpa remarked: "Except I'm not made of wood!" Comrade Axe tried to apologize: "What are *we* s'posed to do?" Then he said: "We've already got a quarter of a square meter of bathroom tile for every family!" Grandpa asked: "What do we do with a quarter of a meter?" Mom tried to console him: "Even that's good, 'cause we can save them up little by little, as long as it takes!" My uncle added: "For years I kept a list of women's names—a nice collection, doggone it!" Jovo Axe said: "What do I tell you!" Grandpa scratched his head and asked: "Why don't we get tiles for the whole bathroom, and let the other people be patient!" Mom tried to back this up by saying: "And the way we kept those deadly dangerous books under the parquet floor—doesn't that count for anything?" Jovo Axe explained to her: "That would be the damned inequality we fought against on every front!" My uncle concluded: "So that's that!"

Afterward Jovo Axe opened up his overcoat and shouted: "Looky here!" From under his overcoat he pulled out a really pretty little house, only small. My uncle told everybody: "That used to be in the Vlada Mitić department store window, only a grenade hit it then and broke the glass!" Everybody started examining the little Builderbrand miniature house, constructed before the war, for advertising purposes. The house had everything you'd need to live in it, only midget-sized. Grandpa looked the little house over from all angles, then announced: "What good is it since we aren't dwarfs?" I said: "Maybe we *will* be!" Mom threatened: "I'm gonna smack you one, even though I feel bad about it!" I explained: "How did Karik and Valya get little when they swallowed that pill in the novel?" My uncle told us: "In Russia anybody can get smaller or bigger if they need to—they just get in a certain machine and somebody else pulls the lever!" Grandpa concluded: "Well, that's *them!*" Right away I wanted to open the door on the little house, but they slapped my hand. Mom said severely: "It's not for playing with!" They left the little house sitting in the middle of the table and looked at it really long. I kept trying to console them: "Maybe we'll find a little man two inches tall, which I've been wanting all my life!" Grandpa admitted: "I'm not giving it to anybody!" My uncle told us: "I saw so many dwarfs before the war in various bottles!" Grandpa commented: "Those are cheap tricks I don't believe in!" Mom insisted: "Medical books are full of pictures of various freaks that are born looking like darning eggs, or something even worse!" Dad finally realized what was going on around him, rubbed his eyes, and said: "What's the point if they can't survive?" My uncle protested: "That isn't true, they just put 'em in denatured alcohol, where they're better off than out in the air!" My aunts commented: "All those freaks that are just a foot or two tall, they only exist so people can gape and laugh in a circus tent, that's all they do for a living!" Comrade Abas looked at us with some sort of pity and said: "Is *this* our goal?" We ourselves didn't know. Dad sobered up completely and said: "Things are cockeyed all over the place!" I confirmed: "Uncle is when he looks at the tip of his nose and practices being crosseyed!" Mom warned again: "Just let him end up that way—he'd be better looking!" My aunts suggested: "We think the answer is for us to learn Esperanto and understand everybody from all over the globe!" Lieutenant Vaculić confirmed: "We're going to create a garden where others wanted to slaughter and kill!" My uncle asked him: "I heard we're gonna change our lives even if some of us lose 'em in the process!" Comrade Abas corrected him: "No, we won't, only we're going to have everything in common—thoughts, feelings, and other internal things!" My aunts whispered: "That's what we were afraid of!" Grandpa proclaimed: "Better to be healthy and rich than sick and poor, but it doesn't always happen that way!" Jovo Axe consoled him: "One day life'll be full of honey and milk, according to what I read in one toilet stall!" Mom concluded: "The whole key is human nature, which is corrupt most of the time!" Mom herself started laughing at what she had said. Comrade Abas instructed us: "We must succeed in laughing even when nothing is the least bit funny!" Right away everybody got serious, very. Jovo Axe tried to cheer us up again, by saying: "Better if I assign each person what to do so there won't be any mixup!" My aunts commented: "The best thing of all is if our lives get over with as quickly as possible so we can see what we've done!" Comrade Abas tried to explain: "It's always obvious who ought to sing and who ought to scrub the stove!" Mom said: "If God had given me talent, I'd play and sing to beat the band!" Jovo Axe went on: "But somebody's got to clean the toilet!" Mom said: "I knew it!"

XV

Thus were the many duties divided up, from premier on down. For the jobs of the most responsible sort, Comrades Pijade, Nešković, and Djilas were picked. In our family, things looked like this: I was for propaganda and poetry, Dad for the alcoholism question, my uncle for the women. All of us were keen on advancing our work, our specialty, the family one. We worked as if we had learned roles in a play called *Family Life,* even though no one told us to. All of us carried out our tasks, the family ones. The words we uttered were spoken loud, as if someone was supposed to hear us and say "Bravo!" Mom kept saying: "I haven't got anything to hide!" Then she went out on the balcony and told the neighborhood gathered there: "Yes, he drinks, but he's a peach of a guy!" The neighbors replied: "Wow, listen to her!" Mom went on: "And my brother lays all the gals in the building, as you yourselves know better than anybody!" After this the neighbors shut up. All this looked like a performance in a theater, even though it wasn't a real one. Our life flowed along daily, without any interruptions. All of us participated in that life; we collaborated on that work as best we knew how. Dad kept saying: "It's not bad!" Grandpa would object:

"As long as you don't know there's anything better!" Mom repeated: "We aren't any of us blind, or have syphilis, or f'rinstance, stutter!" Grandpa said: "God forbid!" Mom added: "While those things are very common all over town, and everywhere else!" We were a family with very healthy members, despite a shortage of other things like, for example, money, food, and clothes. Mom kept explaining: "I'd be happy to go around in rags, which isn't the case, so long as I don't get varicose veins or mumps, which are hard to cure nowadays!" We worked all day without any visible results, and then we would go to bed and dream the same thing, that is, that we were still working, like machines of some sort. Grandpa claimed: "I dream I'm inventing a chemical formula for parquet-floor polish, which I can't remember afterward!" Mom told us: "I dream I'm acting in the most enchanting movies I can't say anything about in front of the child!" Dad tried to explain: "In my dreams nobody keeps me from drinking even the worst drinks, but I never get poisoned, which is odd!" My uncle said: "For a while I recorded my dreams in a diary, but then I stopped!" We would wake up and do those jobs over again, both the ones around the house and those other ones, for all mankind. We kept doing house-work that didn't bring any results. Captain Jovo Axe said: "Someday I'm going to bring a proletarian brigade in here to clean this room for you!" My uncle answered him: "You should, since you're the one who gets it dirty, coming here whenever you feel like it!" Grandpa turned to my uncle: "As if your gals wipe their shoes!" My uncle said: "I'd say that's a different matter!" We were a family with an indefinite number of members because of everybody who kept coming to see us and sit with us, sing unknown songs, knit mittens, and so on. Mom tried to explain: "Our family is the whole world which I'd like to hug!" Grandpa warned: "What a bunch of malarkey!" Mom asked: "What do you mean?" Captain Jovo Axe declared: "There are a lot of people in the world who ought to be strangled, 'cause they're the source of all the unhappiness!" Mom admitted: "Well, then I don't know!"

XVI

My uncle had an ocarina, my aunts had a phonograph, and I had a Mainel und Herold–brand accordion. We played various melodies. My uncle couldn't play until he poured a little water into his instrument. When he played, the water burbled like some bird. Afterward the water would be warm. Mom suggested: "Come on, perform something!" Ordinary life was never enough for Mom, so she was always wanting to see something artificial, in other words artistic. In between two rooms my aunts hung up a dress, like a curtain. They put a lamp down on the floor; right away that gave the room a more magical look. Behind me they set a palm tree in a big flowerpot. Then they said: "This'll be Hawaii!" I took my accordion and played a piece called "Like a Nice Dream!" While I played, a palm branch tickled me on the neck; I kept laughing. Mom asked me: "How can you laugh when it's such a sad song?" We put on a sketch with a barber in it; my comrade named Kalafatović thought up a play in which he sat on a chair and somebody else smeared him with beaten egg white. We got the egg from our neighbor lady Darosava; right away Grandpa said: "She swiped it somewhere!" The sketch consisted of Comrade Kalafatović licking all the egg white off his face each time he was going to get shaved. I invited Elias Alhalel and two others, gave them some prewar calendars that had a conversation between Sarah and Moshe, or some such, and then I ordered them: "You're going to perform this, and I'll play the accordion!" When I signaled, the actors yanked open my aunts' dresses hanging in the doorway, and right away they stumbled over the palm tree, but they didn't knock it over. Everybody was happy. When I signaled again, Elias Alhalel read: "Say, Sarah, my wife, why are you cheating on me with Kohn?" Captain Jovo Axe quickly stood up and asked: "Who wrote that?" I replied: "An unknown prewar writer!" He said: "It's disgusting!" I started to perform the cheerful Russian song "When Stalin Came Out Into the Courtyard!" on my accordion. After this people applauded. Comrade Abas agreed: "Now, that's it!" I explained to him: "We took the old play about the girl who's swifter than a horse and made a completely new sketch with fighting in it!" Vaculić told me: "We're going to remake plays they used to give by inserting positive passages to improve the population's nervous system without anybody noticing it!" Grandpa asked: "What do you mean?" He answered him: "We just want to show you what all there is ahead of you you haven't even heard of yet!" This was right when we were giving a party in honor of our neighbor, Branko Pevjanić, a high-school senior who was leaving for the front. Branko Pevjanić, who was real young, danced with my mom; because he was so tall he leaned down and said in her ear: "This is harder for me than final exams!" The party also had other talking, turning off of lights, and kissing. At the party was the daughter of a lacquer manufacturer who was now in prison. The manufacturer's daughter kissed everybody, but she couldn't get close to me because of the accordion. Afterward Mom wrote something like an excuse to her mother. The note said: "Your beautiful little girl was at our house for a light snack!" Other times Mom would say: "Music is the only balm for my soul, which is completely lacerated!" My aunts acknowledged: "If we'd had the guitar earlier, everything would've been a lot easier to bear!" I declared: "Most of all we like to sit and talk nonsense, like in some play!" Mom replied: "We're a far cry from that!" Vaculić asked: "Why?" She said: "The theater is unique and sublime, but our life is shabby and completely uninteresting, as you can see by my face, which is always unhappy!" Vaculić tried to console her: "That doesn't necessarily mean you are!" Mom claimed: "I can't remember the last time I dressed like a wife and mother and everybody admired me!" Grandpa interjected: "Put it out of your mind!" Mom agreed: "But then poverty has inspired many artists — like myself, for instance!" Vaculić acknowledged: "There, you see?" I was finally satisfied and said: "Everybody says whatever he wants!" Grandpa said: "The freedom to state opinions, even the dumbest ones — that is our greatest wealth!"

But the nicest performance was held on the occasion of the liberation of Šid, a very beautiful town in Slavonia. I promised I would write a play of my own, but I didn't. Comrade Abas asked me: "What are you so irresponsible for?" I said: "I don't know!" Grandpa stated: "He's still a child!" Captain Jovo Axe fumed: "What did we invite Comrade Abas and all the other comrade delegates for?" My uncle said: "You'll have to improvise the best you can — there's no getting out of it now!" We all changed into various garish costumes, both men's and women's. Vaculić tried to encourage us: "How you look doesn't matter, it's what's on the inside!" Grandpa and my uncle fought over an old derby hat. My aunts dressed up like Hawaiians. Mom wrapped herself up in the family's flag; the star ended up in the middle of her chest; underneath the flag she didn't have anything on. When our comrades arrived — the delegates, students, as well as my best friend Voja Bloša — we all started pounding our chests and uttering lots of things we hadn't had the slightest idea about earlier. Everything we recited was unintelligible, but mainly concerned the world revolution and our role in it. Grandpa took off the hat and announced: "I shall open the door to thieves — let them steal everything that has existed in this house, which provokes boredom and other bad features!" Mom said: "I shall trample all the flowers and pull out all the grass, which is unnecessary and directly harmful in the coming circumstances!" Dad claimed: "I'll walk on my hands, if need be!" but he got tangled up among some chairs and fell on the floor, because he was drunk. Mom got daring and shouted: "I'm going to go out on the street naked, to make up for everything in my dreary and joyless life!" My aunts joined hands and said: "We're going to invite soldiers into our bed, even if they're unshaven — why, even ones who don't look anything like the heroes of famous movies!" Grandpa shouted: "We're gonna go crazy, and that'll be our salvation!" Mom added: "I'm already crazy, and that's why I'm happy the way they are in novels!" My uncle dressed up like an American millionaire, the kind who later falls into a mud puddle. Then he said: "Going crazy is like going from a lower stage to a higher one!" Dad concluded: "The crazy guys are our fellow man, that's for sure!" We said all these things very noisily, to the accompaniment of my accordion, and of Voja Bloša constantly shouting: "That's right!" Grandpa told him: "Who asked *you*?" but Vaculić demanded: "Just go on!" Our neighbor Darosava wanted to announce something, too; she kept pulling her skirt up over her head and trying intently to show us some place on her body, but Grandpa warned her: "Now you shut up!" I understood that this show was entirely ours, our family's, and that all the comrades, both the delegates and the ordinary soldiers, needed to keep quiet and listen. My uncle got up on a chair and yelled: "This is victory day for reason and all the positive inventions of the human mind over darkness and the underworld!" Grandpa bowed and said: "I'm gonna shit in the middle of this house and set it on fire!" Dad got tripped up over his tongue but still said: "I'm gonna be king and get drunk as a horse!" Voja Bloša finally managed to shout: "I'm gonna grab the first female by the tit and see what it's like!" Right away Grandpa answered him: "Beat it!" My aunts announced: "We're going to go out of our minds and later we'll write our memoirs!" My uncle said: "We're going to get killed, every last one of us, and we're not gonna be the least bit sorry!" Grandpa proclaimed: "We're going to turn to begging, and I'm gonna enjoy it!" Mom confessed: "I'm going to start whoring and donate all I earn to raising neglected orphans, which is my lifelong dream!" Grandpa concluded: "We're going to be the most famous family of all mankind, which is done for in any case!" At the end Mom said, but to herself: "I'm gonna get another headache and it won't go away for three days!"

XVII

Lieutenant Vaculić asked us: "How come you don't go and give blood, which is badly needed right now?" Mom said: "Not again!"—thinking of all the bloodshed in history! He replied: "As long as they need it!" Right away Dad stood up and announced: "*I'm* going!" Grandpa cautioned him: "They don't need alcohol!" My aunts went to the military hospital, but they both fainted; they got returned without any blood being taken. Comrade Abas reported to us: "The most important thing now is to clear the streetcar tracks and catch the enemies of the people!" Mom told him: "Our only enemies are the bedbugs, which we destroy with a spray gun!" Our secretary, Comrade Simo Tinhead, assembled us in the former Promenade movie theater and demanded: "We've got to divide up and find out who thinks what about newly emerging events!" I said: "Mom and my aunts always eavesdrop through the hole in the wall on what the neighbor lady's doing in bed, who's a whore!" He said: "There, you see!" Then he explained: "Let everybody pick out seven people of their own and follow them around closely!" We all agreed. Right away I started keeping a notebook entitled *About My Seven,* in which I decided to record statements and observations about the comrades in question, as well as a few poems on the same subject. Earlier the black cover had "Ćosić, Grocery Store, Virovitica" written on it; later I scratched this out. Mom warned: "Who said you could take your poor father's precious expense book?" Grandpa helped me out: "What good's the book when there isn't even a can of sardines left of the store?" I again started writing out the homework assigned to me by Simo Tinhead, our secretary, who was some sort of new teacher, only much more dangerous. The assignment said: "Who celebrates their patron saint's day, or wears American shoes?" Here was my solution to the assignment: "Nobody wears shoes, I wear my great-grandmother's felt ones, and Eichenbaum celebrates his patron saint's day!" Simo Tinhead started chiding me: "What patron saint can Eichenbaum celebrate, for God's sake?" I explained to him: "The day he got out of the camp alive!" He thought it over and gave his approval: "All right!" Afterward he asked me: "How are your seven coming along?" I said: "Excellently!"—although the only one I'd written about in the notebook was Voja Bloša, my only friend. Grandpa saw me underline something; he came up to me and asked: "Another dumb poem?" I said: "No, I'm keeping notes on my best friend and what he thinks about various issues!" Grandpa asked: "Who cares about that?" I said: "Simo Tinhead, the secretary!" Grandpa started pacing the kitchen; then he whammed the doorjamb so hard with his fist that everything shook: "Aren't you ashamed it's your best friend?" I ripped up a whole page about Voja Bloša and put it in the pouch, in the john.

Simo Tinhead informed us: "Tonight instead of sleeping we're going to hold a meeting about the most important issues!" First Comrade Abas started talking about the case of a shameful interpersonal event between one girl comrade and a boy comrade we didn't know; afterward he went on to an item that was called "Criticism and

Self-Criticism." The item consisted of everyone saying something about themselves, and then about everybody else; this resembled some parlor game. Everybody mainly said about themselves: "I'm stubborn." Comrade Abas kept insisting: "Go on!" but we didn't say anything. Only Comrade Kalafatović, who thought up the sketch about the soapsuds, admitted: "My father is from a petit-bourgeois family and I masturbate!" Comrade Abas said: "That doesn't matter!" We started dozing off, leaning our heads on each other's shoulders; afterward we would wake up the one whose turn it was to speak. Later the secretary made a sort of circle with a red pencil on an old map of the city. The line connected all the houses we lived in, and the secretary explained: "This is an information chain!" None of us said anything. Then he told us: "The first one informs the second, the second one the third, and so on—after that everybody knows!" We asked: "Knows what?" Kalafatović lived a little farther away, so because of him the circle bulged in one place. The secretary demanded: "Each person say some word of a secret nature to the one next to you, to try it out!" To me this resembled the game Broken Telephone, another very fine one. In that game my uncle would always think up the oddest word, which we would whisper to each other until it ended up something else entirely in the end. We had different assignments, like "culturo-educational," "ideological," "Ping-Pong," and others. Afterward the secretary would call the roll, not with our names, but just like that: "Ping-Pong!" "Musical!" "Hygiene!" We all answered, except the girl comrade in charge of hygiene was sick; the secretary recorded a dot in that place. The worst thing happened to the comrade who was called "Ping-Pong," in the Japanese style. That comrade didn't do his duty at all, because an unknown boy and girl comrade made that baby on the table meant for the game, and broke it in the process. This was all very dangerous, but fun. My uncle explained to me: "Socialism is the childhood of the human race!" Dad agreed: "That's right!" Vaculić told how they do this in Russia: "There everybody laughs!" Mom cried, but because of autumn. I kept on carrying out assignments.

Comrade Abas told me: "You better start checking out that writing in the john!" I went to the school bathroom, not for my own needs, but to ascertain whether "Long live the king!" was written there yet again or not. I shoved one door open with my foot; inside Voja Bloša was sitting on the pot and shouted at me: "Let me crap!" I went home and kept on recording various things about my stubbornness. My aunts asked me: "Is that chemistry?" I replied: "Who cares about chemistry now?" Mom thought very hard and stated: "My dear child, I just don't know!" At night then I would copy over some lists, with the names of people who were suspicious but unknown; they all had very odd names like Šonda or quite ordinary ones like Petrović.

I wore an armband; the band, which was completely red, said "On Duty." I talked about the transition from the capitalist way to the communist one, through a fight to the death. This was in geography class, instead of the lecture on the roundness of the Earth's globe, since everybody knew the part about the roundness. I made a paper model of our district with all the apartment houses, even the ones that were destroyed. I played the piano for Dragica, who performed a Russian folk dance, a wedding one. I used the spray gun for exterminating bedbugs to write the slogan "Life Is Great." I first poured the poison out of the machine, then poured in red ink. I played the second partisan in the sketch *Two Partisans*, with gunfire. I wrote a poem, "Lone Fighter," in acrostic form. I wanted to play on our Young Pioneer unit's first soccer team, but they told me: "You be on the reserves!" The leader of the soccer movement in our organization explained to me: "You may be the smartest one, but you haven't got a clue about soccer!" Grandpa tried to console me: "They're fools and thugs!" Mom said: "My poor child!" My uncle added: "What did I tell you!" Afterward they lined us up to find out our natural height and how much we had developed in the course of carrying out all the assignments; I stood on my toes a little. Afterward we sang a song about the commander hero Chapayev, who I saw live in a movie. Mom looked us over and said: "How skinny you all are!" My aunts cried. Grandpa concluded: "You burst into tears like a drunk bursts into song!" That girl comrade we discussed at the meeting regarding the broken Ping-Pong table, her stomach started to grow. Vaculić admitted: "I've kissed a lot of girls, but *this?!*" The secretary Simo Tinhead said: "I'm really amazed!" My uncle asked me: "Want me to take you to visit the riverboat captain's wife?" I answered: "I really don't know!" We also held a meeting on the question of Comrade Elias Alhalel, who had begun to show signs of insanity due to a shortage of the opposite sex. Comrade Simo Tinhead explained: "We've given you all freedom, but we can't do everything for you!" Afterward he asked: "Would one of the girl comrades be so kind?"—but none of them said anything. I led a girl comrade delegate from Prijedor through the still-unlighted streets to a certain address. There a man in glasses came out and said: "I don't have any sleeping quarters—I'm an engineer!" Afterward I took her to some tailors' place, and instead of going in she kept standing in the doorway and asking: "Honest, you've never kissed nobody?" I replied: "No!" Afterward I recounted all this; my aunts felt sorry for me and said: "How awful!" Vaculić wished we would go on to something else, so he told about an operation with an ordinary pocketknife dipped in brandy, right at the front. Mom said: "Man is like a horse when it comes to endurance!"

We left to go break the display windows of the American reading room in connection with some public demonstrations; books and pictures of Americans in uniform came falling out of the windows. I went out to shout: "Bloodsuckers of the people!"; this was at some rally. I got my sleeve torn there; my aunts did a so-so job of sewing it up and told Mom: "Prepare yourself for the worst!" She shrieked: "Did he get hit by a car?" My aunts said: "No, it's his sleeve!" I had a comrade, a Partisan courier, who talked like a Bosnian, carried a real pistol, and smoked already. There were words I didn't understand at all, like "expropriation," "ejaculation," and so on, but I acted like I knew them. Our secretary Simo Tinhead cautioned me: "That's all well and good, only don't get carried away!" The movie theaters were showing the film *A Great Life*, as well as the film *The People Are Immortal*, which was absolutely true.

Then we assembled in the gymnasium; there some shady types were getting thrown out of school because of their parents being enemies of the rest of us. We spit on them; Voja Bloša climbed up on the balcony and pissed down on them from above. Everybody said: "That's what they had coming to them!" Afterward we beat up two guys who were selling newspapers; the newspaper was called *Democracy*, but it was untrue, devious, and against everything we stood for. My uncle assaulted a girl called Rosie in the basement; she said: "Watch out what you're doing, sir!" but then gave in. Grandpa later warned me and my uncle: "When are the two of you gonna calm down?" I realized all this was getting in my way.

There was also a comrade with one leg, likewise very angry. He would ask us: "Aren't you embarrassed you've all got two legs and I only have one?" Grandpa replied: "No!" and then: "That's the luck of war—a lottery, in other words!" The one-legged comrade, who was very handsome otherwise, drank with my dad, recited some love poems with my aunts, then said: "Fucking luck!" We had the same opinion. Vaculić smiled at all this, nicely.

The comrade with one leg undid his artificial leg, threw it down next to the stove and said: "It's easy for you all to laugh!" Grandpa folded up the wooden leg, and said: "The times are like that now!" We engaged in very serious tasks, but most of all we enjoyed occupying ourselves with things like conversations, singing, reciting, and also playing completely new games. Grandpa admonished me: "You're never going to grow up!" I answered him: "Can *I* help it?" Mom tried to defend me: "He doesn't have time to!" I kept constantly trying to grow up like other people, but right off something new would happen and we'd be left the way we had been all over again.

XVIII

My secretary Simo Tinhead came rushing in and right away started bawling me out: "Where you been, you motherfucker?" I said: "Here I am!" He shouted: "While you're warmin' your ass by the stove some bums went off with all our chorus uniforms!" I said: "Can I help it? They prob'ly unlocked 'em!" Grandpa tried to console us: "They probably haven't got anything else to wear!" My comrades really did start coming to school in the chorus outfits, state-owned ones, without having anything to do with singing. I begged them: "Take those off or I'm gonna get skinned alive!" They answered me: "Everything belongs to everybody now!" Simo Tinhead warned me: "I'll sell yer family's last stick of furniture if I have to, to pay the damages!" Mom declared: "Anything but my meat grinder, I won't give that up under threat of execution!" My uncle said: "In the future, all you're gonna have that's your own is your toothbrush anyway!" Grandpa thundered: "Then you can have the fucking toothbrush, too!" Vaculić said: "All right now, it's going to work out somehow!" I suggested: "Let the ones who took the uniforms sing, and that'll be that!" Mom spoiled it all: "Even the ones with a tin ear?" Vaculić went to Headquarters and started pleading on my behalf: "It isn't his fault, honest!" They told him: "All right!"—but they didn't believe him.

Apropos of my birthday Mom told everybody else: "Let's all go together and buy him a watch or a fountain pen, which is essential for his development as a gifted person, or at least a pair of pants!" Everybody answered her: "What do we have to go together for?" Mom said: "Then forget it!" For my birthday I got a notebook with graph paper that said: "To a diligent pupil in the mathematical sciences, to help you do even better!" Mom said: "My poor kid!" My comrade David Uziel invited me: "Let's go shoot arrows at each other!" I replied: "Let's!" David shot an arrow and hit me in the forehead; afterward his mom said: "Excuse us and come have some little pastries!" Grandpa interjected: "What do we want with their pastries?" This was right at the time a major lecture was being held on "How not to lose our bearings amidst the multitude of ideas!" My forehead was bandaged up because of being hit by the arrow, but I said: "I wasn't afraid of the dark even when I was little!" The secretary Simo Tinhead told me to my face: "Yer ma prob'ly still gives yuh yer bath!" A girl comrade with braids maintained: "He isn't male *or* female, since he writes poetry!" My uncle added: "I heard that in Russia everybody writes poetry, but afterward they kill some of 'em!" Mom hugged me tight and said: "God forbid, better you be a locksmith!" My comrade Kalafatović suggested we play Germans and Partisans; the scene was filled with all sorts of choking; afterward we noticed that our clock for waking up the household—our Wecker, we called it—was gone. Mom called Kalafatović in and complained: "Here we give you our last plate of potato paprikash and you do a thing like this—who's going to wake us up now?" Kalafatović said: "I have no idea!" The girl comrade with braids told my secretary Simo Tinhead: "He kneeled down in front of me!" I admitted: "It's true I wrote her a stupid love letter which should be roundly condemned, but the kneeling part's a lie!" People started telling a lot of bad things about all of us; it was all quite dangerous but totally untrue. The neighbors gossiped: "Who knows what they're up to?" Mom reminded them: "But when we loaned you our meat grinders, then you thought we were nice!" Others said: "They've got a real whorehouse in there, only heaven knows who does what to who!" I asked Raul Taitelbaum: "Is a whorehouse a voluntary association for purposes of art and progressive thinking?" He replied: "I don't know, I wasn't in class!" Then they left us alone for a while, but then started in again: "You sing too much, that's the thing!"

I had an uncle, aunts, and a grandpa; other people also had all this. However, what got said of the others was: "They're a fine family!" but about us just: "They're scum!" We were living at the end of a great war, at the close of an occupation, at the beginning of entirely new days; we used various articles like beds, spoons, and cologne; all this was like what other people had. I don't know where the differences came from. What got said of the others was: "They've got it all!" but of us: "Vagabonds, in rags and tatters and not a penny to their name!" On the tenants' list someone wrote "lover boy" after my uncle's name, "sot" after Dad's, and "fool" after mine. There wasn't anything after Mom's name; she complained: "Poor me!" My aunts kept wondering: "What's everybody hate us for?" Grandpa took the view: "Because we get along well!" My uncle protested: "The hell we do!" We went on living in the family, as before. Then Vaculić brought Comrade Jovo Axe back again, only now he was very distrustful. Comrade Axe looked over the remains of our dining-room furniture that wasn't torn apart yet for kindling, and asked: "Whar'd you get this?" Grandpa replied: "Three hundred years ago!" Jovo Axe inspected the photographs on the walls, mounted in various frames, then wanted to know: "Who are these?" Mom replied: "Dead people, relatives from the last century!" He said, astonished: "They were all priests!" Grandpa replied: "Right!" I asserted: "At the committee they told me just to shove ahead and not worry!" Mom patted me on the head and told Jovo Axe: "He's up to his ears in work, and he eats so little!" Jovo Axe was pleased, and reassured her: "That's how the steel was tempered!" Then he thought of something and asked us: "What were you doing during the occupation, while we were still far away, on our weary horses?" Grandpa readily answered: "I made shoes out of wood and ate shit!" Mom said: "I ate my heart out!" My uncle admitted: "My friend, I better not tell you!" Jovo Axe looked at us in some astonishment and asked: "What do you know about the notorious fascist murderer Erwin Dunkelblum?" I declared: "We only know Mr. Hartmund, the pencil manufacturer, and not any other!" He went on: "Did those hardened bandits of German affiliation Deutsch and Krvinski used to come to your house?" I said: "All I know are Meinel und Herold, the makers of my portable little accordion with sixty bass keys!" Lieutenant Vaculić fidgeted in his chair, then whispered to him: "I told you so!" Axe only said: "Don't worry!" and right away asked us: "Who here did business with unfortunate Jewish souls for mercenary purposes?" Mom explained: "I made a little jam sandwich for Rudika Froelich, my son's best friend, who is dead now, when he was leaving for a camp, because I didn't have anything else!" Then a soldier appeared with some sort of papers and a pencil in his hand, and he asked: "Your occupations, but in complete detail!" Grandpa readily answered: "We live and struggle along, that's our occupation!" The soldier said: "That doesn't count!"; he tore the page out of the notebook, then left. I knew we were a family, by way of a profession, but I noticed this wasn't enough. Mom would protest: "Somebody can bang on a pot with a hammer and right away they put him down as a worker!" Afterward she would add: "I can break my back doing housework and nobody cares a whit!" Lieutenant Vaculić informed us: "This has to do with the manufacturing of merchandise that comes from a factory!" Grandpa didn't understand, and so Vaculić went on: "Merchandise is everything that's packed in boxes, like shoes, for instance!" Grandpa got mad: "Why do I have to be a shoe man?" I said: "In a book by Friedrich Engels it says that all nature is a factory that produces people by means of monkeys, and other necessary things!" Lieutenant Vaculić confirmed: "That's absolutely right!" Dad interjected: "All the things in the world have to be made by *some*body, whether it's flowers or white mice!" My aunts said: "But that doesn't mean we sit around with our hands folded!" Mom said: "We should be so lucky!" Dad interrupted again: "There's merchandise that gets manufactured without anybody noticing it, like propaganda, for instance!" Everybody went speechless; only Grandpa said: "To say nothing of getting drunk!" My aunts added: "As well as having love affairs, which doesn't leave any traces in the form of a product!" My uncle said: "What about the babies?"—at which my aunts blushed, both of them. In nature-study class we drew sketches of all the jobs in the family, like in some store. Mom told me later: "What you use your brain for—it's awful!" I said: "All we do is follow events in this kitchen like they were happening in space, or in nature!" Mom stated: "Just washing the windows, putting up cucumbers, and mending my drunken husband's pants is more than I can handle!" My uncle said: "Anyway, you don't have to go out in the rain and snow like soldiers do, for instance!"

My aunts complained: "We'll never make it into some of the progressive professions like tailoring or barbering!" Right away my uncle declared: "I can shave with my eyes tied shut, in front of everybody!" Mom claimed: "I can take Dad's old suit and make four little ones out of it for children that don't even exist!" Grandpa said: "Who's asking you to?" Lieutenant Vaculić noted: "Unfortunately, it's true!" Everybody worked in different factories, in fields and on ships. We worked in our own kitchen—in our family, in other words. That was the absolute truth. Mom maintained: "The stuff I can do with my ten fingers, you couldn't cram it all in one book!" Afterward she told us: "I often head downtown and don't know what I was going for, I've got so much to do!" Grandpa commented: "That's tremendous!" All of us were doing something, but it was taking place at home; the neighbors talked pretty scornfully about this. My talented aunts would produce little pictures of nonexistent scenes, and then, at dusk, wipe their tears with a handkerchief, for reasons unknown. My dad, at one time a Soko champion at doing handstands, kept finding ways to drink as much alcohol as possible and not show it. Mom did the best job of keeping from falling off the tall ladder whenever the kitchen got whitewashed, which she always wrote something about in the margins of a newspaper they'd already read. My grandpa would start pounding nails in various walls, even where they weren't needed at all. My uncle kept trying to shine his shoes so he could see himself in them; all this went on a very long time. I kept trying to make a man two centimeters tall that could move around using a rubber band; afterward I kept imagining this man was going to come to life. At school they would ask me: "Is it true all your family does is do the laundry and hang up photographs on the walls?" I replied: "That's right!" Then they asked me: "You all think you're so smart!" I said: "That I don't know!"

We started doing other jobs, too: Dad kept trying to sober up, Grandpa to make artificial butter, and Mom to feed us on very small pieces of bread. Family life looked like some sort of movie—exciting, unusual, from time to time utterly boring. Family life kept being reminiscent of some sort of story read earlier and forgotten, with unclear passages. Family life consisted of events; the events took place almost every day, even on Sundays. The events that happened in the family were called "life," a word used very often and only rarely understood. We all had great faith in that word, as well as in the reality that word designated. As for life, we always felt it was enchanting; other people put it this way: "What a pile of crap!" Everything we set about doing looked much better to us than to other people; we couldn't change anything there. We were a family. Within the framework of our family a whole range of human activities, humanity's trades, and tasks of overall benefit got performed, but even so in our case the most important jobs were paternal, maternal, and, in general, ones that relatives do. Almost everybody was against our jobs; only a few people spoke on our behalf and that was more out of comradeliness. I listened to all this. After it all I still think there is such an occupation as being a family, which is so laughed at. In spite of everything we remained convinced we were participating in the very important work of building a new society in an indoor, at-home, kitchen sort of way. It turned out everything there was to say about our life got said in my homework assignment on that topic. The assignment got read in front of the whole class. They laughed and patted me on the back, but at the end declared: "Baloney!" It got left at that. I had forgotten many things completely, and the rest of them were jumbled together. It turned out books have a lot more order and organization, or at least they're supposed to. Then that little man in the hat came, pulled some sort of papers out of a briefcase, a prewar, school one, and informed us: "You have to move out, into one little room, and a comrade will be coming in here with his things!" Grandpa asked: "What things?" He explained: "His own!" The comrade with the things was Jovo Axe, who admitted right away: "Well, I gotta have someplace to live, too, I guess, darn it all!" Jovo Axe carried in a big chair himself and sat down on it. The rest of the furniture started getting carried in by other men, who were unshaven and scowling a lot. The men were carrying in a former Nazi bed now unneeded by the Germans; they were in uniforms without any markings. Mom saw that one was an old family friend, and said: "Dear fellow, what are *you* doing here?" He replied: "Hello, my dear, I'm carrying in furniture as part of serving my sentence!" Later he stopped to catch his breath and told her: "Everyone has to pay, my dear, for his enemy work in the area of petty private business!" Mom replied: "That's right, dear man. Here, let me help you with that table!" Later he and the other convicts moved our things, like the piano, the cutglass goblets, the books, and the pictures my aunts had drawn with colored pencils. At the end Mom concluded: "Thank you, dear man, for packing us off so kindly to this chicken coop!" In the new little room, a very pretty one, we went on singing songs, Russian ones and others. Mom made hot brandy for everybody; I drank two gulps and right away I gave a lecture on the defenders of Leningrad, in Russian, despite no knowledge of that language.

In the little room life went on in the old way, except we were all closer to each other. With those two gulps of brandy I switched over completely to Russian as the language of communication. My aunts recollected the prewar movies *Volga-Volga* and *Rasputin, the Crazy Priest;* they started repeating the hit tunes they had heard back then, long before. Dad told them: "Bravo!" Mom kept telling everybody: "We and the Russians are soulmates!" Lieutenant Vaculić confessed: "I marvel at you all!" Grandpa said: "You needn't!" Mom spread open her arms and immediately touched both walls of the room, it was so cramped: "I'd do anything for them—they're like sons to me!" Vaculić commented: "If you just didn't have those priests in your past!" Mom said: "We can't help it!" Dad asked: "Is the Soko movement for muscle-building going to be revived?" Vaculić's very strict comrade Jovo Axe declared: "The only movement will be the movement for the liberation of humanity, and it will be enough!" We strained to get into the flow of the new organization, despite the shortage of food, the fatigue, and other under-minings of the human body. My best comrade was Voja Bloša, but there were others everybody else considered the best. Those best comrades would come to my Mom's for dinner; my aunts would teach them how to recite, how to brush their teeth, and so on. Those best comrades stuffed themselves on the beans, and afterward they would re-count: "His dad's always drunk, and he's a lousy bum and a tightwad!" Mom said: "Good riddance!" One best com-rade asked: "Who'll do my homework so I don't flunk night school?" My aunts sat down and wrote out every-thing he needed; afterward he said: "It stinks so bad at their place you could die!" Another best comrade kept asking: "If I could spend just one night at your place!" We were all crammed together, and he pinched my aunts, both of them; later he said: "Like at an orphanage!" Vacu-lić got an unsigned letter; the letter told about my family collaborating with a major enemy power, and about my aunts' immoral behavior with regard to German soldiers. Vaculić put the letter on the table; my aunts started sob-bing; Grandpa said: "The jerks!" Vaculić was quiet a while, then said: "Let's forget this!" Afterward the girl comrade in boots came in, unbuttoned her blouse, then said: "I wrote the untruthful letter — I couldn't help it!" Mom said: "God is just!" Everybody drank brandy, but it was quite weak. Vaculić asserted: "The future will be dif-ferent!" Mom asked: "Why?" My aunts sighed: "Some moments are unsurpassable, even though they're sad!" Dad concluded: "I'll have to think about that!" The girl comrade in boots asked: "Can I still come here, even though I wrote the letter?" We said: "Yes!" The girl comrade started inquiring about much of the human race's knowledge that had been completely unknown to her up to then, like about knitting, for instance. My aunts tried to teach her to crochet, to speak French, and not to tell lies. Grandpa asked: "I just don't know who she's going to talk French to!" My aunts explained: "Anybody she wants to!" The girl comrade in boots wanted to pay my aunts and the rest of us back for her newly acquired knowledge. Right away she pulled out a little yellow book by Vladimir Lenin and asked: "Who of you has read *One Step Forward, Two Steps Back?*" My uncle concluded: "That must be a tango instruction book!" She said: "No, it's not!" Dad told my uncle: "It'll be clear to you later on!" but you could see it was still muddled and confusing to *him*. All this led in a completely unknown direction, but many people liked it. I announced: "The passage from childhood into youth is like the transition from the capitalist way of life to the socialist one!" Vaculić agreed: "Something like that!" Mom said: "These times have swallowed up many young people, forever!" One girl comrade with braids asked me: "Is it true you're still a virgin?" I started telling her about my experience, of an artistic sort. Comrade Abas tried to assure me: "This won't last much longer!" From Voja Bloša I found out what I should have answered, but by then it was too late. Then Mom started boohooing. They asked her: "What's the matter?" She replied: "It's always like this in the late fall!" I never noticed the seasons. I was constantly writing poetry, sketching Russian tanks, and trying to memorize the incomprehensible Russian poem *The Young Communist League Song*. Vaculić declared: "Just so long as all this doesn't stop and boredom sets in!" Comrade Abas tried to be reassuring: "It won't!" Mom then said: "If November would just get over with, in January I'm already thinking about May coming!" Mom would say: "Today is that bad day!"

Grandpa would ask: "Which one?" With the help of her memory Mom could remind us each day of great tragedies in the past, both family ones and historical ones. She then told the story of the florist's assistant who was just getting ready for a wedding and cutting his fingernails, and one nail flipped up into his eye, which immediately started oozing.

XIX

Mom made a new pouch. It didn't have anybody's picture on it anymore, not Dad's or anyone else's. On the wall beside the pouch Vaculić's comrades wrote the happy line: "Had your hands on Dragica? Chalk one up right here!"; there was no mention of Dad. Except our neighbor Darosava came and announced: "What should I do with him—he's been sleeping in my bed for two days now like a log!" Grandpa suggested: "Let him stay there!" On the backs of family photographs Mom started writing romantic things intended for Dad, asleep in Darosava's bed, which was narrow to begin with. Dad came home, stuck his hand in his pocket, and found Mom's romantic messages there, often in the form of some sort of poem. In the poems Mom told about their mutual offspring, in other words me, and about the revolution that was changing everything for the better, at least on the surface. Dad fumed: "Who's sticking this stupid stuff in here?" Nobody said anything. Dad explained: "I no longer wish to endure the terror of the past in the form of my wife!" Mom warned: "The child'll have a nervous breakdown!" Our neighbor Darosava swore: "We don't do anything, honest, except he reads me the pornographic novel *Arleta* by Stevan Jakovljević, and I listen!" Grandpa concluded: "Aw, come on!" Dad proposed: "Why don't I take the meat grinder and the thermos bottle, and you keep the stove and the ice-cream maker!" We agreed. Darosava carried these machines over to her place, as well as Dad's expense book for 1929, not valid now. Grandpa observed: "You'll get a lot of use out of that!" Mom grabbed me by the shoulders and announced: "You don't have a father anymore!" I thought of Vladimir Ilyich Lenin, the father of the entire proletariat, but I didn't say anything.

In her coffee dregs Mom found some sort of man on horseback and a sunset, but she didn't see how to connect these two events. Mom once again began suffering from autumn melancholy. At first she said little, but later she exploded, retelling every piece of news as if fire had broken out. She would describe events that had absolutely nothing to do with us, her dreams and so on. Grandpa would ask: "Where's the fire?" Then I went ahead and admitted: "I've got a friend who stutters!" My aunts said: "That's from the war!" My uncle corrected them: "No, it's not, his father was a general, and so was his grandfather!" Vaculić agreed: "It's all up to us young people!" My aunts asserted: "In Paris they're making beautiful dresses again, like before!" Mom said: "Oh my, what a far cry we are from that!" My uncle brought home a state lottery worker who was really short and announced: "This is gonna be my third wife!" Grandpa tried to correct him: "And the ones in between?" Mom complained: "We just never seem to settle down!" The short woman maintained: "I don't take up very much space, and besides, I'll tell you what the winning number's gonna be!" Grandpa warned her: "And get us all arrested!" Mom took out Dad's photograph again and showed it to us: "He was wonderful in various gymnastic poses as long as alcohol was unknown territory to him, poor guy!" The riverboat captain's wife kept telling me: "Why don't you just make up your mind to come over? Your uncle did and I didn't bite his nose off—quite the contrary!" Comrade Vaculić tried to console us: "Just wait 'til we abolish private property!" Mom kept telling me: "If I could just patch your trousers!" My aunts said: "If a movie would just come with Beniamino Gigli when he was young!" My aunts started studying Esperanto, the language of the world revolution. Grandpa objected: "How can you say that gobbledygook all mixed up together?" My aunts made me a sweater with a stag and a five-pointed star on the front. My uncle kept asking me: "How's it going with you-know-what?" I replied: "It's not!" The short woman replied: "It's all in man's nature!" Mom told the story: "When I was young, a guy tried to take a peek at my breasts, but your father immediately threw him out of the store!" Our secretary Simo Tinhead kept telling me: "You just keep on dogging the enemies, wherever they are!" Afterward he would ask: "How's it going in your family?" I replied: "Excellently, only we haven't got room to sleep delegates from all over the country, since we're all in one room!" He explained: "It can't be helped!" I went on: "And besides that we wanted to ask where Comrade Abas is, who we never see anywhere anymore, and he was our comrade!" Simo Tinhead said: "Who is he?" I said: "Why, that comrade who kept explaining everything to us!" Simo Tinhead replied: "I haven't the slightest idea!" I also asked Vaculić: "Where's our omniscient comrade Abas?" Lieutenant Vaculić advised me: "Go everywhere and expand your horizons until you've perfected yourself completely!" I went on: "Only I don't know where Comrade Abas is!" He answered me: "Neither do I!"

Voja Bloša told me: "Your dad found a woman, but you don't know how!" I explained: "That's different!" Mom kept saying of me, to the others: "I'm afraid he'll never grow up!" My uncle told her: "It's no wonder, the way you always dressed him in pink and stupid things like that!" Mom answered him: "That was made out of my old blouse—it was all I had!" Grandpa instructed us: "Nature will take its course!" My uncle asked me: "You don't let perverts touch you, do you?" I said: "No, only the secretary Simo Tinhead said he'd like to shoot me because of those uniforms, and for other mistakes!" Vaculić reassured me: "He was just joking!" The professor from downstairs lectured me: "They've crammed you all in one little room, you clown around so much!" Mom said: "I talked straight even to that German officer who was taking me away because I didn't have my ID!" I recounted: "My uncle used to sing the song 'East and West Arise' back in '39 when it was banned!" My uncle protested: "No big deal!" I also asserted: "I never had a toy electric train!" Grandpa asked me: "So?" Grandpa showed us a very yellow photograph of his prewar gardens, vineyards, and houses with balconies, jabbed a finger at it, and asked: "And what am *I* supposed to say?" Mom showed everyone her famous picture of whipped cream getting beaten in that courtyard, as well as a picture of our store from the inside, full of all sorts of things. In the photograph Dad had a big cap on and a pencil stuck behind his ear; a salesclerk in the picture was reaching for some box, so he ended up blurry. My uncle reported to me: "You know what, your father isn't speaking to me on the stairs!" Mom said: "I'm just afraid he isn't warm enough at that hussy's place!" Grandpa tried to reassure her: "I wouldn't worry!" My uncle told us: "It's amazing, I spent so many nights at the bar with that guy, and now look!" Mom reminded him: "But what about when he won millions from that poor Nuremberg goods dealer in a card game, and gave it all back to him the next morning!" My uncle said: "Like a fool!" Mom corrected this: "That's not true—he had a heart!" Then she wondered: "Is the sea still there like it used to be before the war, when I saw it at Kraljevica and other places?" My aunts said: "Ah, ah, if street musicians would just appear again with our favorite repertoire!" Mom announced: "I've finally decided to have all the bad teeth out that have been killing me and get completely new ones instead!" Vaculić kept saying: "That's what we fought for, isn't it?"—but a bit jokingly.

My aunts recommended: "Why don't we start some parlor game and forget about everything that's happening!" Mom explained: "Many examples of a hard life have already been told about through books, but man still goes on suffering, without knowing why!" My aunts told her: "That's 'cause books are smarter than people!" My uncle's short woman confessed: "I used to think I would hate men, but I don't anymore!" Vaculić whispered to me: "If this thing turns to shit, remember it wasn't supposed to!" I promised him: "I will!" Most of all Lieutenant Vaculić loved to shove his cap back off his face and sing "My Melancholy Heart!" Vaculić was steadily losing his hair, especially because of that cap that was constantly on his head. Mom maintained: "He showed me his picture from before the war and his hair was so bushy you couldn't get a comb through it, but now look!" My uncle recalled: "Gone are the days you could swipe a whole cart full of leather right under the Germans' noses and sell it for a million!" My aunts kept saying: "If only we'd known how to use our lives for something nicer!" Mom said: "If I'd only known then . . . !" Grandpa said: "If only I had wings!" Mom concluded: "Looking back just ruins our mood—and our mental health in general!" That was the truth. Lieutenant Vaculić brought us flowers and urged us: "You've got to go outdoors, it's springtime out there!" Grandpa objected: "As if we were just sitting around!" Mom got sad: "Which means that before long the days'll start getting shorter again!" Vaculić said: "So let 'em!" Then he advised us: "You ought to exchange experience with the rest of society, which is different!" That wasn't true. The neighbors had fights, banged on the wall, and sang. Grandpa maintained: "There are crazy people over there, too, only nobody else realizes it!" Mom said: "We listen to the radio, so we know everything—we don't need anything else at all!" Grandpa added: "All we need to know we learned from our forefathers, who are dead now!" Mom declared: "It'd be easier for me to die, but instead I'm fated to watch all these awful things going on in life and around it!" Grandpa concluded: "Anything can be fixed if it still hasn't reached the final consequences, in other words—death!" Vaculić tried to encourage us: "Someday it'll have to get better!" My aunts said: "Everybody has a cross to bear, and we do sketches!" Mom kept saying: "They really do have a lot of talent!" The riverboat captain's wife told me: "See—it doesn't hurt!" Mom kept saying: "I've made everybody different pastries and knitted them sweaters and wrote the nicest verses in their albums, and they stick a wooden snake in my bed!" Vaculić explained this to her: "Find a man!" Mom went on ironing everybody's trousers; they kept calling her funny names and putting tacks on her chair before she sat down. She would chide them: "That's the thanks I get for going blind darning your socks!" But most of all they liked inviting her to play blindman's buff. During the game everybody took off their blindfolds and watched Mom feeling her way around, knocking the furniture over. Mom's favorite game was "playing drunk," which was full of stumbling. My aunts, my uncle, and everybody else participated in it. Earlier Dad had watched this rather scornfully; now it was like some sort of remembrance of him. Some things were finished, others were getting ready to start. Then Vaculić told me: "Why don't you write down everything about your family, since you've got such nice handwriting!" I asked: "How?" He explained to me: "Get each one to admit everything about themself, the comrades will like that!" I asked: "Which comrades?" He told me: "All of 'em!"

XX

We were a family, in spite of all the admonishing. Everybody else diligently sat at a shoe-repair bench or tended bar; we were the only ones that constantly hung around our little kitchen, although we didn't have any reason to. Everybody else manufactured bicycle pumps, office stamps, and shoe brushes; we were the only ones who didn't produce anything, which you could tell right away by looking at us. We were constantly saying things, in the form of a conversation, instead of being quiet and listening to other people, even if they *were* dumber than we were. Grandpa was always telling everybody a lot of things to their faces, which was absolutely wrong. Mom often cited horrible but true examples from history, instead of forgetting about those and substituting nicer ones that hadn't happened at all. Our views into the future were often much less clear because of books we had read in an earlier period, and this was our own fault, impossible to rectify. They tried to teach us it was best for the human body if we rode the streetcar standing up, didn't salt our food, and slept on a hard surface, but we just didn't believe it, even though we should have. We went on reading from thick novels, mostly unillustrated ones, instead of taking them all to the home for blind children, who couldn't get corrupted by them at all. We kept being warned not to use idiotic things from the old days, like umbrellas, toothpaste, etc., but we did it anyhow, out of spite, even though we didn't have any excuse to. We got asked to eavesdrop on what the enemies in the neighborhood were doing, but we refused to out of innate stupidity, and hence allowed this work, the enemies', to go to impossible extremes. We saw many terrible scenes of the professor man getting thrown out of the apartment one of our comrades had moved into, but the worst part was that we kept telling about it later on. Comrade Jovo Axe tried to patiently explain to us that we didn't see what we had seen, but we resisted and this kept leading to undesired consequences. We could never grasp that certain events didn't take place since they hadn't been predicted, and this was only because of our previous habit of seeing everything. Comrade Jovo

Axe tried to teach us that the only things that happen are the ones that are good to have happen, and no others, but right away Grandpa asked: "How can that be?" and thus spoiled it all. We used to think that a family of seven was worth more than one lieutenant, a young one with his arm bandaged up from being wounded, and we just couldn't convince ourselves to the contrary. Mom often watched how white bread got distributed to officers' families at a special store, and on account of that she would mention our neighbor Darosava and her whoring, which in fact didn't have anything to do with it. Many times we connected the most important things in historical development with unimportant whoring and card-playing in our neighborhood when there was no need to. I kept getting requested to write down everything Voja Bloša said in geography class and elsewhere, but all I could remember was his message to the riverboat captain's wife: "Here, take me by the tummy handle!" which didn't matter to anybody at all. I would remember very well what our secretary Simo Tinhead spelled out to us when he made assignments, but I would still hold to it the next day when the assignments had been changed completely. I asked him: "How is it Comrade Abas was our closest comrade yesterday but today he's enemy swine?" which I shouldn't have asked at all. I went on explaining everything about Comrade Leon Trotsky's life, following Comrade Abas's recommendations, even though I got told clearly and distinctly: "He never existed!" We kept remembering the worst examples from our own lives and other people's instead of going out for a walk and forgetting everything once and for all. We would often ask after various comrades who used to sit around our kitchen but later on never came back again, although we shouldn't have. Many times we got scared about big changes that happened overnight in regard to various students and their fate, but that was quite mistaken and totally unnecessary. Mom would always utter her very reckless sentence: "They're flesh and blood people, too!" but later that proved to be untrue. We maintained that many people were alike, but later we ascertained that this wasn't so, either in regard to rank or with respect to height, the size of the head or the brain inside of it. Later I realized we should have formed a commission to establish the fact of my dad's boozing, my grandpa's crazy talk, and the use of awful expressions on my uncle's part, but we didn't. Even before that I was supposed to report on all those tales of my mom's about tuberculosis and the other dastardly things in our building instead of just listening to it all without doing anything. We simply couldn't see why a bald comrade in a cap had to be handsomer than Ronald Colman on horseback, but it turned out that he did, and my aunts simply couldn't see why. We were unduly astonished when one comrade declared: "It's a good day!" and we simply couldn't grasp the grandeur of this declaration. Comrade Jovo Axe was constantly trying to convince us we should say "koferentsia" and "apateka," and we argued with him groundlessly and kept showing him what it said in a grubby book that wasn't in use anymore. We kept being urged to sing the prettiest songs we knew, but right then some important comrade of ours that we'd never heard of died, and because of that we were rightly told: "What are you yelling for when the whole country's suffering?" We thought comrades don't die, but later we turned out to be wrong. First I got asked to describe certain things that had happened in my family, but later, when it got read, I was warned: "Don't you ever pick up a pencil again, or else . . . !" Even before, I had recorded various great thoughts of my grandpa's and my uncle's, but many fewer of my dad's. Grandpa discovered these slips of paper, cut them up with the big kitchen knife, and put them in the pouch we kept paper in in the john. Mom reassured him: "Somebody put him up to it!" I kept noticing many occurrences that were happening around us, but whenever I wanted to recount them in a written composition, Mom always looked at me and said: "You haven't the foggiest notion!" I tried very hard to make my composition a kind of homework assignment on a particular topic, but then new events appeared and the thing got jumbled up. People were endlessly coming to see us, telling us what to do and then leaving. In the meantime different jobs got done around the house; some happened often, every day, others utterly rarely. All this had to be differentiated and learned by name. Grandpa would protest: "What a screwed-up madhouse!" All this used to happen before; later it kept starting all over again. Mom would complain: "How long is this gonna go on?" Nobody knew. This was what our family life consisted of, somebody asking something and the others answering or not. It was also what the contents of my homework assignment consisted of, called "Our Cursed Life in the Form of a Vicious Circle." Mom thought up the title, but the inside part was entirely mine. Mom kept adding: "Our troubles are never over!" In writing my homework assignments, which looked like some story, only an idiotic one, what mattered most was living through it, and then remembering it all, later on. As for the living-through part, that was all right, at least for now; it was the other part that turned out much harder. Lieutenant Vaculić, age twenty-three, kept saying: "Our lives really couldn't have gone any better!" My aunts agreed with this. The hardest thing for me was to keep all the names and other people straight, because of the door to our apartment, which was always open. Grandpa admitted: "Our place is like a grade school, only I don't know what's getting learned!" People kept coming and going, but then they'd come back again; we never even got a chance to take a decent walk with all these types around. Mom assured us: "Better this way than at other people's, where it's dull as a crypt!" My uncle would add: "I tell you there isn't this big of a crowd at the insurance company!" In spite of all these outside interferences Grandpa went on with his talking, Mom wiped away her tears over the autumn equinox, and my aunts poked at their needlepoint. The only thing was that the silk thread my aunts needed ran out later on. Thus my uncle's efforts at whispering in female visitors' ears were noticed the most, and Mom's efforts, that is, Grandpa's, which consisted of telling dumb things and shedding tears. We did all this in the pleasant space we got for our use instead of our six rooms, which were old and stuffy. Our rooms went to Comrade Jovo Axe, who was very tired from the wartime hardships. We also ate some sort of noodles, perfectly dry ones. We started going to visit other people to eat the same noodles and talk about politics. We were a wreck of a family with a lot of nice photographs. We lived in the middle of the twentieth century, a little before and a little after that middle. We were in the front ranks of various campaigns such as snow shoveling, literacy, and the implementation of friendship among people. We knew some people that were the finest in our country and some that were perfectly horrible. First I was told: "You're one of us—shove ahead and develop artistically speaking to the farthest limits!" Later they told me: "What are you blabbering for? Don't make us wring your neck like a canary!" I had a father who drank the largest quantity of alcohol in Central Europe in a given amount of time. We were housed in a room crammed full of things and got told: "It's plenty for you—it's *too* big, really!" I was a child a very long time; afterward all the rest began. I wore my mother's fur coat, my grandma's shoes, and over top of it all, a windbreaker from an American pilot, now dead. We lived together like some military unit. The main things in our life were drawing, cooking, and watering flowers, which also were wilted. I thought at first that babies were born by the stomach getting cut open. I thought babies were made with a little rubber hose and a pill which was kept hidden in a box that said "Death." I thought that after freedom was established, alcoholic drinks would stop being sold. I hoped I would learn to play the violin, but I didn't. I had parents who said "Pussy-cat!" to each other at the beginning, but later on "Damn you, you bastard!" I was shown pictures of a female body getting used, but I didn't believe it. Our secretary Simo Tinhead kept telling me: "Yer grubby books are one thing, but real-life events are somethin' else again!" We saw pre-war officers, German soldiers, Partisan commissars, and Russian tank crewmen. Before the war my dad had a Soko uniform, but that was another matter. I dreamed I had won a toy car with pedals, but when I woke up I saw that reality was different. Plumbers, piano tuners, university students, and Lieutenant Vaculić, my comrade, all came through our apartment. All this was earlier; later some-thing different started. Mom kept asking me: "Why can't you go on being a child?" I replied: "I don't know!" Voja Bloša asked me: "Are those your first long pants?" I replied: "Yes!" At the beginning everything was clear and simple, but afterward more and more confused and inex-plicable. Many people used to come and visit us, later just a few. At the beginning I knew only a few names, but afterward almost all of them. I don't know how long all this goes on. My uncle asserted: "These are powerful mo-ments!" My uncle changed professions twenty-seven times, not counting the most important one—ladykiller. My uncle kept count of the women up to five hundred, then stopped. Mom counted up her Alexanderwerk-brand kitchen appliances; Grandpa counted and recounted the matches in one box, a very small one. This was all in a big turmoil. It was in a pandemonium of some sort, but this is how it was. Like this, or even worse.

■ □ ■ □ ■

RUSSIANS BY TRADE

IN 1936 IVAN PONOMARYOV, A BANDLEADER, WENT BERSERK and murdered four members of his band, and then hanged himself. The same year Yasha Sevitsky, an unemployed engineer, built a stove that would burn worthless, useless stuff — that is, shit. The Russian Cossack general Pavlichenko, in utter defeat, fled from the Soviets into our country, on a horse, and gave lectures about it all; the horse later died. At about the same time Lidia Przhevalska, for whom another horse was named, from the nature-study course, fell under a streetcar, because her nerves were frayed. All these events happened in our country, and yet they were carried out by foreigners, members of the émigré community — Russians. Grandpa protested: "They're all we need!" We had two names for all the bugs around the house: the black ones we called Krauts and the yellowish ones Rooskies; the Krauts were always bigger.

I had friends named Rudika Froehlich, David Uziel, Isaac Abinum, and so on, but there were other ones, too, like Nikita Gelin, Lonya Bondarenko, and Igor Chernevsky; this last one wore glasses. Nikita Gelin had a woman's blouse that buttoned on the side. At his house we drank tea out of a saucer; Mom said: "Heaven forbid!" but I thought it was great. I called Nikita by his name; everybody else called him "Roosky goose!" My friend Igor Chernevsky showed me a notebook; in it someone had written: "I might kill myself!" I asked: "Is that out of a novel?" He said: "No, it's out of here!" and pointed to his heart. Then he asked me: "Haven't you ever thought of killing yourself?" I answered: "Never!" My friend Igor Chernevsky walked along the ledge outside the sixth floor with his arms outstretched. His mom fainted. Voja Bloša admitted: "I wouldn't dare!" Lonya Bondarenko's mom wore big hats, frightful brooches, and dresses that were really gaudy; Grandpa said: "She's gonna poke somebody's eyes out with those pins!" My aunts marveled at her style, but still they declared: "A dog wouldn't have anyplace to bite her!" Lonya Bondarenko's mom suffered from a great shortage of money; all the same, she smoked through a long cigarette holder and was always saying: "Ooo-oo-oh-h!"—which was the best Russian word of all. My aunts asked her: "Is it possible we might some day see the famous and handsome Nijinsky who dances *Swan Lake* and is crazy?" Lonya's mom only smiled, sadly, and immediately started explaining how to make butter by shaking spoiled milk. We marveled at all this, but Mom later said: "If she just weren't so vain, and besides, she never takes a bath!" My aunts objected: "Russians are very fine people, such as Mr. D. M. Kuzmichov and sons, the tea merchants." Dad got carried home by a baggage porter and put down on the couch; he mumbled something and smiled, gently. Grandpa declared: "He's dead drunk!" but Mom put it differently: "He's drunk as a Russian!" My aunts asked: "When are we gonna go hear Olga Yanchevetska, the Russian café singer, perform with a flower in her hand?" Mom replied: "We don't need anybody else hanging out at those joints!" She was referring to my dad, of course, which everybody understood right away. My uncle explained: "I know Miss Yanchevetska-Azbukin personally, and also a lot of girls she teaches who sing excellently in Russian even though they're from our country!" My aunts told him: "Nobody can keep up with you!" My uncle brought home a little book called *Zosya, the Pretty Russ-*

ian Girl; it had a lot of drawings that were excellent but absolutely forbidden. My friend Isaac Abinum stated: "I think Russian women know how to take their clothes off better than anybody in the world!" There was another forbidden book, *The USSR in Words and Pictures,* that showed a big tank going over a little Finnish house; my aunts kept this book behind the stove; because of this the tank was a little yellowed. Then Lonya Bondarenko's mom offered to make us a lampshade, an amazing gadget for lighting up an area very cheaply. Grandpa concluded: "That's so you don't see how dirty their place is, since it's half dark!" While the movie *The Mannerheim Line* was being shown, an usher came out holding a flashlight and said: "Don't anybody shout 'Long live the Russians!' or you're gonna get arrested right away!" In the same movie when Finland was being liberated by big Russian tanks all the Russians were in white lab coats and were very large, but the Finns were quite small. Of all the Russians in that film the one I liked best was Joseph Stalin, who was always smoothing down his mustache as if he had just eaten. I thought everybody in Russia had a mustache and ate food that was rich and greasy. Stalin also smoothed down his mustache during the best newsreel in artificial color, with Mr. Ribbentrop, a German general who came to Moscow to shake hands with all the Russians. Grandpa warned me: "I'm not gonna let you watch that nonsense!" Then Lonya Bondarenko's mom tried to plant a love in us for raising flowers, which we didn't need then. She also showed us a thick book called *Vegetable and Flower Gardening* by L. Muratov, which said: "The blossoms are blue. They blossom in June!" Right away my aunts said: "That's a poem!" My mom said: "What I care about is having spinach and leeks to feed my child—forget about your chrysanthemums!" Lonya Bondarenko's mom found a picture in the book entitled "Pearl Leeks" and pointed it out, but my mom stuck to her opinion. Lonya's mom finally said:

"*Nichevo!*" and it ended there. Right at that time my aunts learned to perform two Russian songs, to a guitar: "Those Green Eyes of Yours" and "East and West Are Red," both of them sung while crying. Grandpa asked them: "You have a pain somewhere?" The way I understood it, all Russian singing signified some ailment, like a cold or maybe worse. Every time Mom told the depressing story of the Russian countess who was seduced by the cavalry junior sergeant and jumped in front of a train, she would say: "Life is sad, especially for women, Russian women!" Undoubtedly this was out of some book, too. My uncle asked: "Then what do you throw Mrs. Bondarenko out for when the woman wants to show you how to crochet?" Mom replied: "What's it to you?" Afterward she told him: "You want to catch some Russian disease!" but nothing like that happened. Voja Bloša only asked me: "If you know Russian, then what does '*Davaj spičku da zakurim*' mean?"* We could have asked Igor Chernevsky about this, but we didn't. Igor went on hovering up there in the air, going along the ledge like he was sleepwalking. I realized that every Russian's life was full of dangers but was utterly unthinkable without them. Lonya Bondarenko's mom confirmed this over and over again by sighing a lot in the presence of my uncle, whose hair was always smoothly combed. Lonya's mom came to see us many times and offered to do us some favor or other, but my mom usually turned her down. Lonya's mom offered to make something useful out of silk, but mostly she watched my uncle, who was reading a book. My uncle kept interrupting his reading and saying something inaudible to Lonya's mom; afterward Lonya's mom would run to the door and stand by the wall, breathing heavily. I noticed that Russian women mostly run out, stand out-

---

*A bastardized version of "Got a match?" It sounds off-color in Serbo-Croatian. — Trans.

side the door, and breathe, very heavily. At one time it appeared that our whole life depended on the Russians who lived in our neighborhood and knew about everything. I am referring to their reports on various appliances and flowers, and also this thing about the breathing. All the Russians had famous names; some of them were made up. In our neighborhood there were four would-be daughters of Nicholas the Second, who had been sawed in half, and twenty-seven countesses. Their names all ended in "ov" or "ski"; they knitted shawls and crocheted and things like that for a living. Lonya Bondarenko's uncle could multiply any two numbers together from memory; his name was Lebedev but nobody believed him. Lebedev worked at a bank, while Nikita Gelin's dad was the best one at making artificial letters out of lead at a print shop. We used the Russian word *kvalifikovani* for all of them; this got on my mom's nerves most of all because she didn't think it was a real word. At that time I thought being a Russian was some sort of trade, one of the most important ones. In any case, the Russians were similar to my dad, my uncle, and everybody else, except that they wore glasses, kept looking at the sky, and pretended they were sad. Russian people and our people were very similar in their drinking, swearing, and their particular love of one sex, the female one. The Russian language was similar to ours, only it was stretched out in some places. Russians talked the same as our people do, only when they're drunk. All this was very exciting for us, especially my aunts. They kept complaining: "Why weren't we born Russian?" Mom tried to explain to them: "Right now you wouldn't have any bread to eat!" They replied: "So what!" This was when Lonya Bondarenko's mom taught my uncle how to write the old Russian letter "Ъ," with a little hook. She admitted: "It doesn't exist now!" I concluded from this that when Russians talk they use letters that don't exist, and that none of us except my uncle knew what they were.

RUSSIANS BY TRADE

In 1937 the would-be countess Yevdokia Krutinska asked us to sign some paper she needed in order to get a job with a steamship company. Dad signed it, but the countess still didn't get the job. She stayed home and took care of nineteen cats, and then would come to visit us with thread and hairs all over her coat. Grandpa protested: "Just so I don't find a cat hair in my soup!" In 1942 the countess brushed off her coat, put a swastika on her hat, and announced: "We are occupiers, too!" Grandpa recalled Ribbentrop, who shook hands in Moscow, and asked: "Is this because of him?" but nobody answered him. In 1942 Mom nevertheless said, in a hushed voice: "God bless the Russians and their cavalry!" My uncle asked: "What?? After all your talk about how Mrs. Bondarenko hangs her laundry in her room and never changes clothes?" Mom replied: "You're lucky you don't understand!" I noticed that the Russians suddenly became great in spite of the fact they dried their laundry in their room, on a string. Lonya Bondarenko's mom kept on coming to visit us, but didn't offer to do much. My aunts looked into her eyes and complained: "If we could only be that sad!" Mom tried to explain: "That's because the poor wretch doesn't have a husband!" Grandpa told them: "You always have to be nonsensical!" Lonya Bondarenko's mom really did keep looking mournfully at one spot, nobody knew what for. Dad claimed: "I've heard that every Russian drinks like a pig and then cries like a baby!" Mom said: "They've prob'ly got some reason to!" My aunts said: "It's because nobody understands them!" Lonya Bondarenko's mom would often start telling something, then change her mind and stop. Grandpa said: "They all keep wanting one thing and another, and that's how they spend their lives!" I also noticed that Russians would do something and later regret they'd done it. That's the way it was with my friend Igor Chernevsky, and with Nikita Gelin—the one where we drank tea out of saucers—and with Lonya Bondarenko's mom, who was so nervous. Grandpa warned: "Each nation has some direction it's going, but them—God forbid!" Even before then some students had told us: "All people are brothers, but the Russians are our biggest brothers!" Grandpa said: "How can that be?" I asked: "Is it because of those tanks that knock down a Finnish tree in that one movie?" The students advised me: "Forget that now!" My uncle said: "That's right, we saw that at the Casino Theater, where they had tables!" The students said, kind of severely: "We're still gonna be one of their republics—the best one, too!" Mom concluded: "The poor masses!" Mom herself noticed everyone was constantly talking about sad things in Russian life and our own. So she announced: "I'd just like to know what I'm going to die of and be able to see it like in a glass!" Grandpa answered her: "And that's enough?" Later Mom said: "I envy anybody that falls asleep and never knew he was alive!" She thought that by doing this she was sharing the serious mental illnesses our Russian neighbors had, but this wasn't so. My aunts kept constantly trying to cheer up Lonya Bondarenko's mom, but then they remembered such bad things out of novels, which were also Russian, that they themselves began to cry. Mom finally took pity on Mrs. Bondarenko and asked: "Could your brother show my son a little mathematics? He's stupid as a horse in it!" Lonya's mom gave a short answer: "*Da!*"

When Lebedev, who was once a refined gentleman from the field of banking, arrived at our place, Grandpa commented: "What can he know if his elbows are worn through?" My aunts said: "They're all that way!" Lebedev started trying to explain the secret of the square of the hypotenuse to me, but he gave up right away and started singing "Ah, Woe Is Me!" Everybody hummed along with him, almost inaudibly. Dad's heart melted and he said: "There's a good one!" My dad never drank more alcohol than when he heard Mr. Lebedev the mathematician sing "Ah, Woe Is Me!" So the work on mathematical science stopped, completely. Grandpa agreed with this. He said: "Who cares how much three workers drink in six days if they drink five bottles of beer apiece, and other stupid things?" I myself noticed that arithmetic problems take the worst examples from human life, except in the end they draw a line under it all and add it all up.

Later, Lebedev got his sister to show us a ballet figure she had learned from Madame Nina Kirsanova, the queen of this art. Lonya Bondarenko's mom lifted one leg up very high, way up in the air. She looked like a compass opened up wide; it was as if this were also in honor of mathematics, that very neglected science. Everybody was dumbfounded. Lebedev said: "*Nu, vot!*" and pushed his glasses into place.

This story ends in October of '44. We went down on the street to see the Russian tank crews who were smiling from the turrets of their big iron machines as they went by. The soldiers on the tanks were eating bread and jam—black, plum jam, and their ears were all smeared with it. People looked at the friendly faces of the tank men from Kuibyshev smeared up with jam, and also at the would-be countess Yevdokia Krutinska, who was up on this machine, too. The countess had replaced her swastika with a very large hammer and sickle; Grandpa said: "There's that woman again!" It was then that Lieutenant Miron Stepanovich Timiryazev, aided by vodka, the highly valued Russian drink, walked the whole length of Queen Natalia Street on his hands. Dad immediately announced: "He's my man!" Dad and Timiryazev sat and sat at the table, a very long time; the Russian kept telling Dad: "You are my friend, my friend are you!" Later he vomited a lot into his sleeve, so it wouldn't be noticed. Here's how it sounded: "Bwah!"

Then Lonya Bondarenko's mom started staring at the many people who were going past our building, both the ones on the tanks and the other ordinary ones, with the rifles over their shoulders. Lonya's mom took off her hat and lay down in front of the biggest tank; no one riding on it noticed a thing. My mom later asked my uncle, crying: "I didn't even know her name!" My uncle replied: "Neither did I!" This all confirmed that every Russian remembers everything he ever did in his life and then later, at the end, adds one more thing to it, like a punishment of some sort. Russian women especially.

THE ROMEO'S TRADE—
A MAJOR ONE

MY UNCLE BEGAN TO COUGH IN '43, IN THE FALL. HE SET HIS water glass up high on the buffet and told me: "Don't you touch it!" Mom said: "Just so he doesn't start spitting up blood!" Right off she started listing all the awful TB cases she had seen on a visit to the Živković sanitarium. Then she said: "Poor devils, even when they do get a winter coat they can't wear it, they're so weak!" My uncle lazed in bed in his little room and hummed: "I'm feeling fine!" Neighborhood girls started going into the room and saying: "Here's some bread and butter for our patient!" Grandpa asked: "Where'd you get that?" Mom warned Grandpa: "Shush!" My uncle would bolt down the badly needed food, which was from before the war, and then demonstrate the trick where you take a piece of toilet paper and poke a hole in it to stick a finger through. The girls were completely enchanted. Mom asked them: "Aren't you afraid of getting infected?" They said: "No!" Mom said: "I'm going to ask the doctor man if you should be coming to see him at all!" My uncle told the girls about his dangerous work as a conductor on the Zagreb streetcar, and about Fanika Ilerova, an actress he was also acquainted with. Later he claimed: "I personally saw Mr. Konjović, the greatest member of the prewar upper class, sitting on the terrace of the Hotel Esplanade and drinking liqueur with two young ladies, Beba Prpić and Branka Rot, both of whom were wearing silk stockings!" The girls clapped their hands: "You don't mean it!" My uncle kept coughing, eating 100 percent white bread spread with butter and honey, and showing everybody an obscene little toy he had made himself. The toy was supposed to be a man ten centimeters tall, one part of whom was unnaturally large; moreover, this part could move—upward. All the women squealed, I didn't know what for. Mom screamed: "Not in front of the child, hide it under the covers!" and then, much more softly: "Damned war!" Later my uncle went ahead and put his toy into operation under the covers, but by then they'd already thrown me out of the little room for good. My uncle knew how to make other movements with his hands, too, such as the one with the pointer finger under the nose. I knew this was forbidden, too, but by whose side I wasn't sure. Right then a waitress came in and pointed to my uncle: "He makes a baby, then acts like he's crazy!" My uncle said: "I've never laid eyes on her before!" Dad said: "That doesn't mean a thing!" Mom first asked: "Who is the young lady, if I may ask?" and then afterward: "Don't you see he's at death's door?" The waitress slammed the door and shouted: "Have it your way!" There was no mention of any dying. My uncle kept on eating the excellent food from the neighbor girls and women, and his color improved; he played dirty songs using a comb and cigarette paper, and then he started repairing watches, very small ones. First he took apart our neighbor Darosava's watch, washed the tiny parts in gasoline, then put it back together again. He did this using a magnifying glass that he held up to his eye, very adroitly. My uncle complained: "If I just had tweezers!" My aunts said: "We're not giving you ours—we need them for our eyebrows!" Darosava was in my uncle's room a while; some squeaking and other shouts could be heard in there; Grandpa said: "That's his tweezers!" Mom immediately started singing an operatic aria and threw herself into window washing — the kitchen window. Darosava came out of the little room, pushed her hair back with her arm, and announced: "Works like new!" Grandpa replied: "Obviously!" After that the police clerk's daughter came and said: "Could he repair the alarm clock that wakes my father up to go to the police station?" Grandpa said: "That'll be a snap for him!" Later the clerk's daughter was also in my uncle's room for a pretty long time; they told me: "Get your roller skates and go outdoors, only don't fall under a streetcar!" My uncle fixed all the clocks in the building, both the small ones and the very biggest ones; Mom waited for my uncle to finish work on a clock belonging to a bookkeeper who was now a prisoner of war, and then she whispered to his wife: "Not you, too? The wife of a proud bank clerk who is rotting away behind barbed wire?" The banker's wife answered: "Mind your own business!" They sent me out to buy half a liter of vinegar, which they didn't need at all. I was always having to go buy something at the grocery store, so I never did see my uncle finish any of his repair jobs. My friend Voja Bloša told me: "Boy, does he fleece 'em!" I said: "How do you know?" Dad kept asking: "Who knows how he fools them?" Grandpa answered: "Ordinary dirty tricks!" Dad went on pondering: "The only thing is I don't know what he tells them first!" Mom said: "Why should you care about that?" I grasped that only my uncle was allowed to work with clocks, because of his illness, of course. Dad hung around the kitchen, heard what was going on in my uncle's room and later said of him: "What a Romeo!" I asked: "Is a Romeo somebody who fixes things?" Right away Mom sent me out to split wood for kindling, but she said: "Just don't chop your finger off with the hatchet, or all I did'll be in vain!"

At this same time Nikola, our relative in the shoemaker's profession, started coming to visit my aunts. He sat with them at the dining-room table and kept whispering something to them, pretty quietly. This seemed to me to resemble my uncle's watch repairs, but I didn't understand why. Nikola kept constantly pulling slips of paper of some sort out of his pockets and showing them to my aunts; after that he performed the famous botanical trick involving the cutting of an apple. He picked up the apple ceremoniously, respectfully, and cut it across; a five-pointed star made out of seeds appeared on the surface, like a sign of freedom—a natural one, no less. We all were amazed. Nikola said: "It's nothing—there's a star in every one!" Mom asked: "Is this punishable?" but nobody answered her. There was another trick that had a star in it. On a plate Nikola made a five-pointed star out of toothpicks that were broken in the middle. From his pocket he took a lemon, a very rare fruit, and squeezed drops out of it onto the plate. Those precious drops made the star broaden and swell up; we all burst into applause, but quietly. Grandpa started muttering: "He'll drive them completely mad!" Mom wiped away a tear and said tenderly: "Let him!" Nikola continued to visit, but he always looked behind himself on the steps. He would haul in all sorts of mysterious books like *Sacred Misfortune, San Michaele,* and the nicest one of all, the book about Jussi Björling, the Scandinavian revolutionary. Nikola sat with my aunts clear till dusk, showing them pictures of some sort; later I saw one such photograph of a man on horseback with a flag above his head. Grandpa complained: "When are they going to lay off these pornographic things?" Mom asked him: "What do you think's the matter with them?" Just in case, though, she took me into another room and showed me how to draw an elephant, even though I'd known how for a long time already. I was sure somebody was making some sort of love here, too, except I didn't know who was doing it with whom, or why. Especially because Nikola was very cautious and would immediately climb into the clothes closet as soon as someone rang the doorbell. A man from the ground floor came in carrying a poker. He asked Grandpa: "Where is that bum?" Dad addressed him politely enough, even though his tongue was tangled from alcohol: "Say there, fellow, friend, brother, and neighbor, let's not be that way!" The man with the poker was trembling: "How dare he grab my daughter's tit?" Mom tried to explain: "It's a terrible misunderstanding!" The man said: "Don't let it happen again, or there'll be blood!" Mom asked: "Isn't there enough of that on every front?" The man said: "No!" My aunts rashly added: "But all he did was fix the spring on her kitchen clock!" Again the man lunged at the clothes closet, shouting: "He's in here!" Out of the closet came Nikola and said: "They haven't done anything wrong, you have my word on it!" The man looked dumbfounded at Nikola, who was holding an apple cut in half; then he said: "Who's asking you?" I screamed: "He's a hero of the underground front!" but right away I got a punch in the nose. Everybody went speechless. Then Grandpa asked the man: "What do you think, how are we going to get rid of the Krauts?" The man put down the poker and left, dejected.

Later the daughter of the man with the poker came back, very out of breath. She didn't say anything, but only breathed heavily, walked by the closet, which was now empty, and rushed into my uncle's room so she could look at him. My uncle asked: "What do you see in me?" She answered: "I don't know!" My uncle went on: "I'm not right for you, since I'm so sick and you're as fresh as the dew!" First she said nothing, but then she did say: "That doesn't matter!" My uncle brazenly told all the women: "Leave me alone!" after which they breathed even more heavily and kissed his hands, over and over. My uncle was constantly amazed: "Why me, when there are so many others?" Dad protested: "Fools have all the luck!" That's how that went.

Later Darosava ran in and reported to us: "Here they come!" Policemen shoved their way into the kitchen and immediately began threatening: "Where is he?" First the policemen opened the closet where Nikola had been earlier, but they didn't find anybody. Mom stood in the doorway of my uncle's room and stated: "Better you should kill me!" The policemen shoved her out of the way; my uncle was lying in his room with the wife of the bank clerk who was now a prisoner of war. The policemen asked him: "Aren't you ashamed of yourself?" He replied: "Why?" The policemen started rummaging through my uncle's things, and they combed through the drawers with the watch-repair tools, shouting: "Where are the weapons?" My uncle, who was still naked, asked: "Is this it?" The bank clerk's wife covered him up with the quilt. The policemen found a lot of photographs of naked black women and a man who had a top hat on his stomach, even though he wasn't holding it with either hand. The policemen said: "We are requisitioning this!" At first I thought my uncle's work, which was fun and full of giggling, also had its dangers; this was true, but only partly. The policemen left, laughing.

In '44 I had already written my famous poems "Why Is the West on Fire?" and "The Swallow," devoted to the sunset and the migration of birds to warmer regions. In spite of my youth, people began to regard me as a poet, given the many similar attempts on the part of my aunts — failed ones. I would sit at the kitchen table and describe everything that was going on around me; Mom asked: "Where am I going to chop onions when you've ensconced yourself this way?" I wrote with a Hartmund pen — a prewar ink one; later it was just impossible to get it repaired. My aunts begged me: "Write about Errol Flynn and make him a pirate, since he's our idol!" My uncle asked me: "Can you write me a few words for that little hairdresser Rosie?" Finally Nikola arrived and whispered to me: "You could think up fancy words for a proclamation, since God gave you the talent!" I immediately rejected the topic of pirates and Errol Flynn as stupid; the other thing I tried to write without any rhyme, in the form of an article, with passages inserted in it about love. The neighbors kept threatening to pour club soda in Nikola's eyes; however, they frightened my uncle with something much worse—the police. I grasped the similarity in the secret doings of my uncle the self-proclaimed watch repairman and Nikola, the expert at playing with a lemon. In '44, in the fall, I tried to describe every example of secret love forbidden by the police as well as by other people—deceived husbands, angry fathers—in short, by neighbors. I wrote about the fearless heroes of the mysterious trade of the Romeo, which wasn't entirely clear to me but was very nice. About the way they all lie in bed, naked, and hold some kind of flag that the enemy shoots at. Grandpa helped me by declaring: "This is the whorehouse of history!" and such. I admit that I myself didn't entirely understand what I had written on the flour sack that had been emptied and then ironed a bit.

A week later, bareheaded Germans in retreat raped a little neighbor girl, in the courtyard, in front of everybody. Three weeks later, the Russians came into the city on tanks, smiling, happy, and swearing. Three months later, my uncle took me to visit Rosie, the hairdresser, who showed me the parts of her body and what they were used for. After several years I came to understand almost all the words I had written in my famous proclamation of a patriotic nature, in the great year of the Romeo, '44, in the fall.

■ □ ■ □ ■

US AND THE ELECTRICIANS

MY FAMILY, WHICH LIVED IN THE MIDDLE OF THE TWENTI-
eth century—which was filled with wars, a revolution,
and other universal human events—respected all the elements of nature, like water, air, and so on, but most of all
we counted on an artificial force of an electrical nature,
that is to say, electricity. My uncle tried to explain: "Electric current flows like water through a wire that's in the
walls!" Grandpa immediately said: "Don't lie like that!"
Mom added: "Really, though, why don't we hear it when
it flows?" Dad informed us: "I know a man who can cure
all kinds of illnesses by using electricity, only you have to
grab hold of a doorknob!" Grandpa said: "Nobody could
get me to do that!" My uncle said: "The only time I feel a
current in my heart is when I get my hands on a sexy
babe!" Mom lamented: "We know how to repair everything in the house that needs fixing, only not the electricity—not on your life!" One of my aunts said: "Death from
electricity is the worst kind, because the person turns all
blue and doesn't know what's what anymore!" And the
other aunt said this: "I feel electric current when I accidentally bump my elbow!" Mom explained: "I used to
think: if only my son doesn't become a judge and have to
dispense justice and death, but now I pray God he won't
touch electric current and other things that could cost him
his life!" Grandpa said: "I suppose he isn't crazy!" My

uncle told my mother: "Didn't you see how Ljudevit Durst the repairman always stands on a board to insulate himself?" Dad added: "Or else they use some trick that only they know!" Mom said: "The worst thing to me is, I never know when it's going to strike me, since my hands are always wet from washing dishes and doing the laundry!" I declared: "In school we studied about electricity using a drawing nobody understood!" Grandpa answered me: "So much the better for you!" Dad said: "I'll bet you I can take hold of a wire with my bare hand and nothing'll happen to me!" Everybody shrieked: "Don't!" Dad insisted: "I dare to do things that people much smarter than me don't!" Dad climbed up on the sewing machine and began to unscrew the lightbulb. He said: "Now I am going to stick my finger in the socket!" First we started grabbing him by his legs, but then Grandpa screamed: "If you hold on to him you'll be killed, too!" We all got away from him fast and into the corners of the kitchen; Dad stuck his finger in the electric outlet, and nothing happened to him. Grandpa concluded: "That's because of the alcohol!" All this was in '44, at the end of the war; electricity, the voltage of Hitler's Europe, where we too were located, had weakened greatly, and the secret and unknown elemental force that flowed through the wires didn't so much as scorch my courageous daddy.

Then the electricity was turned off completely, and we started burning prewar candles that we had taken the little saints' pictures off of, which were absolutely useless now. Even in the impenetrably dark night we could still make out the movement of history, the horse cavalry of that history, and the men on those horses. My uncle said: "Those are the Russians!" Grandpa said: "Surely there are Serbs, too!" Everybody kissed each other. Mom whispered: "It's like some sort of current is going through me!" Lieutenant Vaculić came into the cellar carrying a lantern. My aunts said: "There's the light of the new era!"

No one was even thinking about the movement that used to flow like water through wires in the walls. The wires had been yanked out and used to tie up naked Germans in the courtyard. Afterward they were blown to bits by a little bomb. Some bits of the Germans were left hanging on a wire, along with an electric switch that had been forgotten. My uncle declared: "Even in the dark we'll find our freedom, won't we?" The soldiers warned him: "Don't get carried away!"

All this is a story about electricity, a force none of us had any notion about. It all happened in '44, a year with many events, which were often completely incomprehensible. Lieutenant Vaculić noticed our perplexity and explained to us: "The point is that the current of the new life, the source of that current, will take us in the direction of all that is positive!" Mom added: "If someone could just put a stop to the accidents during repair jobs!" Everyone told her: "Are you really still in doubt?" She said: "Yes!" That's how it was left.

This was supposed to be a story about Victor Merta and Miloš Obušković, who were electricians and experts at making repairs, but it's not. I used to think of electricians who come and replace a shorted wire in five minutes as some sort of magicians, but this story doesn't have any of those. Instead, the story has my dad, my mom, and my grandpa, as can be seen. They weren't all that skilled in things of an electric nature, but they did succeed in entering into the current of the era—high-voltage, gleaming, and very dangerous. Many times it happens that a story starts about one thing but turns out to be about something else. This is such a case.

■ □ ■ □ ■

OUR EMBROIDERERS

WHEN THE WAR BEGAN, MY FAMILY WAS LIVING ON THE fourth floor of an old building; from then on we just stayed there. In the vicinity, right in our neighborhood, lived people of various occupations — waiters, carvers of official seals — tradesmen, in short. My uncle tried to count them up, but he couldn't, so he switched to adding up his conquests in love; meanwhile, the people went on doing their various jobs, many of them completely unnecessary. Grandpa asked: "Where do they get the money to run a store nowadays?" Mom said: "What's a girl trying to prove, sitting and doing embroidery called azure-plissé?" Grandpa asked: "What on earth is that?" My uncle answered: "That's when they embroider a monogram on my shirt so it can't be stolen!" Grandpa said: "I don't know who's stopping 'em!" Mom recalled: "I used to have something embroidered on every dress, but now there isn't a thing!" Grandpa told her: "Be glad you aren't naked!" In '43 the job of embroiderer of expensive dresses, women's dresses, seemed to be long gone, yet in our neighborhood we had Miss Flora, who was red-haired; all this could be seen on her sign — both her hair and her name. Grandpa asked: "What do they have foreign names for when it's all a lie?" Mom answered: "Her husband was French, before he left her, the beast!" Grandpa continued: "How can she sit and keep scratching with that needle?" Mom explained:

"One time when I was there she stood up and showed me her leg that was cut off by a streetcar!" In '43 very few women from our neighborhood went to Miss Flora to get their dresses decorated; all the same, she kept on sitting and pricking something with a needle, mainly because of the tragic event with her leg that we hadn't known anything about before. My aunts said: "We can do a little needlepoint of Lake Bled any time we want, but a monogram—now that'd be a lot of trouble, for sure!" Grandpa said: "It's good you admit it!" At the beginning of the occupation German junior sergeants kept coming to Flora's and saying: "You make voman's name for us!" This went on a while, but then it stopped. My uncle started saying: "Better if she switches to making Russian five-pointed stars!" Grandpa warned: "Yes, and get herself bumped off!" Dad added: "Well, she's a fake anyhow!" My uncle said: "You know, sometimes gals with a leg like that are the best ones at you know what!" Mom shrieked: "God forbid!" It was '43, a pretty weird year, a war year; in school they told me to embroider my name on a piece of cardboard! Grandpa screamed: "They want to turn you into a milksop!" Mom protested: "I don't have enough thread to mend your trousers, much less for that sort of foolishness!" My uncle explained: "When I was little, a sewing machine needle went rat-a-tat-tat through my finger, and afterward I could hardly get it out of the bone!" Dad commented: "A Russian machine gunner has started rat-a-tat-tatting over our roof, do you hear him?" This last thing was absolutely true. Then the machine gunner shinnied down the downspout and said: "*Zdravstvuite!*" Mom promptly started to mend his sleeve where a German shell had gone through it. My uncle announced: "Now we'll kick Hitler's ass and sew things up once and for all!" The Russian said: "Rrright!" Men jammed into Miss Flora's shop, shouting: "That floozy that knitted sweaters for the Krauts, we're gonna fuck her mother!"

She asked: "What sweaters?" What they threatened the mother with, they did to the daughter, that is Miss Flora, personally. They said: "We didn't know she's only got one leg, but she's still great!" My uncle said: "What did I tell you?" Women came to pull apart the unfinished embroideries and steal the expensive floss made in England before the war. The floss was called DMC; all this was incomprehensible, but of great value and excellent for stealing. Miss Flora began to die in the evening; in the morning people said: "They really hollowed her out, poor thing!" Somebody said: "They could have sewed her back up!" Mom said: "Poor wretch, if she'd known what was going to happen to her, she wouldn't have sat in the corner all her life!" Then she added: "Or maybe she would have!" In '44 in our neighborhood, any friendship with Germans was severely punished; this was especially the case with embroiderers, waiters, barbers — service jobs generally — the common people. Lieutenant Vaculić tried to explain: "Everything has to be in proper order or else not at all!" Grandpa asked: "Who's going to do monograms for you now?" Vaculić replied: "Coats of arms and things like that aren't what matters, what matters is what's in the soul!" And in the soul — his, mine, all of ours — a completely new sign was beginning to appear, an emblem for the future, a monogram for far distant years we didn't have the slightest idea about then.

■ □ ■ □ ■

HOW THEY FIXED OUR HAIR

OUR LIFE IN THE CELLAR BEGAN THE THIRTEENTH OF OCTO-
ber, 1944, a leap year. When it burst upon us we jumped
out of bed and started bumping into each other in the
dark, which was practically impenetrable. Grandpa first
thought of Dad and shouted: "Lord, the guy farts like a
horse!" but later realized he'd made a mistake. My uncle
and I kept trying to put on the same pair of trousers, but we
couldn't do it. Mom kept shouting: "Where's my child?"
An airplane flew low overhead, whining. Mom dropped a
bundle of rags of some sort and immediately threw herself
on top of me. I yelled: "You'll smother me!" Afterward I
got out somehow and found my shoes. The Russian attack
started very early; Dad hadn't managed to sober up yet.
They carried him down the steps anyhow, gently and
painstakingly.

We dragged everything downstairs—beds, pots and
pans, quilts. Grandpa kept elbowing neighbors he didn't
recognize. He yelled: "Watch it!" and things like that.
People were shouting, knocking things against the wall
and crying. Somebody grabbed the janitor's daughter by
the tit and she shrieked. My friend Voja Bloša said: "This
is great!" They tried to pull the umbrella maker's wife out
through the door but couldn't, because she was overly fat.
Mom said: "It's elephantiasis, an elephant disease from
Africa!" They left the woman where she was. The umbrella

maker locked his wife in, turning the key twice, presumably to prevent a robbery; all he took to the cellar was a book, which was also fat. Once my uncle calmed down he started grumbling: "Damn it, I didn't get to shave!" Grandpa consoled him: "Isn't this a close enough shave for you, for God's sake?"

In the cellar we pushed the coal out of the way, threw out my sled, and immediately made up a bed, the brass one. My uncle pointed at Dad and warned: "Don't anybody bury him while he's unconscious!" Grandpa said: "He'd be better off!" Mom said: "Horrible!" and immediately went on fixing up our new apartment in the cellar. Grandpa ran around labeling everything like the logs, the baby buggy, and so on with chalk, in case we survived. Then above the bed he pounded a nail in the wall, which was sooty, and hung up a picture of Saint George, on a horse. Rosie Milivojević the hairdresser came in, took a look at the saint hanging there, and asked: "Do you have room for me in the storage closet?" Grandpa gave her a short answer: "Get lost!" She reminded us: "You're forgetting how I used to come to your place and cut your hair—for free!"

At dawn the Germans came, stumbled over some old men who were wrapped up in shawls and had already fallen asleep, and lit up all the corners with a flashlight. The umbrella maker was sitting under the stairs reading his fat book by the light of a candle. The Germans didn't say anything. They kicked at some dishes that were lying there, shoved away Rosie the hairdresser, who had been standing in the middle of the room, and cocked their machine guns, but they didn't shoot. I thought the Germans were only checking to see how we had gotten settled. They were nicely shaven and completely sober.

When they left, the umbrella maker started talking about Nostradamus, and golden cows that come from the East, and other disconnected and awful things. My uncle warned him: "Don't talk gibberish!" Then he turned to Dad, slapped him on the cheek, and whispered: "Come on and sober up—what's the point?" Dad said: "I will—just a sec!" but he didn't. Shells continued to fly over the rooftops, both Russian and German ones. Mom kept wondering: "Did I close the three-door cupboard?" My aunts added: "If we'd at least brought the manicure kit to do our nails!" Rosie Milivojević whispered: "And if I'd only brought my hair clippers!" Grandpa immediately answered her: "Did anybody ask *you?*" Our neighbor lady Darosava was stammering something and constantly crossing herself. Voja Blošak's mom kept hitting her head against the wall as if she had a toothache, but she didn't. You could see right away that all of us were a little bit drunk, even though only one of us got accused of it, that is, my dad.

The next day Dad started saying: "The whole place is swaying, for God's sake!" but nobody believed him. The building really was shaking, though, from the ground up. The people with diarrhea, and also some others, were fighting over the basement john and trying to take it over. Dad declared: "I wouldn't think of mixing with the riffraff!" He left to go up to our john on the third floor, in spite of the shelling. My uncle concluded: "Not worth getting your brains blown out just to take a crap!" Mom screamed: "He'll get killed!" Grandpa tried to reassure her: "God looks out for the drunks!" Dad stayed in our comfortable john a long time; the umbrella maker insisted: "The guy's dead!" My uncle tried to reassure everybody: "You don't know how long it takes him!" Dad came in buttoning up his trousers, with a newspaper under his arm, an old one in tatters it had been read so much. Then he reported: "Nothing's moved an inch—even the ashtray's still on the table!" He was swaying a little and yelling loud, though, because a shell had exploded near his ear. My uncle went up to him and ordered him: "Blow!" Dad blew, right in his face, but there wasn't any smell.

Then in ran Vujo Dingarac, a man without any hat on but with a torn sleeve. First he said: "They about skinned me!" Then he started looking us over, caught sight of Dad, and rushed right into his arms: "Lazo, you old son of a gun, what are you doin' here?" Mom said: "Can this be Mr. Dingarac who composes beautiful songs about so many events?" Vujo replied: "Who else?" Mom always said of Vujo: "He's a jack-of-all-trades," even though we were never able to determine what his real profession was. Vujo sang a song about the terrible occasion in our bathroom when a pair of Dad's pajamas caught on fire and burned up. Another excellent song of his was about when Mom was baking a cake, but was sad. This time Vujo described the taking of the famous Delini pharmacy by Russian troops and also the sound gunshots make when they buzz near your ears. At the end Vujo said sorrowfully: "And Teodor Graočankić's great little bar is in ruins now—razed to the ground!" Grandpa said: "What a shame!" but you could see right away he didn't think so. In the evening Vujo started entertaining us by holding his fingers upside down in front of a kerosene lamp and making shadows. Just by using his hands he could do a mountain goat leaping, and an unknown bird flying, and an elephant's trunk; all this came out looking much larger on the opposite wall. The umbrella maker protested: "Don't get it on me!" Later, Vujo showed us a live mouse made out of a dirty handkerchief. Right away Mom said: "That's just a piece of cloth!" but she squealed anyhow, just in case, and backed away.

Later it began to seem to us that life would go on. People started getting fidgety; each one needed something or other they didn't have. Little by little everybody began to envy my dad because of his trips to the john, but that was as far as it went. Rosie Milivojević kept hanging around us and saying: "You could all stand to have a good haircut and a shave!" Nobody said anything. Even before the war

I refused to get my hair cut, saying: "I won't—it hurts!" Mom kept promising me: "The man'll be careful, and then I'll take you to a movie!" but I wouldn't go along with it. At that time Mom started rolling her hair up in little pieces of newspaper; she called them "papillotes." I thought this word was prehistoric, in other words, Greek. Mom tried to explain: "You've already read the old newspapers, so my hairdo won't cost a thing!" My aunts found a piece of metal called a curling iron, a gadget for artificially making hairdos like in the movies; they would heat it up on the stove; I burned my fingers on it and didn't go to school for three days.

Now, in the cellar, Rosie Milivojević looked around her at our shaggy hair and all the stubbly beards. Sighing, she said: "Oh, to be back at Mr. Krasić's salon or Mr. Kaćansky's, who might not even be alive anymore!" Grandpa said: "Yes, and hustle the men while you cut their hair!" She said: "Me? God forbid!" Then she described the shop by the name of For Ladies and Gentlemen, longingly. Mom consoled her: "It says that on restrooms, too—don't mope about it!" Then my uncle joined in: "Is it true that hairdressers all go around feeling each other on the butt?" Rosie replied briefly: "Why, sir!" After this Mom and my aunts breathed a sigh of relief. My uncle continued: "As for me, I've always had a girlfriend do me, privately!" Right away Grandpa said: "I don't doubt that!" My uncle said: "I had enough brilliantine to last if the war went on ten years, only I left it upstairs in the bathroom!" Mom said: "There, you see?" My aunts complained: "With our curling iron we used to be able to fix all the hairdos from the prewar movies, and some we did even better!" Dad told them: "I'd bring you all those dumb things from upstairs if I knew where they were!" My aunts sighed: "It's hopeless!"

I still thought the best moment of a haircut is when the barber bows and says: "There you are!" For quite a while

I thought the barbershop was putting on performances of some sort, like royal or palace ones. The barbers were always talking in a low voice when I would come for Dad, who was getting shaved under a towel. I thought their conversations were from some French play, a very naughty one. Barbers always bowed to their customers and showed them a mirror as if they were expecting some sort of applause. The barbers often trimmed each other's mustaches; this happened later, though, after they had put the blinds down and gotten paid by the owner. I knew all this from hearing Dad tell about it, earlier. Whatever Dad told about, he always left something out; it seemed to me that there was something more about the barbers' trade that I would only find out about later. Then we heard the treads of Russian tanks, very close by. Right then somebody remembered to say: "Where's that young lady, that Slovene that's been screwing Krauts all this time?" We found the Slovene girl, a drugstore clerk, in a corner; she was half-done powdering herself, and was shaking. The umbrella maker said: "If we had one of those gadgets right now I'd know what to do!" Vujo Dingarac straightened up; from his inside pocket he pulled out clippers, which were quite small, but shiny and nickel-plated. Everybody's face lit up. They sat the drugstore clerk on a chair, in the middle of the cellar. Vujo ordered: "Lights!" Rosie Milivojević protested: "What am I here for?" Nobody answered her. Vujo took the clerk by the hair and started shearing her — gently, deliberately, expertly. Her white skull began to show, a bit wrinkled. Reddish, dyed hair fell on the cement floor. My uncle picked up a few strands between his fingers, pulled out his cigarette lighter and set them on fire, squinting merrily. Vujo blew on the teeth of his clippers, which meant the job was done. The young lady looked like a boy, repulsive and phony somehow, with painted-up lips.

We heard somebody's voice at the gate, a commanding,

inquiring voice. We headed out and right away saw a skinny young Partisan in a German tunic with a British machine gun over his shoulder. We said hello. The fellow pulled out cigarettes, offered them to the people around him, and then asked: "Any of ya heard'a this gal wrote here on m'pad?" The fellow showed us a slip of paper with names on it written in ink in big letters. The soldier jabbed a finger: "Thar, ra' thar!" Everybody took a look but nobody said anything; the young man turned around nervously, looking the women in the eye. Then, flustered, he came up to the janitor's daughter, who had dark hair. He asked: "Is it her?" Everybody said: "No!" I touched his pouch, a real soldier's leather one; he told me: "Beat it!"

Then they brought out the Slovene girl, the drugstore clerk, with her hair shaved off. The skin on her pale skull wrinkled up. The fellow stood where he was a minute, blushing. Then he took out his pen, spit on it, and crossed off the name.

The fellow turned to leave, but his machine gun bumped against the wall. Out of the barrel spewed a thin stream of fire—bluish, then rosy. The burst destroyed a mosaic in the floor; one bullet embedded itself in the electric meter, others hit the janitor's daughter in the stomach. The girl bent over and kneeled on the pavement. We saw her greasy black guts and her eyes that were all white. They lifted her up on crossed arms and carried her into the cellar.

The fellow stood there, at a loss; he took his cap off. Vujo Dingarac shrugged his shoulders.

Somebody called from the street. The fellow hurried to leave.

Meanwhile, Dad was reading good news of some sort in an old out-of-date newspaper, way up on the third floor, above it all.

A STORY ABOUT
DOGCATCHERS

LONG BEFORE THE WAR BEGAN MOM USED TO CAUTION ME: "Don't you dare let a mad dog bite you, or they'll give you a shot in the stomach and you'll start foaming at the mouth!" I had no idea where the mad dogs lived then, but I wished I could see how they looked. All I ever saw was one time we watched the dogcatchers chase a little white doggy across the playground, then hang him by a wire noose and throw him in a cart with bars on it. Mom said: "Poor gypsies, the way they have to do all the nastiest jobs!" I asked: "Why do they?"

In general, everybody at that time was opposed to dogs that barked on the street, stole sausage, and then bit the professor man's son on the leg. My aunts started telling what life was like downstairs, between a husband and a wife; they said: "They fight like cats and dogs!" All this was sometime around 1937, a bad year for animals. I had a rabbit, in the kitchen; it ate the broom, Dad's slipper, and things like that. Afterward they hit it over the head with a piece of wood and made paprikash out of it. Then they wanted to take me to a movie about Pluto the dog, but I said: "No, thanks—it's okay!" The only dog that was well thought of was the one that belonged to Mr. Popović the salami manufacturer. We ate salami from his factory while the dog sat on the rug and growled; even so, Mom kept saying: "Isn't he darling?" I knew Mom still hated dogs, and animals in general, only she kept it secret. She could never bring herself to stick her finger in the book that had pictures of different wild animals, especially at the page where the snakes were. She immediately threw the book on the floor and tied a towel around her head to stop the pain. Later on, she crammed various parts of animals into a big cooking pot and made soap out of them; the rest of us went outdoors because of the stench. She kept explaining to us: "You've got to wash or you'll disintegrate from the dirt streaks!" This was during the war and we understood.

Several years later I asked: "Where are those people that go down the street with a noose and hang dogs up by the neck?" Grandpa explained: "They've been hanged now, too—the same way!" That was pretty much true. All during the war I only heard about this line of work once from Voja Bloša, who knew about everything. Voja had been watching what was going on with the riverboat captain's wife while a vinegar and liqueur manufacturer was visiting her. All of a sudden the woman came outdoors completely naked and slapped Voja in the face. Voja clutched his cheek and shouted: "Dogcatcherfucking bitch!"

The first few days after the liberation Dad wasn't at home. Right off I asked: "Has he gone to get artificial butter, or is he at the bar?" Mom told me: "He should be so lucky!" I kept asking: "Why?" Nobody said anything; then Grandpa whispered to me: "He's chasing mad dogs down on the wharf!" Mom immediately started wiping away tears: "Him—and he wouldn't step on an ant, poor guy!" I only asked: "Does he have a noose?" My uncle said: "Of course!" This was true, too. Soldiers had ordered unemployed people, city shopkeepers, and others to come to headquarters; there they gave them boat hooks and other pieces of wire, and said: "Rid your own city of the beasts— it's up to you!" Dad and the others chased after the starving dogs, which had crept into shell holes and burned-out tanks and were barking from down inside, menacing furiously. The people threw stones at them and beat them with poles, and anything else they had. Mom just went around the kitchen wringing her hands and saying: "Horrible!" I asked: "Is Dad gonna get bitten by a mad dog, and then foam at the mouth afterward?" Grandpa explained: "He's mad already as it is!" Mom warned him: "Don't say that while his life is hanging by a thread!" In the debris on the wharf and in the German forces' broken-down bunkers there were still some Germans, too; they were wounded, frightened, and quite pale. The German soldiers, starving and mad with defeat, were also barking. Dad asked: "What do we do with these?" The commander of the unit—a civilian, dogcatching unit—said: "Same thing!"

This is a story about those things from that year. It can't be all that nice a story, considering the subject matter and the main characters, who are mostly animals. Lieutenant Vaculić tried to explain to us: "This won't last long—just a few days and it'll be over!" I kept asking: "Are all of them mad?" He answered: "All of them!" I was asking about the dogs; Vaculić meant the Germans, the ones left behind, but it didn't matter.

Dad kept coming home in the evening all bitten up. His only trousers and his skin had been ripped in many places by the teeth of frightened dogs, and also the teeth of our city's last enemies. Mom would rub him down with brandy; Grandpa protested: "That's all he needs!" In spite of it all Dad didn't foam at the mouth, and he didn't bite any of us, either—on the contrary. He did talk in his sleep and bark, very quietly. One day he opened up his coat and pulled out a puny little pooch, white and shaggy, with an injured leg. He admitted: "This one I just couldn't!" Everybody started to cry. Those evenings I kept noticing that many chores were being neglected, even the roughest ones, and that everybody was thinking about things that were ordinary, old-fashioned, and long-forgotten. I watched the very hardworking and devoted members of my family crowd together like drunks, hug each other, and look at the floor, at the circle in the middle of them, without saying anything. Mom cried a little and then said, as if reading out of a book: "When will all this stop? When will this cursed dog's life be over, and a life that's human begin?"

IN PRAISE OF YOUNG
PILOTS AND OTHERS

IN 1944, IN THE SPRING, AMERICAN AIRPLANES WERE BLOW-
ing up Romanian oil wells near Ploesti; returning to their
bases near Bari, Bizerta, and on Sicily, they would fly over
us. Patriots, barbers, out-of-work piano tuners, and amateur builders of all sorts all looked, beaming, at the Americans' shiny, rumbling machines, stuck high in the sky.
The Americans, the great victors in the battle with the
Romanian oil rigs, scanned the Allied cities they were flying over, all the while hating the Germans, the occupiers
of those very pretty cities. The Americans, the men who
set the brilliant days-long blazes on those key Romanian
fields, later began, whether out of carelessness, boredom,
or by accident, to drop a few things on us, too. They
dropped shoes that had pinched, and empty whiskey bottles, photos of Italian whores and photos of Betty Grable,
the most famous American actress. This city eager for
friendship and freedom began to get pelted with fabulous
shoes that were made of fine-grade oxhide, but were too
tight. Later, from time to time, a bomb would also fall.
People looked at the tinfoil airplanes and were proud of
the Allied armed force, that force's main female, the
Romanian oil that had been set on fire, and the bombs that
put the occupiers of our pretty city in a bad mood.

Up above in the rattling cabins of the Liberators, bare-
footed and sweaty American pilots, scorning the oppres-

sors of the friendly peoples, began to unbuckle their trousers and undo their buttons with the US insignia on them. Down onto the beaming, freedom-loving city fell nervous captains' too-tight shoes, whiskey bottles, bombs, and human excrement—American pilots' shit. Onto the sunlit roofs of the theaters and museums, onto the stupid plaster figures lined up along those roofs, onto the noses of those figures shined smooth by time there fell fragments of bombs and Allied armed forces' shit, the cargo of upset and anxious soldiers of freedom who were tired of flying, war, and the fires that sprang up underneath their wings. Ruddy, talented pilots, mainly young, very well nourished in their field hospitals near Bari, Bizerta, and on Sicily, and fattened up with excellent Italian spaghetti, chocolates, and the bitten-off ears of SS men, relieved themselves with blissful inspiration above our city, a city stubborn, dilettante, and very proud all at the same time.

Our neighbor Pavle Bosustov, a democrat, reader of Remizov and a Russian, a great expert on the human heart, would go out on the balcony and here, under the rain of bullets, deliver his fiery lectures in support of the Allied air force. The heroes of the American air fleet, ruddy fellows from Mississippi, would empty their bowels over our city while Bosustov, an émigré from Odessa, spoke elegantly, eloquently, fearlessly, and in a very dignified fashion on behalf of this act.

My grandpa, a personal enemy of the deceased German general Potiorek, also went out on the balcony. He went out cautiously, like a soldier, curious, trying to find out what was going on. Through the uproar of the antiaircraft artillery cannonade he caught fragments of a heavy Tolstoyan sentence from Pavle Bosustov, who was delivering a speech to the residents of our beautiful, enslaved, plundered, shat-upon city. My grandpa, who was deaf already but whose other senses were very acute, inquired about the smell that had spread over our capital city, a city unique in every regard. "That is the smell of friendship," said Bosustov, "the smell of victory, the splendid smell of a victorious air force. It is the smell of human understanding, the smell of human kindness,"* preached Bosustov, an expert on many great languages, English among them. Fragments of that grand holiday performance, rubbish from the Allied airplanes, from the pilots in those planes, from the digestive organs of those pilots, kept on falling onto the roofs, onto the streets with overturned streetcars, and onto the solitary orators on the protruding balconies.

An attack happened about dinnertime; they pulled Grandpa by his coat to get him back to the table. There my father was sitting, somber, hungry, and very nervous. Grandpa was talking about corpses and about history and the uproar it made out on the street; articles from the American air force began to drop through the fallen-in ceiling. Plaster and Allied pilots' shit began falling onto the empty plates at my family's home—an infernal meal, one of the most infernal in that drastic season. "This place isn't fit to eat in anymore," my father said, aggravated beyond measure. He kept swearing and shoving starved and startled family members around. They went through the rooms that had been decorated by the American air force and rolled things up in bundles.

My father hired a coachman, and from the fourth floor they hauled down the sewing machine, the pillows, and Grandpa, who was grumbling. Sitting in the coachman's carriage, with our junk and sacred books falling out of the sloppily made bundles, we floated down the streets of the freedom-loving city, which was smoky, scared, and horribly stinky. Before long other people left the foul-smelling city as well.

Life in the suburbs did not get off to a happy start. The year, a whole long season, was devoted to an air force of

*This last phrase is in English in the original.—Trans.

American origin and its brilliant, surprising performances up above, over our heads. Nobody felt like going into town, which was frightened, and decorated with numerous objects of varied nature; only my father went, after dreaming up fantastic excuses; he was always seen off as if he would never come back. Mornings went by in trembling, in a distant roar, and in trying to hear the radio. The radio either was silent or played the same dumb aria about a Nibelung tank driver, or told about American airplanes passing overhead—in Romanian at that. In the evening my father would come back covered with soot, tipsy and happy, with a sack on his back. In the sack was salami of dubious color and ham of unusual dimensions. We didn't eat the salami or the ham—my mother had gotten wind of their terrible origins. Out on the street there were minstrels and traveling circus artists, very hungry ones. The high-wire artists and the others told about underground salami factories down in town. There wasn't any meat to make the salami out of, so they used children. The minstrels had a song about this; as they played it on their mandolin, they brought tears to my mother's eyes, the tears of the mother of an only child endangered by illegal manufacturing. The year was devoted to pilots, brave ones and young ones, but the minstrels told of other things as well, and people believed them. In the desolate city, deserted even by the occupiers, the few residents that there were seized suspected wooers of little girls, with candy in their pockets, and harmless homosexuals who were sighing over some boy or other, and strangled them, without a trial. Since there weren't any contraptions usable for criminal purposes, not even ordinary meat grinders, in the homes of the humanists, homosexuals, and horticulture devotees, the horticulture enthusiasts and pederasts died senselessly and innocently. Still, we didn't eat the salami, despite our very great hunger. Grandpa kept leaning his ear to the prewar-made radio, where warnings could be heard in

Hungarian, Romanian, and Turkish about American bombers. Grandpa kept expecting something would finally be said about the salami that was being made out of children, and he pounded furiously on the radio out of revenge.

I started wanting to go back to town. The city, brim full as it was of weird things, constant location of my father's inexplicable dealings, began to preoccupy me with its mysteriousness. My father got into the habit of displaying many artistic leanings: he recited pornographic verses with wonderful flair, he walked on his hands without getting red in the face, and I — to enter into the same spirit — tried to write poetry. The poems were about autumn, snow, and trees; they were musical; they left my father cold; he made a sour face. Still, he did appreciate the effort; finally he decided to take me with him. Mother cursed as she saw us off, my aunts composed two short funeral sonnets, one for each of us, and Grandpa raised his arms in surrender, unable to understand a thing.

In town there weren't many people. My father pulled out a bunch of keys; worried, I thought of thievery, and gallows — the awful things that awaited us. My father smiled gently and said: "It's nothing. There are friends all over." In the city, deserted and left in disarray by the Allied air force bombers, there weren't any people, but the best things of all were still there: fearlessness, fun, and comradeship. The comrades had ten or so apartments apiece, completely deserted, with the stage and set of a previous life. Into the spacious parlors decorated with dust and debris from antiaircraft shells the comrades brought little girls, awakened princesses from the enslaved capital city, hungry and dirty but utterly enraptured. In these littered parlors people had long been playing cards for imaginary stakes, making love in front of everybody, and eating the choicest meats anytime they found any. The small population of the deserted city — the cardplayers, the lovemakers, snack bar managers and comrades—lived a fun-filled, happy life and were full of bravery. The city kept being showered with hot cargo from the Allied air force; the year was devoted to the aces of Europe and America's air forces, but all the same, people made love the same way: the woman would lie in the pieces of plaster and the man would go out undressed on the balcony showing the lofty pilots his sign, which was an unmistakable one.

In one salon in the capital city, on the fourth floor on Laza Pachu Street, I got my first lectures on art, which is fearless and insatiable even in the worst of times. In the middle of the room stood a man in pajamas, a great expert in his line of work. His skill was simple: eating a chicken with his eyes closed. Girls sitting side by side on sofas, cardplayers, and mandolin players all stared at this, the nicest number on the program. The chicken was conquered, the man in pajamas bowed, and a relative of the host's, Jovan Milić, nicknamed Mile, stated in a voice that was touched and full of awe: "All I can say is: very good!" The others began to applaud.

In a city left to people who were bold filled with an appreciation for beauty, beautiful performances and regular amateur theater productions came to evolve. At these performances I saw all the parts of the human body for the first time, both male and female, I heard poems by great poets, traveling ones and classical both, and I watched many drills from the prewar Soko movement. The year was devoted to the air force, the American one, so that was taken into account as well. Here and there bombs fell along with other cargo from a great air force; friends of my father's and thus of mine played various aviation games, they made paper airplanes and threw them out the window, confusing the German artillery. Homemade but very authentic planes made out of dog-eared pages of checkered notebook paper took over the city sky, leisurely circling, borne by the wind, the wind of freedom; the

Germans, gathered around their batteries, badly judged the altitude and shot randomly, fearfully, completely aimlessly. In the salons where the newly formed friendships were, no one even mentioned the funny cannibalisms; the tightrope walkers, alcoholics, and pederasts who survived the stupid pogroms were reading books about aviation and admiring Lilienthal, his name and his deeds, as well as Mermoz, who also disappeared during the heyday of flight. A girl they called Milkica, in a pale violet dress with tinsel, thought up a poem about Voisin, who was also a pilot. The year was an air force one, a weird one; performances took on unusual winged markings of their own. Ignoring my mother's worries and Grandpa's curses, my father, who was utterly fascinated, and I along with him, stayed for an evening performance. The sky over the city was starry, and the girls came there with no clothes on; all they had on were little wings made of heavy wrapping paper stuck on and brightly painted. In 1944, the year of the air force, in a city destined for destruction on the part of the Allies, I caught sight of representatives of a heavenly air force, an angelic tribe of little sweethearts, musical, bold, and ready for anything. As the only child there who had survived the terrible stories about salami manufactured out of newborns, I was carried on the wings of these enchantresses, watched over, and pampered greatly.

Lev Konstantinovich Gelin, a former printer, did not attend the performance. The first bomb had wiped out Lev Konstantinovich's family, his apartment, and his designs for a newspaper printing press, an unusual plastic one. Lev lived in a room that had been abandoned; he only came out for acts with food in them. They would give him what bad performers hadn't been able to eat blindfolded. After the major accident of aeronautic origin Gelin switched over completely to aircraft mechanics, to fearless and astounding designs for improbable aircraft. The room nobody went into was crammed with sketches;

the sketches looked like a child's, but were promising; they were completely covered with explanations in Hebrew, Old Church Slavic, and Finnish.

In the morning I woke up in the lap of one girl, my father in another's. Gelin came into the salon unnoticed by many who were still groggy. Gelin was wearing a funny suit cut out of old quilt covers; when he opened his arms out wide, something resembling wings appeared underneath them. On his head he had a yellow shoe, a pilot's shoe. On August 27 of 1944, the year devoted to the air force, Lev Konstantinovich Gelin waited for the first attack by the American bombers and then, determined to join them, went out onto the balcony, which had a broken-down railing. His flight was magnificent and astounding, if brief. Spreading wide his Slavic arms so accustomed to stretching, Lev Konstantinovich, a failed designer of our civilization, threw himself into that expanse that was filled with Liberators, with the struggle being waged by the human race, and with the uproar of war, and after a moment in that ghastly position, he plummeted to the ground wrapped in the oddly cut quilt cover. Jovan Milić, nicknamed Mile, went to the window and said: "All I can say is," but he didn't say anything. Somebody else added: "Why a quilt cover?" Meanwhile, the Americans, this century's young and thoroughbred pilots, who were on their way to our definitive victory, kept on flying.

■ □ ■ □ ■

DIARY OF AN APATRID

HACER TIEMPO, "TO MAKE TIME," MEANS, FOR THE SPAN-
iards, to hope. So says José Bergamin, in 1937, in the war,
the civil war, for whom hope, *because of intense hoping, is
often hopelessness, despair.* Hacer tiempo, time made, is a
book by Marko Ristić about another great slaughter, of
human beings, fifty years ago. The final volume of Proust's
mammoth work has a similar name, Le temps retrouvé,
Time Regained.* *One of the first evenings after my return
in 1916,* it says there, *wishing to hear conversations about
the war, which was all that interested me then, I went out
after supper to visit Mme Verdurin,* just as I am visiting my
own Mrs. Verdurin almost daily, during the mild end of
Rovinj's summer, *because she, along with Mme Bontemps,
was one of the queens of wartime Paris,* and accordingly, a
princess of the Rovinj hill in this war, the Croat-Serb one.
And while the ladies from the beginning of the century
wore *straight Egyptian tunics to be patriotic,* and *long
gaiters resembling those of our dear soldiers,* my Verdurin-
Bontemps ladies enter into the conversations about the
war as if they had graduated from West Point, and it's just
as likely they could take apart or put together a Kalashnikov with their eyes closed. I, on the other hand, am quite

*All the quotations from Proust are from the ZORA-GZH edition,
Zagreb, 1977, translated by Vinko Tecilazić.

weak in this discussion, so I say I am reading an old Arab philosopher, Averroës, and, if I may say so, along with that, a few chosen pages of Proust. *The Louvre is closed, as is every other museum,* not only those in Paris but our skimpy museum in Rovinj as well, so thus the prevailing style is *elegance amid a shortage of art,* and a paucity of conversations that would deny the topic of the war even a minute of the attention it deserves. But Proust wrote about this recent and current war, quite precisely, nearly a hundred years ago, so I am simply taking quotations from his book, ones that, already written long ago, are true today. Mmes Verdurin and Bontemps, of Rovinj, say that all anybody needs to read are the newspapers, and there only the reports of what we have already thoroughly accepted and established in our conversations. The newspapers report what everybody already knows and what everybody (and we are always "everybody") has gotten down pat already; surprising as it is, the newspapers don't report anything new, but rather, in the newspapers and with the help of newspapers, we reassure ourselves that we know about the only things that matter, that is, war ones, and that we knew about them before we even picked these big thick newspapers up. This is why newspapers shouldn't come out at all, since what is in them is in all our heads in practically identical form, in each one separately and yet in all of them together, as though it were a matter of a printed text, a truth established in advance and issued in print form. So the newspapers can't be untrue when there is nothing in them except what each of us imprints in them before they are printed, so in fact in some strange way each reader is offered "his own" individual reading material, a text as it were that he himself has dictated to the man at the linotype machine. My remark about Proust should thus be discounted because it may seem sacrilegious *to strict republicans that we are occupied with art when coalition* Serbia *is besieging a territory of freedom.* My downfall is obviously that of Proust's character Saint-Loup: *antipatriotism, atheism, anarchy.* The other day I read a peaceable and decent writer's call to war, while a psychiatrist showers a television audience with his curses against pacifism, which is worse in me than in Saint-Loup. We ought to have done once and for all with such peacetime nonsense, in other words, *because it was the fashion to say that the prewar period was separated from wartime by something as deep and ostensibly as long as a geological period.* Thus we all leave the impression of mammoths suddenly excavated from the iceberg of history, and whether we were alive at all during a relatively long period is difficult if not impossible to prove now except by paleontological means. Because where we used to be doesn't exist anymore, except that we left our lives behind in that period that is nonexistent today and, much much worse, also the memory of that life we had lived. The new democracy, in contrast to the strictures of communist organization, brings a new sort of forgetting, of that which happened, as if it really hadn't happened, and we who were there hadn't been there at all. We really, er, let's see now, I mean we were there only because we didn't want to be there, and the fact that, honest to goodness, we really and truly never did want to be there, that is proof of what we maintain now, that we weren't there, period! The only ones there were "them," those few who truly wanted to be there, while the rest of us, "everybody," we weren't there—it was just empty space. Communism is truly very skilled at handling empty space as if it were full, except that one question gets asked regularly— where were we, then?—and the answer is geological: our prior history is a picture of hibernation behavior, while the event that followed corresponds to an event from the story of Snow White. That is to say, my country got awakened as if a little piece of apple had been dislodged from its throat, and after that the glass coffin broke of its own accord. On one outing, a decadent, solipsistic, and totally pacifistic one, we went to see a Magritte* exhibit in Verona, and there, in the city in which our patriotic prince was unable to awaken the sleeping Juliet, is a painting of a chamber filled with a huge apple, so huge there isn't room for anything else but the apple. The country I was born in is filled with the country I was born in, such that there is nothing else in that country except the country I was born in, just as there is nothing in Magritte's chamber except the apple that fills up this space, of the apple's. This painting is called *The Mute Room* [*Gluha soba*] and the country I was born in is mute even though everybody can talk, because they all talk at the same time and because they say exactly the same thing. Saying the same thing, therefore, can only turn into silence, not the silence of a decadent and pacifistic idiot such as Saint-Loup, but the silence of an expression that, expressed by a group in identical fashion, expresses nothing.

Our journalism is a special kind of journalism, though.

*One philosopher-poet here, though, has referred to Surrealism as a movement of crazy intoxication that brings uncontrolled outpourings, primitive ones, in contrast to our light, clarity, sober thought, and culture, which is loftier, of course, than any Parisian-Flemish morons can produce any of their opiate paint jobs of. So, too, my cadet Saint-Loup speaks in vain, although even in his falsetto he is telling part of a truth that everyone knows. Because if the clarity and daylight thinking of the philosopher-poet are muddled and foolish, a jolt, a poetic one, from Breton's era can make a kind of sense that we in our magpie's hideaway can only dream of. We are clear, we think sensible daylight thoughts, only we thought this way for nearly fifty years under the influence of just such foolish daylight thinkers and antipoetic interpreters of our reality. As a matter of fact, this war began in part when our smartest literary critics began to promote nonsensical reading material in our bookstores that was "simple" and, in the daylight, "clear," but if one gave even a bit more complicated and complex thought to it one could see for the umpteenth time that it was a useless and futile business.

It isn't like "their" journalism, which actually can hardly be called any sort of journalism at all. Because if somebody wanted to learn what journalism really ought to be, he really could study that directly every day from our journalism and our newspapers. Really, nobody's journalism is the ideal journalism that "we" would like to have for journalism, but under "the given circumstances" and "taking everything into consideration"—what we have is actually the best in the way of modern European journalism that we can have, all in all! This is also the thinking of Proust's characters, who, by some miracle, surround me these days, in the war. *The Germans will no longer be able to look Beethoven's statue in the face; Schiller must have trembled in his grave; the ink that initialed Belgium's neutrality had barely dried; Lenin speaks, but the steppe wind carries his words away all the same.* This is how to be open and intelligible to each ordinary man of ours, who is ordinary partly because his entire life he has been consuming newspapers of this sort, which encourage the ordinary man to be ordinary, and if he already is ordinary, then he will incline our ordinary but quite truthful truths to his ordinary heart in the most ordinary and most intelligible way! For example, *our command knows how to keep its eyes open; we want to win and nothing more; as for us, we don't hide the truth; nor will we say land has been taken if it hasn't; Germany wanted war and now it's got it—the die is cast!* In such really quite simple sentences as these there is something every reader of these sentences discovers as if he had written them himself, and therein lies the great paradox of all real journalism, that what it, as journalism, reports, every one of its readers already knows beforehand, so it turns out that he really didn't have to read these real newspapers at all! Instead, inside the person sits that big devil who wants to ascertain how that reading matter he is already familiar with as it is is familiar to him in "thus and such" a way and not some other! Just so long as some newspaper reader of today doesn't "someday" put me next to *one of our generals who are waging war because of the war horrors and in order to punish a people who foster an ideal that they themselves, fifteen years before, had viewed as the only sound one.* Because generals always wage war for war's sake and not for the sake of the ideal that, like some sort of alibi, stands behind their warring. And the language in which this warring is justified and promoted is always the very same: *Germany uses so many of the same expressions France does that one might think she was quoting her.*

Maybe I'm just imagining I'm not biased, and maybe my only target, really, is "our" cause, not "their" cause. But to this I say to my Mr. Verdurin, of Rovinj, that I'm not for one side or the other in this war at all, but am only listening to the conversations that we are conducting in the course of this war, and that reflect the social climate created by this war. And that I am discovering this same climate in a society from back at the beginning of our century, as it has already been depicted in the book I am reading, along the way, in the course of this war.

The belief that life is created for enjoyment is shameful, the poet Blagojević quotes Alfred Rosenberg as saying. *We must root out this weakness. The strength of our nation will overcome this temptation,* even at the cost of this nation's strength—and that nation itself—ceasing to exist entirely. A nation as such always has some mission, but from time to time, under the influence of national theoreticians, this mission leads to suicide and total national necrophilia, our poet goes on to conclude. The panic that comes with martial law roots out enjoyment while attempting to get another impulse to take root—a self-destructive one. Because if we eliminate the hedonistic obstacles, we are already on our way to eliminating man himself with his natural strivings, and an individual with no natural strivings would be the ultimate goal of this pernicious doctrine.

A siege atmosphere, a sense of doom and the end of the world—these, then, are what my circle, the Rovinj one, my Verdurin gang, is living on, here on the cape of our kingdom, which is already one foot in history, was something once upon a time, but practically is no more! We are excavated relics, resurrected to talk like idiots and like witnesses to the past, in the same way that the carbonized inhabitants of Pompeii speak this language of the past. *What documents, my book says, for future history, when asphyxiating gases similar to the ones Vesuvius spewed out, and ruins like the ones Pompeii is crammed with, preserve untouched all the last imprudent women who haven't fled yet to Bayonne with their paintings and statues! Indeed, haven't we been looking at clippings from Pompeii for a year now every evening when these people run into their cellars, not to bring out some old bottle of "Mouton Rothschild" or "Saint-Emilion," but to hide themselves and their most precious possessions?* In other words I, as I get out my evening wine, already belong to that region of shadows and that sequence of history which has taken place. Talking as I drink that same wine, about things that aren't directly related to our status as mummified and Pompeiicized witnesses, I am a shadow myself, and I talk to myself as if to my shadow. But how can it be, my Mr. Verdurin asks me, that I, a man of the moment, with some supposed daily inspiration of my own and the savvy he says he expects of me, that I should suddenly turn into a shadow and a piece of the past, which is already over? That, I say, is because these events we are present at really don't interest me, because I know about them from reading a book written long ago. What we here are living through is a pastiche of what other people went through almost a whole century ago. What I'm saying is that I have no desire to repeat what happened, so I am occupying myself with my own dreams and my own utterly anachronistic misery. He and they can go ahead and be synchronic with events, but let me be asynchronic and anachronistic, because the only person who can be nonanachronistic is one who insists on being very much up-to-date—something rather strange to me. That which is is not, one of my characters has been saying for almost a whole decade, and, taught by him, I hold to the same. That which is is only thought to be, but in fact already was, and was so in a much more worthy form. From out of my own anachronistic state, which permits me to know more than others about anachronisms, I am watching what is happening *now* and is a part of a past that manifested itself in a manner that was much more honorable. *Yes,* our Baron de Charlus says, *all of us have gotten bogged down in dilettantism,* which means that we are imitating and copying someone or something already known from history.

I don't remember what I've told you about how M. Norpois marvels at this war, but the fact that in our native land philosophers and poets and journalists and psychiatrists and art historians and clerics with revolvers in their belts are all marveling at the war within our homeland, a liberation war—of that fact these same marveling journalists inform us day in and day out at the top of their lungs. *Right off, have you noticed the burgeoning of new expressions,* the flood of neologisms that will find their place at some session of the Academy group for language and literature, almost certainly? Because inasmuch as *the wartime philosophers have proclaimed that all ties to the past have been broken,* I emphasize this same sentence from "my" book with special emphasis, who knows why, and our Mr. Verdurin, of Rovinj, can't stand it any longer and has to have it proven to him that it was Proust who wrote this utterly up-to-date phrase and that all I'm doing is reading it, perhaps at the wrong time, and giving it some "special" emphasis. Because what did that decadent have to do with our bloody reality since he looked at the whole slaughterhouse of Europe from the position of an asthmatic and invert degenerate, whereas I think it's no wonder he talked about his own war as if he were talking about ours, and a human being, unless it's Proust's M. Norpois, ought to regard every war with the same attitude, whether it's a war of liberation or not: because for a war to become a war of liberation someone has to christen it that, and when a war has been christened and properly blessed, then it can be only what it is titled, so that its further course, no matter how bloody and inhumane, will have acquired its normal state and its meaning—for history, of course. However, that human heads also roll like watermelons in historic wars of liberation remains virtually a routine and utterly accepted fact for even the most humanistic of thinkers. And one mother journeyed several thousand kilometers across Europe to try to free her son of a hated enemy uniform so as to clothe that same son, with her blessing, in just such a military uniform that is now "ours." This mother weeps on the doorstep of Europe, she even renounces her maternity, for she tells those in the north of the continent that *they are our mother,* that we haven't given birth to anyone, but, rather, that those fine people have borne us all, we are their obedient and endearing children, and toward the child we ourselves bore we will be what we can be, which is to say Medea. In fact, in other words, we will go on with our European confusion in which we try *to Europeanize Turkey while not Montene-groizing France,* we'd like to be where we still can't be, except that we can in our Montenegroizing way, which is Medea's. We'll fall to the last man, and when not one live person is left in this pretty homeland of ours, someone will be able to say that it was indeed pretty and that we fell to the last man for it. And since *people from high society are more naive than is thought,* even those who really aren't from such high society repeat this nonsense even to our last man fallen on our homeland's last rampart. The high and mighty are naive, our writer says, but that doesn't mean our godparents and peasants who have lived through things of this sort in their plebeian lives have to be that way; however, now we plebeians, too, are partially up there riding high, on the Promenade, just as we already were during this half-century; indeed it was to some extent because of our own resourcefulness that we lost Valent Vudriga,* and how Vudriga, had he survived the casemates of the kingdom, would have behaved as a cabinet minister or a second-in-command in a government that was truly ours, that we can know only by analogy. Which is to say, maybe we really are the children of Europe whom Europe simply won't allow to grow up. You just stay here and play nicely with your little guns, and when one of your mothers comes to our doorstep, she herself will admit that she is our child and that she doesn't know what she's doing. And we who in fact are from a much higher society than the one Proust tells about, we gonna figger out what in Christ name to do wit' ya! Because nobody knows what to do with you, not even we ourselves, and nobody knows because with you the way you are, you yourselves don't know what to do with yourselves! Because behaving inhumanely toward the human race doesn't refer only to when we treat others that way, that is, inhumanely, but also if we act this way toward our own selves. This is what a philosopher from our neighborhood, Agnes Heller, says looking at something else but seeing what is happening right here this very moment. Man can commit an innumerable number of inhumane acts toward those close to him or not close, but what he is capable of committing on himself and his already disturbed brain, his human one, would be hard to commit on someone else. So that what you do to others, do to yourself, as in the folk proverb, except that it looks simple in a folky and proverbial way only at first glance. Unsettling our own

*A folk character of Krleža's.

soul can be done in an almost unbelievable number of ways, and yet we are capable of employing an even greater number of flowery phrases to justify this disturbance of our own mind.

We need to learn, says Heller, *to seek the best—as much satisfaction as possible—from this life, because we have only this life, and we shouldn't use ourselves as a means, either.* Because by pressuring others to do as we wish, to think as we think we think, to write as it seems to us we write, and to voice their opinions as we suppose that we voice our opinions, daily and excessively, we not only are deprived of any human satisfaction (other than that equally "human" impulse to pressure others) but we are using our own selves directly in a necrophiliac, hurtful, and murky deception whose direct impact on our own lives we seem completely unaware of. *He who feels satisfaction will not despair. He who does his duty has a right to hope,* says the historian. But history has very bad examples in it of doing one's duty, and a sense of satisfaction is, as we see, a very problematic, elusive, and, at its worst, fickle sense. Perhaps the most acceptable emotions are those that range around cheerful resignation or "unsatisfied satisfaction," as she herself says. Because *neither the narcissistic nursing of one's own ego nor activist self-sacrifice at the altar of the future is an attitude that can be easily generalized or is acceptable.* Perhaps we are obliged *to live* according to some idea *but always imperfectly.* This is where the philosophy behind our war comes in, as well as the spirit behind that philosophy, which is every bit as antireason and counterhuman as the philosophy itself is. And yet we keep on devouring the basest expression of that war spirit, which appears in the newspapers: *the Germans will no longer be able to look Beethoven's statue in the face; Schiller must have trembled in his grave; the ink that initialed Belgium's neutrality,* etc. For General Pau from Proust's book wasn't the only one who shouted on the day war was declared: *"I've been waiting for this day for forty years!"* Inasmuch as, worst of all, this day was also awaited for forty years by those who are only nineteen years old and who will never reach twenty! Because for the young men who are nineteen, that day they will fall has been awaited much longer by men who have many more years behind them, and who have been appointed by history to have that historic memory, for themselves and for others.

But philosophy, of war, counts on only the enemy's death, inexorable and total. *And because of just one death on our side it will be necessary to kill every last Kraut. And what they did in Louivian, cutting the hands off the little children!* Proust's hero would sooner let his *snout be peppered with bullets than submit to such barbarians; those aren't human beings, they're real savages—we're not about to say they aren't.* While I, as a former, estranged, and forgotten son of that tribe, ought therefore to keep my silence. Really, I should have said something when it needed to be said to testify that the tribe I belong to by origin is barbaric, but when I didn't do this and only the apostle of our spirituality, a confused builder of sacred structures, found the strength to say it, then I should also keep my silence today when it has occurred to me to say not only that my own clan is barbaric but that the clan waging war with it is also barbaric in large measure, and that the time that frames this battle is without any doubt barbaric as well; maybe I wanted to say all this of my own free will, and not out of any obligation to stand up and be counted. And can a man talk in a composed and reasonable manner about the events of war only if he is a decadent like M. Charlus, Proust's? Because *he didn't say "Krauts," he praised the Germans' bravery, and he didn't put it down to treason that we weren't victorious on the very first day.*

So, *M. Charlus' impartiality was total. Which is to say, as soon as he became a mere observer, everything inevitably drove him to be a Germanophile, because he lived in France but wasn't a true Frenchman.* To look, to observe, and to recollect what has happened is now becoming a passion—a decadent, solipsistic, and almost unpatriotic one—in the war.

I read that the actors of our country are ready to go to the front line, in particular one actor tested in many heroic roles says this. He says that everything that has been is nothing compared to what will be, both in a heroic sense and in that other one, the theatrical one. But I read this in "my" book, too—the old one, Proust's: *Didn't you see that Sarah Bernhardt announced in the paper: France will carry on till the end. The French are prepared to perish to the last man.* Baron Charlus, a decadent and *apatrid* (as I myself am an *apatrid*), throws in his own remark, which is apatridic and decadent at the same time: *I have no doubt of it, only I'm wondering who authorized Mme Sarah Bernhardt to speak in France's name?* And by the same token, who authorized this cabinet minister of ours to say the same thing the other day? To lose one's last man in the name of the motherland (which would thus be left without its last man) is an idea both necrophiliac and in large measure insane, except that, fortunately, from time immemorial it has never been achievable except in proclamations, whether by cabinet ministers or by actors. "All" the people will never give their lives for their motherland, and that is the greatest thing they as people can ever do—not be the last man who will fall for his motherland.

Somebody says our brave athletes are also rushing to the front to engage the enemy, and I say it says the very same thing in Proust: that *some fellows joined the army simply to follow the crowd and take up a new sport, the way one year everybody plays "diabolo."* Famous wrestlers, masters of martial arts, and boxers now want to enter the fiercest battle, and one defense leader is inviting the archery champions to join them. This way the war could well turn into a sort of championship, a European one if possible, and the slaughter in the cornfields would need to be put under the regulations of the ancient Oriental arts, whose morality allows no retreating.

Every thing looks like some other one that doesn't dream it could look like the first one. I am circling around the house because my Mara keeps coming along behind me from one room to the next with her cleaning equipment, and that housework rather reminds me of my own fate, that of an émigré. As soon as we clean here we'll let you be, but for now please go somewhere and find something to do, and then afterward, afterward you can do whatever you please! My countess on her broom chases me from one room to the next and I—I'm supposed to get out and not think!

Mr. Verdurin asks me what kind of book I'm writing, and I say it's a book about a schizophrenia I have. That in fact there's nothing schizophrenic about it except that everywhere it should say "Serb" I put "German," and where it refers to Croats I say "Frenchmen." This is a joke of mine, a writer's joke, in this time of war, and not some game of hide-and-seek, since I make no secret of my "Germanness" nor the fact that I was born in "France." My Mr. Verdurin says writers can't get along without their little tricks, and he marvels I could ever come up with something like that! He believes that writing as a profession requires a certain minimal intelligence, but that when "we" get going with these tricks of ours, he has great doubts about this intellectual minimum. In spite of these admonishments, however, I am continuing my story, however unintelligent it is. Because to live intelligently means such a life needs no story, whereas with this other kind I evidently am living, storytelling is the only thing that, with my lack of intelligence, keeps me alive in any fashion at all. I've just read that my colleague, a poet, gave a speech and that in it he said *Germans* could go on living in *France* on the condition that they show their anticipated constructiveness; but if they have no such constructiveness, then the *French* really wouldn't object to our leaving.

I don't know why I never used to be asked what I do and why I do "that," but now, ever since I've become a *German,* people are constantly asking me that?! Because a *German* among the *French* must be doing something that must be *anti-French*, if only to the tiniest possible extent, and the idea that it might at the same time be *anti-German* to a much greater extent doesn't concern the *French.* What a *Frenchman* is concerned about are the *French* and *France* — and therein is that whole spirit of the *French* that Gide perceived in that train with that peasant woman who was taking her daughter who knows where and who knows what for. The *French* mother is taking her *French* daughter no one knows where, but on that trip what matters to her is that "they're with each other" together, that they're glad who they are, and that they can do without everybody who isn't *French!*

In wartime everybody plays some parlor game of their own, and at just such a time we here are playing *Frenchmen and Germans;* even though we're at war we sit at the same table and converse about this war of ours, kind of as though we were playing a game. And one of our most interesting figures turns out to be Baron Charlus, from Proust, who in addition to being a pederast is half-French and half-German, just as I, were I a pederast and were I a baron, would be an almost ideal incarnation of him among us. I say that every one of us is an incarnation of who knows which character in the novel, because nobody is quite prepared to be outside any book or any story, no matter when it was written.

Another invert, also European — Gide — describes a character of his who is sitting in a train, and in front of him some French mommy is cuddling her daughter, wrapping her up in a shawl, then cooing to her that the two of them are glad who they are, *you and me, me and you, what do we care about the rest,* because we don't need them or the rest of the world in the least! Our motherland is traveling the same way in a train in the full view of some European decadent; and that she is wrapping herself up the same way in the shawl of her own selfdom is entirely clear to me. Because when she grows up, when that almost incomprehensible moment of her initiation occurs and she becomes ready for marriage, her classical poet,* as a contemporary newspaper quotes him, will write in her album that her whole body and her whole heart are of our blood, and that only a true youth of our blood will be allowed to kiss such a dear body as this! The old Grič novelist could be refuted by every recent advertisement for Benetton, in which a black tot, an Asian one, and our pure white European youngster are side by side, giggling, but to our local editor that deceased Grič writer's statement in that album matters more than all the realities of the modern world. We're glad who we are, we are perfectly content on our own, but when our mothers go to visit Europe, to complain to Europe about bad times at home, they will tell those at the German court that they are the Germans' children, and would the masters from this court please be our parents! Because our motherland doesn't want to be a mother either, she wants to be the child bundled up in the shawl in the train car, Gide's.

But then that intelligent Hungarian lady, Agnes Heller, says in her book on history that one nation can't survive by saying of the history of another nation that it's no sort of history at all and that the only history that can exist at all is this one that's "ours" and that has been unfolding "our" way for a very long time already, within "our" nation. Indeed, every day I read in our newspapers that this

*That is, August Šenoa.

history we have here is really and truly the one and only authentic history, while any other history of anyone else's would be very depressing to call any sort of history at all. Our Hungarian lady could teach us a fair amount here as well, because in her view history doesn't exist as an onto-logical system, but only as a scheme in the brain of this or that grouping of human beings. History itself doesn't know it exists; only we who have been pondering it (for the past two hundred years) know that it is and that it's as it should be, however it is. This assumes that *those others* know neither that they are in some sort of history nor how unhistorical that history of theirs looks when it is viewed from our standpoint. In other words, we believe that an historical being exists and that those who house that being are the people with "our" views and of our type, while others are utterly incapable of housing that being in any way at all. History thus becomes some sort of destiny like many others that obsess the human brain and have done so for a fairly long time now.

But what do these articles that stir universal fervor mean? I'm quoting this from my book I'm reading now, in the war, when nobody else is reading anything because we are in that war. But inasmuch as we all—in the course of this same war—are in different wars, differing almost from individual to individual, I who am in "my" war, I read, while the others, who are in their wars, they don't read anything. For if they in that war of theirs were to read what I am reading, it might happen that at least for a moment they would no longer be in their own war but, rather, in one that at least partially resembled the war I myself am in. *M. de Charlus,* the book says, *would get irri-tated at the triumphant optimism of the people who knew nothing of Germany and its strength,* and this wasn't because he himself was of German origin, but because he was *sharp at detecting any false judgment by a patriot,* whether in articles that likewise were patriotic, or in the discussion I myself am conducting, today, at the end of summer, in a Gothic town that may be nothing but a thriving fishing village.

I am probably also an incurable snob and scornful ignoramus, nationally speaking, because I am unable to repeat a single war report of the day, but Mrs. Verdurin and Mrs. Bontemps, my Rovinj one, she can, I tell you, and in such a way that this report of hers is almost more reportorial than the one she is thinking to interpret. Without adding anything, she speaks in a manner that not one of our reporters knows how to do—because she injects the fervor of a person who has virtually no involvement in what is being told about. The only person who can report the news is one who has no direct involvement in what he is reporting—except that he believes that in fact he has a superior relationship of this sort.

But *M. Bontemps wouldn't so much as hear of peace until Germany was reduced to the same fragmented state as in the Middle Ages,* nor does my Mr. Bontemps think of peace either, except he doesn't know what to do with me in this discussion, or whether I am, in our version, a Frenchman or a German. My situation here is quite confused, in that in this German-French discussion of ours I really don't know who I am. Because a German born in France can still choose to be an *apatrid,* a foreigner, a dissident, a defeatist, a republican, or purely and simply a nobleman, like Baron de Charlus is, an aesthete, cynic, and pederast whose last name, *des Guermantes,* is enough of an indictment that he can dare to get involved in discussions of the war. In other words, the only people who can talk freely about the war are those who are in it, meaning the ladies instructed in the parts of a Kalashnikov, inasmuch as *not one duchess* of ours, either, *would go to bed without finding out from Mme Bontemps, or from Mme Verdurin, at least over the phone, the contents of the evening war report, what was omitted from it, what's going on with Greece, and what kind of offensive is being pre-pared;* with the Verdurin circuit boiling this way like a pot, we're practically at the headquarters of "our" forces, and Mme Verdurin would say "we" speaking of France, just as our ladies on the hill say "our side" thinking of the Croats and "your side" when they have the Serbs in mind. But with me things are pretty confused, because "our side" and "your side" in any ethnic sense mean nothing to me; they do mean something to me, though, if I view as "our side" those for whom this ethnic question also means nothing, and "your side" or "their side" the ones for whom this same ethnic question means everything. Thus it turns out that in one very small group of people gathered on what was once an island, later turned into a fortress, medieval and very quiet, that on this very same spot on this overall Balkan peninsula there are "ours" who are really "theirs," and vice versa.

So I sit on my Rovinj hill and don't know who I am. I can't be a *Frenchman,* even though I've been surrounded by *Frenchmen* from time immemorial, but I'm a *German* only in the sense that three-quarters of my blood is *German.* Nevertheless, Mrs. Verdurin tells me: *"Come at five o'clock to talk about the war."* Did Valéry's famous flow-ery phrase have its origin in this sentence? But talking about the war for this lady doesn't mean talking about war operations, over there, in Slavonia, but rather, about how nobody ever talks about war, but how they ought to. In every war there are many people who don't talk about that war and its events, which usually are bloody, but instead talk about events that didn't happen at all in the course of such a war. It turns out that a war has many more events in it than any war can, and that they can't possibly all fit into such a war, even the most capacious one. At the same time, the war "market" has gone into action, that institution that procures nonexistent events as if they had just happened: *on the market every sick ruler is*

dead and every besieged city has been taken. For this reason I am trying to observe these conversations as psycholinguistic studies, if engaging in psycholinguistics during a war is a proper thing to do at all. It turns out that
during a war we can occupy ourselves only with "war,"
and yet I didn't notice during peacetime, which was very
lengthy, that we occupied ourselves with "peace."

A certain professor wrote an important book about
Schiller, and reviews of it appeared in the newspapers. But
before they said anything about him as the author of the
book, they would write, as a kind of "imprimatur," that
he had been on the Marne and at Verdun, that he had
been singled out for praise five times at early morning for-
mation, and that two of his sons had been killed. Then
came praise for the clarity and depth of his book about
Schiller, who was allowed to be called great on condition
that the phrase was "that great Kraut" instead of "that
great German." That was the password for an article to get
published quickly. Because stories have been published
over the decades about our glorious sons not because they
have written some book or other about Schiller (which
they haven't, as a rule), but because they were or were not
on the Marne, they were in exile and in the dungeons of
the former police, but as for whether their own sons were
also killed, that was maybe sometimes omitted. Because if
they just hadn't been in those police dungeons and in that
exile where they worked as garbagemen, they really honestly would have written those books of theirs on Schiller,
but since they were garbagemen at a time when they
shouldn't have been they didn't write these books, so
instead they are writing books now since they didn't get a
chance to write the books about Schiller—but, see, fortunately, today they are writing their testimony as to how
and why it happened that they didn't write those books!
Because if they had written them at that time, earlier, they
might have written something they themselves would view

today as inappropriate, so that what they'd already written, about Schiller, would have to be written over again. Thus it turns out that in troubled times it's best not to write anything, especially not to write a book about some poet from a foreign nation about whom in fact one shouldn't write in any case, and thus, and especially, at a time when one shouldn't be writing at all in any case! There really is something in us that advises us when we should write something and when we shouldn't write anything, and thus, at the moment, our most highly rated writing is that which is written at the greatest length about that nonwriting of ours in the past. It turns out that we had known back then how times would change, and we were waiting for that change, and when it finally and definitively came, then we would have time to write about our previous nonwriting to our heart's content! That nonwriting of ours "then" when we "shouldn't" have written can best be seen now when everybody knows that at this very moment we "should" be writing—and how!—because in this present "and-how!" writing a really totally unbelievable mass of writing is making its appearance—reading matter we ourselves never could have imagined would be ours! Because even though we did write before, what we wrote then and what we are writing now about that completely mistaken writing of ours almost seem to have been written by two people practically entirely unknown to each other, a twosome who hadn't ever met each other even! This is that misfortune of ours as writers—that in one instant we are one thing and in another something quite different, all owing to the cursed times which are so changeable. Because if the times weren't changeable we would always be the same—from that time and this one both—whereas now it's turning out that we're in some sort of schizophrenia, and that we aren't to blame for this schizophrenia at all. Because if anything is "crazy" it's the times, and not we who are quite unwilling witnesses to those times.

What do we care about this or that time, and what's it to us anyhow, and yet it turns out we're enslaved to it in a truly cruel and nasty way.

The soldiers of limited and trite spirit, writing poetry while they recuperated, didn't raise themselves up, to describe the war, to the level of events that in and of themselves were nothing, but rather to the level of the banal aesthetic whose rules had been adhered to before, so that they talked the way people would have talked ten years earlier, about "the bloody dawn," "the quivering flight of victory," etc., while Saint-Loup, a much more intelligent and much greater artist, remained intelligent and an artist, tastefully describing landscapes to me as he relaxed at the edge of some swampy forest, but as though he were hunting wild ducks. Hearing that, this friend of mine asks me again what sort of book this is I'm reading, because such a book really oughtn't to be read as long as this war, the *French-German* one, is going on. Because really such reading material could hamper not only our brave lads who are convalescing (who don't write poetry at all), but especially those for whom poetry is a profession and a duty and who would suddenly begin to write their poems about war problems with a feeling of doubt as to whether anything of the sort ought to be written at all. But I say that a feeling of doubt while writing is the one right feeling, which, in fact, is the only thing lacking in the poets who are writing about the war, here, today. Because if they had that feeling of doubt they would be writing about that feeling and that doubt, and not writing their poems in that way of theirs, totally and almost in principle having no doubts whatsoever!

But it's true that people see everything through their newspaper. Because looking that way, in fact they don't see, nor do they have to—since the newspaper sees for them, and since it is their realest and truest eyes! Perhaps eyes in fact ought to see in such a way that, looking indirectly, like true Marxist theoreticians of the human body, they see not what that philosopher himself thought ought to be seen, definitely not directly, in other words, but by way of another point, and after the looking itself. The question, though, is what remains then, later and after, that is, afterward, from that earlier part, and whether this hasn't been left now in some odd way to intermediaries between us ourselves and our looking, who are no longer of a theoretical nature but belong to the market that trades in news and rumor, a market at which what has happened is announced as having happened this way or that depending on whether the price of the information or news is rising or falling. *On the market every sick ruler is dead, be he Edward VII or William II, and every besieged city has been taken.* So thus the same milieu that zealously talks against surrealistic illusions is submitting most openly to the surrealism of the daily news broadcast and an almost Dadaist playing with elements of events, as if they were pieces of a collage, by Hausmann. Now the world has been cut to pieces à la Tristan Tzara, and as for who will paste these pieces back together and what sort of totality they'll be put together into, that depends. Everybody's obsessed with this children's game of cutting and pasting, and the whole outline of history is unfolding as if it were on the stage of Voltaire's cabaret. Thus the newspapers are presenting an incredible patchwork of what may once have been our "reality," the newspapers are making collages out of elements of that reality, already nonexistent now, while as for what it may "really" be, *naturally the newspapers are ordered not to write about that.* And what the newspapers weren't permitted to write about in Proust's day, which is that underage young men were being taken into the army—*why, they're still children,* for goodness sake!—naturally they aren't writing about in this patriotic journalistic Dadaist time, either. So thus in this wartime autumn we are conversing about movements in art that have already come to an end during our century, as well as about the elements of these movements that are, naturally, still alive in our present-day practice. We have boarded up and sandbagged our churches the way the Bulgarian artist who wraps even the world's largest structures would do, while anonymous fellows from everyday life are, in war, becoming unexpected great men of public life—like what one artist of the "conceptualist" movement dreamed up in his mocking style in our capital city some ten years ago.* And in fact, there on Republic Square as it once was, where he hung up enormous paintings of utterly anonymous citizens of our capital, chosen at random, individuals of that degree of anonymity now appear—saying things that in every sense, including political, are completely anonymous. Anonymity is that final blow to the logic and pace of a time that not only has gotten out of joint but threatens to stop being any kind of time at all. We may now be reaching that degree of trans-Einsteinian fantasy in which time itself may disappear as all the values that are supposedly human become relativized. And the city in which such wise thinking was once done about Heideggerian Being—that it was what clothed every creature who was being operationalized and announced by means of this Being—now sees the camouflage of the armed forces as the sole cloak for any psychophysical human individual, which doesn't camouflage its wearer from the enemy too awfully well, but if that wearer has ceased to be aware of his own existence, it does camouflage him from that existence. Because wearing camouflage can't mean that I am furthering this existence such that somebody else won't recognize me and so thus camouflaged supposedly help me survive this clash, but rather it means that the man in camouflage has camouflaged himself from his own self and that he no longer knows much at all about his until

*I am referring to Braco Dimitrijević.

recently uncamouflaged self. Likewise, a mask on a human face not only shields that face from other people's glances but removes from its wearer some of his knowledge of his own face, because camouflaging oneself means wanting to be somebody else, not only for others but for oneself as well. I am no longer what I thought I was, because what I was I had no confidence in, for one Mishkin-like* reason or another, so let's go be something else now than what we have been, although during that transaction it may turn out that we haven't become that something else, while what we had been we have completely forgotten in this transaction of ours. Thus being camouflaged not only camouflages nothing, but in an urban setting—quite the opposite—it emphasizes the very intention to camouflage oneself, not concealing the camouflaged person from the view of other people, but instead calling attention to him himself and his wish to completely forget the most recent phase of the uncamouflaged period of his life. From time to time it's hard for a person to be completely anonymous with no camouflage (as our conceptual artist showed), so now, wishing to camouflage himself and "hide," he tries to conceal not his precamouflage human status as an individual and subject who had at least some sort of face, but rather the status in which this face wasn't noticed by any-

*In the Croat-Serb war of 1991, one agent of the people armed himself in order to protect his agency with his own weapon, but oddly enough handled his revolver clumsily and wounded himself, twice in fact. This is an example of *a failure to grasp* under "abnormal," wartime, conditions. What I mean is, breaking a vase in circumstances however Mishkin-like is still "more normal" than being awkward with your own body, especially when that body belongs to others as well, that is, to the people. Thus does Mishkin's role get its counterpart, just as his great rival isn't completely free of gestures that are "idiotic." Now the Russian prince, the confused one, is becoming Rogozhin, and his hand isn't controlling his "intentions" either, but is carrying out orders from higher up and according to Thanatos's plan.

one except conceptualist fantasizers! A camouflage masquerade, whether military or not, is in fact an unveiling, a performance that emphasizes, presents, and displays what even a totally unattractive and anonymous person can achieve with a multicolored piece of cloth. Camouflage design is intended to mimic the variegation of nature's colors, to aim for something so constituted, be it a chaffinch or a turtle or a butterfly in their variegated colors, but a crack appears in this intent to mimic: the concealed person wants to reveal himself as not having concealed himself very well and, with this wrapper, having gotten a promotion—a bigger one than if he had gone out on the street with no trousers on. He is now that unconcealedly concealed warrior whose mission hasn't been entirely fathomed by all his brain cells, but who knows at least this part of his intent and has become different from what he had been, such that this act of metamorphosis has likewise been announced publicly, in the square.

On the other hand, there are still quite a few members of our population who would not risk showing themselves but would literally disappear down a mousehole, not just because there is a frightened mouse heart beating in them but because disappearing down a mousehole conveys some of the mouse's shame over the sometimes totally crazy person trying to get rid of it. Because a mouse is gotten rid of not just because it's a pest and because it makes a mess in the kitchen, but also because mice are "supposed to be" gotten rid of and because that is a totally logical and expected daily item in our kitchen schedule.

I immediately thought of Combray, of my fertile little corner of Slavonia, which was even more modest than Proust's Combray corner was for him, and even he once *thought* he would *sink in Mme Guermantes' eyes if he were to admit the modest social standing* of his family, in Illiers. Anyway, life there, a mouse's life though it was, was fertile and quiet; in this rich domain my great-grandfathers performed their divine services, my grandfather settled the accounts of his winery and his correspondence with horticulture companies abroad, and concerned himself with trying to get a certain special seed from one German firm or another for a yellow flower he hankered to have somewhere at the far end of his garden, which was laid out in a totally French manner. All this once was as it was in the book I am reading, Proust's, but then the cannons began to plow the last remnants of these gardens, which had already been plowed up once, fifty years before. Today the little town that bears the name of one of my grandfathers* is under barrage; "our guys" are there and the other "our guys," or "your guys," are firing away in what's left of the garden because they believe this garden, Grandfather's, is "theirs," when only the flowers know who they bloomed for then, practically a century ago, and why. These cannonades not only are burying in cannon fire two nations transformed into one, a dead one; they are burying a different kind of seed in the ground, all that's known about which is that it won't be bearing flowers. There were flowers here once, but now other plantings are being required of us, and an utterly different sort of gardening that threatens once again to become the last. Because every time after the cannons come it looks as though grass won't grow, yet after a certain time it does grow, while the cannon in that grass then gradually rusts and disintegrates irreparably. This is some sort of chemical process that keeps society together, and yet the idea that society may have no reason to stay together I have also sensed perfectly well for a long time now. And I don't know why some people are so fearful they won't be able to keep their own life together, meaningless as it turns out to be. *Everybody tried to keep me from going* there. *They thought I was crazy. As they told me*, says one

*"Changed" now.

lady, of Proust's, *in Paris you're safe, but you are going to areas the Germans have occupied, right at the moment everybody's trying to flee from them.* I, meanwhile, know people close to me who go from here, from our *French* environs, over there amidst my *Germans,* to converse with them and even to do a bit of business, in an almost fantastic way. And this at a time when one cabinet minister from here, in his *French* arrogance, believes that connections with the *Germans* should be severed once and for all. I, meanwhile, am that *German* with whom he wants to sever all business dealings, even though I still live in his and my country. In other words, this could be achieved only if I somehow succeeded in severing my connection with myself through a sudden attack of madness, which, by some real miracle, hasn't hit me yet, but, as we see, has already hit this minister in a merciless way. One of our critics describes his Combrayesque childhood, the locale of his birth, which has now been destroyed, barbarically and unnecessarily. He says, though, that in the immediate vicinity there was another small town whose name was totally unclear and almost meaningless to him, and that all he knows about this *Saint Cauchemar* was that it was where one changed trains, and that if there was anything else of importance about that town he didn't know it. The writer thus reveals his loss of historical memory almost unerringly, because in *Saint Cauchemar*—ours—half a century ago there was a penal colony for members of the enemy nation, and changing trains then meant sailing under Charon's oar. However, if the author of the Combrayesque description demonstrated his forgetfulness, I bear witness to a superabundance of my own memory, only because my grandfather was in that colony, and there, watching priests of his own faith hitched to oxcarts, thanks to his horticultural skill, he designed the great Nuremberg emblem out of Saint Cauchemar tulips, and thanks to this gardening know-how managed to get himself spared, because flowers were highly valued at one time in these gloomy parts.

Intellectuals are (probably precisely because of that superabundance of memory) *the problematic individuals par excellence,* says the historian Heller, and as such they become the scourge of God. But they merely call attention to a problematicalness deep-rooted in humanity as a whole, highlighting this fairly distributed neurosis and experiencing it personally. They are that problem humanity has that, for its own sake and more often than not to its own detriment, it proclaims in more or less precise flowery phrases; so what they do is attempt to convert this loss of memory about the problems of mulling, pondering, and thinking in general into productive knowledge.

These days intellectuals have access to the truth, but they have access to untruth as well, says Heller, *because in the division of labor the creation and implementation of well-thought-through views of the world becomes their task.* Now it is no longer science on the one hand and the state on the other, but rather, says the philosopher Foucault, a symbiosis is formed in the basic form "power/ knowledge," such that he who wields the whip prescribes at the same time what may and may not be known.

Power is what gives legitimacy to the scientific discourse launched under this power, and, as the philosopher Lyotard says, *the "legislator" who concerns himself with this scientific discourse is empowered to prescribe the particular conditions in which a statement becomes a part of that discourse and the scientific community can take it under consideration. Since a close similarity exists between the kind of language that is called science and that other one that is called ethics and politics,* we are now hearing our scientists talk like prophets, while, surprisingly, in the statements of our politicians the "scientific" spirit is being very painstakingly covered up. Science, in other words, is the material that is now being covered up, because of a very pragmatic question—Lyotard's: *who decides what knowledge is and who knows what needs to be decided?*

In one scientific discussion long ago on this topic, as Lyotard says, *Laswell defined the communication process using the formula: Who says what to whom through what channel with what result?* Our present "wartime" television regulations congenially repeat this Princeton study. *Every dialect fights for dominance, and if it is in power then it spreads into all the pores of current and daily public life and becomes* doxa, *nature.* Calvet finds in this *the old target of Barthes' work: the common-sensicalness of false obviousness, (that is) the masks of ideology.*

Once again my Mr. Verdurin is amazed.

Here's what I find bad about the citizens, the citizenry of *France* displaying that famous courtesy of theirs toward authority: they used to be courteous to "those," and now they're courteous to "these," so thus it turns out that courtesy is a general state of affairs and a climate in which the citizenry as such resides. To be a citizen, according to that interpretation, means to govern one's conduct politely, especially toward those who govern, whereas they, on the other hand, in governing their own conduct, have no obligation whatsoever to try or succeed in displaying any sort of "politeness." Because where would a governor get if in governing his own conduct he were guided by his "politeness" and his innate courtesy as, in some paradoxical way, he expects his own citizenry to show?! That the citizenry in some discourteous sense wouldn't be a citizenry anymore at all, that is entirely clear to my Rovinj Mr. Verdurin. I, meanwhile, know some very great European citizens throughout history who never even thought of displaying such an attitude to the governor, so I am finally at a loss as to how to define this "profession" of humanity's that is felt and considered to be citizenship. Because citizenship is also a craft or a trade, and what is turned over and placed into circulation in this trade is this cultivated relation toward people who are completely uncultivated. The citizenry, in the main, believes every government will come to an end sooner or later, and that they themselves with their courtesy and their endless patience will be left to show this same patience/courtesy toward a government that hasn't come to power yet at all. The citizenry is prepared for a government that doesn't even dream it will be coming to power, such is their patience, stretched into the distant future. Because "we" will always be here, but "they," they will keep changing until they make their final change, before our eyes, sooner or later.

And if there is anything at all that bothers me in what is called our citizenry, it is a narrow-mindedness that manifests itself in that citizenry from time to time. Everybody noticed that the leader of the failed Russian coup, Yanayev, was shaking and that he was perspiring immoderately and inhumanly at his only press conference; not many observed what this person, already pitiful, was doing with his pocket handkerchief: though it was folded up, he didn't open it up at all, instead constantly shifting it back and forth from one hand to the other like an object that was almost burdening him. Yanayev's clenched handkerchief immediately revealed a sort of narrow-mindedness he had, his miserable conspiracy, and his awareness that he couldn't wipe himself off and cleanse himself in the public eye. Besides, opened out, this hankie in his hands, which were shaking badly, would have been the final *semion*—the white flag of surrender, the sign of defeat.

So I am sitting on my Rovinj hill, and instead of talking about the war I am reading what Proust said in 1916 about that war then. Mrs. Verdurin, the local one, asks me again how on earth I can read Proust when the whole country is in flames, and I say that Proust's country was also in flames the same way, if not worse, when he wrote what I am reading now. Because the way I see it, someone is always writing something, whether that someone's country is in flames or not, and if this same *someone* didn't write, that country wouldn't be any the less in flames. The question is, my lady says to me, whether Proust in his decadence regarded his country, in flames, as his own country at all, which I understand relates to me and my relation to this country of mine, in flames.

We are all children of the same mother (who sometimes doesn't want to be a mother!), but even so we should all be obedient children, and if that someone from our parental home tells us to black out the windows and go down to the cellar, we will of course do this, but then, *from time to time, defying police orders, some mansion, or even just one room on one floor, looked as if it were all by itself in the impalpable darkness, like a brightly lighted projection, like a specter without substance only because its shutters weren't closed.* Friends really do tell me there is a house in Čakovac that shines this way, decadent and Proustian, in the Medjimurje darkness because its inhabitants, like me myself, do not accept this war and these blackouts of light and sanity, but instead set their lamp out on top of some hill, be it Rovinj's or not, and if somebody wants to shoot at this light, let them go ahead! There's always somebody "more conscientious" than we are, who aren't conscientious at all and leave our light, our island light, shining like a provocation, to the enemy. *Close your shutters—you know that light is forbidden because of the Zeppelins,* repeats that strict warning spirit of the conscience that hovers over all the cities that are under attack, like an all-seeing eye of God, strict and inexorable. But even the frontline soldiers are unconcerned about such phenomena: *No more Zeppelins will be coming. The newspapers have even hinted that they've all been shot down.* But what is it that newspapers, be they ours or not, reveal, and what do they conceal in the very course of their newspapering—deliberately?! *When you've weathered fifteen months at the front and when you've shot down your fifth plane the way I have, then you'll be able to talk. The newspapers are not to be believed. Yesterday Compiegne was attacked and a mother and two children killed. A mother and two children!*

I'm reading about the amazing changes that take place in Proust's characters: the ones who had been for "that" are now most zealously for "this," more zealously in fact than they had ever been for "that." *It's all a matter of chronology,* the writer says in one of his footnotes. Things used to be one way, but now that way's over and done with and something else entirely has come along, but the strangest thing about this change is that the people most energetically involved in the new way had been the heroes of the "old" one and of the existence that got buried overnight. Because it isn't unusual in semi-European countries for a regime to change the school readings used under previous regimes, but it *is* strange when these textbook reconstructions are done by the authors of these same, now redone, books, and when they view this phenomenon and this role of theirs in that phenomenon as utterly natural. We used to be one thing, but now we're something else, but whether we are the same "we" now that we were then, that is a question only a very poised doctor of psychology could ask, behind windows that have been properly blacked out. That same doctor, meanwhile, appears on television and attacks the pacifists in our otherwise very nonpacifist masses, where even the peace-loving poet, out of the depths of his isolation, says that he is for the war and that it must be waged at all costs.

In other words, Proust's society changed (as mine has) such that the cosmopolite Bloch, with his patriotism, all but overshadowed Saint-Loup, the professional soldier. *And while Bloch was displaying the most chauvinistic emotions, Saint-Loup, after Bloch left us, was full of self-irony for not resuming his duties in the army,* it being appropriate now to talk about these things only when

Bloch, the former cosmopolite and Dreyfusard but now an ardent chauvinist, only when such an ardent person has gone away from us and our ironic judgments.

As far as that goes, aristocrat officers encountered that same patriotism in full measure in socialists, whom I heard them charging, while I was in Doncieres, during the Dreyfus affair, with being "without a homeland." The military men's patriotism, just as sincere as it was profound, had acquired a particular form that they regarded as inviolable, and they would get furious when it was disgraced, while patriots who were in some way naive, independent, lacking a particular patriotic belief, such as the radical socialists were, couldn't understand what profound reality resided in what they thought were hollow and hateful formulas. The whole point is, one group thinks the other's formulas are hateful and hollow, while the other group regards those same formulas as the ABCs and the Ten Commandments. And when the group with the Ten Commandments says one thing and the one with the hateful formulas something quite the opposite, it's impossible now (because we're at war), it's impolite today to conduct psycholinguistic discussions and hold forth on the topic that nothing once written is ever the same when we read this writing again; there is no point in our Lacans and our Derridas and our Paul de Mans being here—rather, the one who has reason to be here is named Fyodor Mikhailovich Kalashnikov or some such.

And "I don't know what I am" not because I don't know whether I'm a *German* or a *Frenchman*, but because I'm reading Proust while all anybody else is doing is thinking about how to become *Frenchmen* when they're actually *Germans*. The human being constantly wants to become something other than he is, especially during wartime. Because even pure-blooded *Frenchmen* in these situations want to become *super-Frenchmen* in an ultra-super-French sense. It turns out, in fact, that one of our ladies, from Rovinj, who is particularly notable for her "Frenchness," isn't a "Frenchwoman" at all but is as much of a "German"* as I am. It is ending up that this war is much more greatly preoccupying those who, being *non-Frenchmen*, want to present themselves as *Frenchmen*, perhaps even more than it is those few poised *Frenchmen* I know who don't reveal their *Frenchness* in any way, and would even like to put some of it in parentheses.

Every day my Mrs. Verdurin of Rovinj *marvels at the bravery of the young men, the intoxication of the cavalry assaults, and the intellectual and moral nobility of friendships* in which one sacrifices one's life for another. *War*, which is my lady's main topic, *war is, on the contrary, a passionate love affair of homosexuals*, and not just because our Combray invert refers to it that way. In war, as in sports, a carefree brotherhood of males organizes that the female sex cannot join but is allowed to watch from its theater boxes, through field glasses, which are also for the theater. We all are watching the war from our boxes, and this position is made possible to us by our modern theater technology of the television variety. In war, brought closer and magnified this way, that lily of unisexuality blooms, and on this same television network one evening they banned a film about two young girls who start fondling each other as if in a lyrical Hamiltonian haze. Somebody called somebody else up—or else somebody didn't even pick up the phone, but on his own, of his own accord, rid

*The Serbs and the Croats, it says in The Guardians [Ćosić's 1978 novel—Trans.], will first be brothers, after that enemies, then brothers again and godparents, then they'll take knives to each other's throats again, and finally, act as if they'd never met before. This was written by the hand of the compiler of an eternal calendar whose medium and scribe I was fifteen years ago. A plus about eternal calendars is that the facts stated in them don't go into effect for a long time, a whole "eternity," and then, overnight, they become the authoritative word and a document of history.

our conscious minds of these two little Albertines, because unisexual occurrences don't occur in war, or that is, they do occur, and since we ought not to know they occur for occurability's sake, our esteemed audience won't hear a word about it from us! We are once again here to certify what will and will not be talked about, and what really exists on earth but ought not to! Because what ought not to be will not be, whereas what really ought not to be— there shouldn't be such a concept, the certification one, according to which this certifier of ours determines what exists and what doesn't. Because even if he himself may think this "something" exists, it can happen rather easily that this same "something" doesn't exist at all, and that this existence of the nonexistent is only a figment of his questionable imagination. That is why I am undertaking to talk not about what possibly does indeed exist, but about what may in fact not exist, no matter how much that something has been talked about by my Verdurin and Bontemps ladies, daily. Maybe the reason they talk so much about this or that is because they don't see "this" and "that" all that clearly or the way their intelligence might have expected, so they talk about these phenomena in order—through their talking—to make them more phenomenal and more visible.

Male brotherhood blooms along all the world's fronts, and in the pauses in that frontline torturing and bloodshed so full of senselessness the impulse appears that my classic book reveals like very few others that have set about trying to reveal it. *He was quite pleased,* one invert tells of some other invert, *when he saw that he wasn't being asked to betray his homeland, but only his body, which may be no more moral, but is less dangerous and much easier.* I am reading this episode from a book that is decadent and, according to the standards of one of our contemporary critics, stupid and nonsensical, and in that nonsense I am discovering from the perspective of the

Dalmatian Zagora how the betrayal of one's own body in that bordello, for soldiers, compares to the betrayal of that same cube of flesh, bones, and an occasional thought at the front, the homeland's. There, Mother Earth who bore us is being defended, but in such a way that in her Medea-like outlines we are betraying our own physical system and that little bit of thought that tells us we in fact are some kind of system. A battlefield is a market that is plainly full of cheating and Latin-style dangers, where we exchange that tangible little piece of reality that can be substantiated through meditation, for meditation with no physical substance behind it. Because the homeland isn't a piece of territory that used to be somebody else's but now is ours and one day will be who knows whose; the homeland in this mercantile semispiritual or one-quarter spiritual trivial academic discussion would only be some sort of aura, the breaking up and dispelling and clearing up of which would bring to light that this halo actually has no light in it. The aura that surrounds our discussions about the homeland is a piece of trickery, from a street fair, in the hands of those who deceive the eyes of children, there on Pincije. There they also spin dolls in a little box, and the children of the homeland, its future sons and soldiers, watch this spectacle with amazement.

But I can't take part in these conversations by dint of my *Germanness,* because what sort of *German* would I be if I rejoiced at some *German* defeat, while as a *Frenchman* by the country of my birth I lack that enthusiasm, for warring, that every *Frenchman* ought to have. In any case, if this tale of mine smells of a deficit of national consciousness—*others would call it Kike internationalism,* perhaps in part because it reflects my sick *liberal culture*—then part of the blame falls on the author I am quoting, who, as we know, was a pacifist, disdainfully anational, a desperado in his everyday human existence, a snob, decadent, and pederast. *M. Charlus's situation changed,* however. Be-

cause all sorts of things happened as a result of his "quirk-
iness," manifested in that he was less and less tolerant of
those whom he had no obligation to tolerate, and that he
stopped accommodating the pace of his personal life to
anyone else's, even that of history. I feel all this, intimately,
as though it were a description of my own circumstances,
in this war, a senseless one. And just as the baron *lived in
relative solitude, of which he was not the cause,* so, too, do
I notice that I myself am surrounded by *emptiness,* which
most interestingly of all I am almost enjoying. In fact I
came to this former island in order, if possible, to test how
the people who until recently had been close to me would
react to this intention of mine to come to this island. Telephone connections, now cut off, even before they were
cut off had gotten cut off by my absence and by my deci-
sion, the island one, and the formerly very important individuals in my theater have now been reduced to a mono-
drama, à la Beckett. We are in this garbage can of history,
and what we are mumbling from inside this can can scarcely be understood even by those with the best of intentions. Nevertheless, I believe in some sort of hermeneutic
skill in the people of the future that will make sense of
even that mumbling, which is illusory in a Beckettesque
sort of way. *M. de Charlus,* owing to his *ill repute that
was now widely known,* was left "alone" and *people who
didn't know better thought those who weren't visiting
him were ones whom he had arbitrarily refused to visit.*
It's always this way: I've gotten tired of certain people,
intimately; my ever more chronic negativism no longer
encounters that little flicker in them that ought to flicker
at least from time to time with intimates, in order for
them to be that—intimate, and it has turned out that that
negativism of mine is completely called for, because these
above-mentioned people have also begun to get tired of
me, whether or not there had actually ever been this flick-
ering, of a reciprocal sort. Except that *M. de Charlus mul-*

tiplied the quarrels he had with his family, foreordaining the quarrels his present reader of these quarrels is having, almost word for word. The loss of cordiality, and then of almost all human contact between what had once been my family and their son, the prodigal one, who fled to a former fishermen's island, falls at the moment of my disinheritance, a complete one, by my mother country and my hometown, which is becoming permanent. Because, *what nationality is he really?* asks the baron's close friend, Mme Verdurin; *isn't he Austrian?* He's actually German, or he isn't German, but see how he lives here among us *French,* and the most interesting thing of all, moreover, we *French* put up with him, a *German,* very charitably. And where is it written that a group of *French* people have to put up with an individual *German* when it's well known that individual *Germans* are always plotting against our lives even when we aren't plotting against theirs, as individual *Germans,* at all? This is how my Verdurin ladies of Rovinj could talk about me if they knew about this excuse, a quite interesting one, which I am discovering, in Proust. Because *the Queen of Naples told me—surely you know she's a horrendous spy—*but anyhow, *that if we had a more energetic government, everyone like that would have to be in a concentration camp.* So these, camps, weren't invented in "our" time, of history, but were anticipated in the dreams of these ladies from the Faubourg Saint-Germain a century ago. People are either "on our side" or they're not, but the ones who seem to be "on our side" but aren't are just about the worst of all. And for these really rather mixed-up individuals we ought to develop some sort of antidote, one for spies, because it's almost certain of the baron that *surely the Germans had assigned him to make the preparations for a submarine base here,* because somebody like that—an invert, decadent, utterly suspect from a national standpoint—is fully capable of selling off an entire bay belonging to our homeland for the use of enemy torpedo boats and what in our childhood was called "sou-marens." True enough, *M. Charlus was a poet of high society, the one from his environs who knew how to salvage a certain type of poetry that contained history, beauty, picturesqueness, amusement, and a frivolous elegance,* but aren't these precisely the earmarks and characteristics of the anational, the antinational, and the treacherous in a high degree? Because the intellectual, the educated person—the "mind," by the criteria of any patriotism—is that suspect dimension of human existence, that utterly inconstant and unreliable individual brain mass that goes "this way" today and "that way" tomorrow, and worst of all, this this way–that way will most often be aimed against whatever is collective, unanimous, and socially useful, which is to say against "ours" in the "our-est" sense of the word! An intellectual, be he also deformed in his sexuality or not, is always somehow barraging himself with questions, and is somehow confused about himself, right when there's no time for any confusion or barrages of questions, lest the time for love of our homeland slip away from us along with our home itself, and not a thing remain of all that is sacred to us! Thus did our poet of the immediate, which expressed itself in picturesqueness, a frivolous elegance, and amusement at its own beauty, find himself the target of society's single-mindedness, and now here am I along with him, thinking how I, too, could very easily find myself a target, for similar reasons. Because I, too, believe that the time for frivolous elegance, pretty picturesqueness, and the nurturing of beauty has not withered in the times that are around us—wartimes. The more I read this old book, the more circumstances, people, and phenomena I am discovering in it that exist around us, in this season that is not only not peacetime but is confused in the extreme. And part of our confusion comes from thinking we are living as people who are alive and in existence when we are only characters in a book written at the beginning of the century. But since books are written by their authors at a time that is almost indefinable and indecipherable as to the level of psychological relevance, maybe this book wasn't written then at all, but instead, by way of our conversations, actions, and our bad dreams, is appearing in its final version just now, and right now, partially owing to us ourselves, as some sort of very crazy extras in it.

Baron de Charlus was a person gifted in the art of life and living, yet at the same time he committed one of those improprieties against this life that only a particular class of people commits, in that he was too occupied with spiritual matters and aspects of culture, and in keeping with this, he threw himself into that same life from the "wrong" side, as a decadent, invert, and pederast. But aren't we who shun the "naturalness" of a certain expected allegiance to the state, the nation, and social regulations also inverts of a special sort, and hence outcasts, not only in a "moral" sense? Because being "natural" nowadays means finding your mate in a person of the opposite sex, and additionally, being committed to the idea, the one and only one, that hangs over this nation and this country like a rain cloud. In other words I am being promiscuous, not with a soldier of my own sex who has by some chance deserted the front, but rather, with my own idea, which is the idea neither of that soldier nor of any military whatever. Because my idea, an antimilitary and antifront one, turns out to be really inverted, since I have no desire for that same soldier, physical or spiritual, either one. Because to me *he* is the invert with his completely approved of and "natural" impulses to sin with his mother homeland, against which I, from the depths of my own inversion, can have nothing either. That soldier of mine is an abandoned child and the unfortunate offspring of a father he never fully knew, and in putting on his camouflage, he has decided to lie with his own mommy homeland, forgetting every other physical, spiritual, and maybe even intellectual impulse. There's always much that is intellectual about lying with one's own mother in any case, as Hamlet's neurotic dilemma shows us well enough. It is impossible to lie with one's mother without having this intellectual and intelligent idea, but with this idea it is practically impossible not to lie with her. So let my warrior of the same sex lie with his own homeland mother, but let him leave me, also an individual profoundly of the same sex, alone to commune with my idea, whence I may have had my origins earlier and more truly than I did from the woman who bore me in this country once upon a time, long ago. Because even before I came out of her womb as her earthly and human product, I had already been produced by my mother idea, being older even than that human earthly parent of mine who was bloodied by my arrival in the world. And now I am returning to it, or into it, with the incestuous passion I would feel returning to where I had been before I had ever been at all. My incestuous inversion can thus stand up to scrutiny because I am avoiding another sort of incest, the one promised to me in my mother homeland's bed. Perhaps our version of this picture, a lastingly unnatural picture, can be glimpsed now when the daughters of the homeland commune with their promiscuous mother: this can be seen in their homelandish faces and their getup, the suit with its mannish look, showing signs of our widespread national practice of women passing for men.

Now I, too, am the potential target of lampoons of the sort that dogged Baron de Charlus's suspect national consciousness, as they were described in the book that, in spite of the war, I am continuing to read. Because *as soon as the war began, not only the baron's inversion but also his supposed German nationality came under attack: "Frau Kraut" and "Frau van den Kraut" were M. de Charlus's usual nicknames. One article of a poetic nature had this title, borrowed from some of Beethoven's dance tunes: "A German Girl." Finally, two novellas: "The Uncle from*

America and the Aunt from Frankfurt" and "Intrepid Hero in the Rear," which the circle of intimates read in galley proofs no less.

He who isn't one of us must be made of some special material—human, semihuman, or even "animal," as one musicmaker, or musician if you wish, says, speaking of the nation he thinks finds war to be that way—musical, I mean. And since I am of that "other" nation that our tunester has deigned to call animal, I am trying to think like a beast that not only behaves in a beastly way but in its beastliness often feels quite endangered by man. Because man is the one who rules over nature in a, one might almost say, natural way, but we who are other, or in other words beasts, ergo animals, we also—oddly enough— have a thinking process of our own, albeit an entirely animal one. In other words, animals think even when it is thought they don't know how to think at all, while that equally animal man who believes only he knows how to think, he thinks as has just been spelled out. People can in fact become beasts, although even under "human" conditions they will try to behave in a way that, based upon our common humanity, everyone hopes we won't behave, because even among "us" who have almost completely human form there are people of different colors, there are vegetarians, numismatists, and horticulturists; there are flutists and Jews, inverts, both male and female; or if nothing else, then just highly sensitive individuals, aesthetes, decadents, drug addicts, neurasthenics, melancholics, and outright madmen, and children. These assemblages of people, naturally, aren't some elite that human society expects will exist until the end of the world and the ages as an elite and compact whole in and of itself; rather, they are that unpleasant ballast that disrupts and spoils such a picture, so then in spite of ourselves we set about our lampooning and our satirizing, or in fact satanizing, of the antihuman aspects of our true panhumanity and superhumanity, whence these handy little items in written form by the names of "Frau Kraut" and "A German Girl." In other words, I am one such German girl, not because I have any feminine characteristics or that by the very fact I am *non-French* I have immediately acquired a deviation, a sexual one, but rather because in my writing I don't adhere to that "homosexuality" that our musician who craves war— war against a pro-animal nation, at that—has. I just can't fathom that same "homosexuality," even with people of my own language, with whom I ought to be in similar circumstances, linguistic ones, be they human or animal! Because what I have been saying to these fellow tribesmen of mine for quite a while now, these fellow tribesmen of mine are unable to understand, and the ones who don't consider me to be their fellow tribesman may even sense something in my speech that's doglike and roosterish. I am a lingual pederast who doesn't use his organ, of speech, the way any "normal" man from my tribe uses his, but rather, I use and employ it as only a total invert, depraved and warped, knows how. Because every tribe knows the proper way to talk (just as it "knows" how we should behave publicly, sexually, or religiously), whereas I, in the altered church of my language and in the depravity of my lingual sexuality, talk the way they do only in a brothel and in the reversible bordello in the book *Fabian*. In it young men play the virgin to their aging but manly females; Baron de Charlus, Proust's, pursues soldiers who have deserted the French-German front, and I, in my daily pen-pushing routines, write as I ought not to and as no one expects that I as a "normal" writer would be able to. Because a deceitful and insidious trait we inverts have is that many people don't know we are inverts, given that not every homosexual goes down the street wearing lipstick, but instead, perhaps, hides this lipstick-wearing of his deep in a corner of his depraved heart. By the same token my writing, which appears undepraved, is probably depraved to a high degree, yet to get at that depravity would take an elite team of linguistic police, of the sort that unfortunately is still in its infancy here. I am more of a case for the bewilderment of my Mrs. Verdurin, of Rovinj, who sees that there's something wrong with my writing, but what it is that's wrong with it she still doesn't quite know exactly. Many of my things, which she sometimes even reads in manuscript, she actually likes, in fact; nevertheless, in her own fondness for them she finds some possibly latent and certainly still undeveloped sin. But then any reading is sinful, especially the reading of someone else's text that is some sort of more or less unconcealed sexuality, and my lady assuredly senses this, in a vague way. I am making love to her through this reading matter, but she doesn't realize that by reading it she is making love to me. So if I am of a completely different class of zoological phenomena of the world, if I am a vampire who is revealing myself as a vampire through my vampirish manuscript, then she is all but delightedly entering into a liaison that is just as utterly perverted if not completely forbidden. She knows that war is "unbearable," and that during a war one ought not to be reading, not even something by same-sex, same-nation writers, and yet at the same time she grabs up my *German* written Eros like a forbidden object, like something sinful, in other words, of an Eastern sort. Because I am an Eastern sin not only when someone from the West is reading me, but even when I, by some miracle, and in tiny little alveoli of readers, am read in the East. I'm not read "the way authors abroad are read today," on a massive scale, in huge series, and this, too, is my sin as an introverted, and probably quite sinful and wicked, figure of the sort used for frightening boys with. The daily literary masturbating I and my readers do thus goes on in the seclusion and secrecy of almost every word I have written, because masturbating on the public square is only for political jargon, which pours out its bodily substance from off some balcony like out of a bordello chamber pot. This act, in other words, this inverted literary action of mine, is utterly morbid in nature and falls within the pathology of a national system that is practically *as big as Mont Blanc,* because *there exist huge organisms, assemblages of individuals called nations; their life merely repeats and magnifies the life of the cells of which it consists;* a nation is an almost single-celled creature, and those few microscopic counterproteins and other pathological substances to be found in that huge macrocell, those are those poor alphabet letters of ours and those concepts of ours—repulsive, inverted, pederastied, and masturbated to pieces—that someday in the healthy supercellular future of this same nation-cell probably won't exist at all!

M. de Charlus, who had exceptional moral traits, who was given to compassion, who was generous, capable of being loyal and devoted, at the same time had no patriotic feelings, for various reasons, among which the reason that his mother was a Duchess of Bavaria may have played some role. Because of this he belonged just as much to the body of France as to the body of Germany. This is the fate that shadows half-breeds and national inverts, even if their history isn't thoroughly baronial. To have a little part of your body be *this* and the rest of you *that* is a fate, however, that contributes to a clarity of mind and thought unknown to monolithic human individuals, who only imagine they weren't the locus of ethnic compilations and national interbreeding in the distant or more recent past. The only difference is that some people learn the identity of their ancestors several centuries back, so they know exactly which Orthodox priest married a German woman, an Austrian, or the daughter of which lesser Croat landowner and when, while the others, who hardly know their grandfather's name, can't tell their grandfather's grandfather from their grandfather himself. This is why it's easier for me to follow the moral dilemmas of Proust's baron, in this book I am reading, injudiciously, as time goes by — wartime. Anyhow, there was this character of the writer's (who was to some extent the writer himself), and he was *bright, while the largest number of people in any country are dimwits; there is no doubt German fools would have angered him—had he lived in Germany—because they were defending something unjust in a stupid and passionate way, but since he lived in France, he was just as angered by the French fools for defending something that was just, in a stupid and passionate way.* Because being right doesn't necessarily mean that the one who is right is immune to stupidities that can turn a thing to folly similar to the madness reigning on the side of the unjust. The just and the unjust clash over the justice — which is problematical and difficult to establish in any case—of this or that issue, but in that consequently unjust struggle they usually use the same means, because even the juster ones, in the desire to promote this justness in the others' eyes, start up such a bunch of stupidities that the justness itself gets fogged over in that fervent and utterly idiotic effort. A wise man, though, in his anational isolation and in his cursed outcast state, simply doesn't get involved in the struggle between categories of justness that are difficult to establish, not because some personal limitation or cowardice is holding him back, but because he parades the limitations of his ignorance, and his uncertainty about having the right views on issues of planetary importance, as being his most authoritative message and his most precious possession. I who don't know what's what in a quarrel between two people—man and wife, father and daughter, son and mother—how would I know what the trouble is between two nations, even if they are very homogeneous and monocellular in their makeup?! I can't understand the reason they are quarreling, nor can I be the judge in a hearing that, full of sound and fury, has been going on since Macbeth's day. I marvel here at the thoroughly thought-out solidity and purity of the logical conclusions reached by our vicars, our doctors, our academicians, and our scientists, who know where to find what in an index/table of contents that does nothing but count, enumerate, and list, when that list and that overall articulation of the problem not only aren't fully articulated but can only be talked about in a state of delirium or under some sort of hypnosis. Life is a dream once again, particularly when people are going into battle as if they were dreaming it, without anybody actually understanding a thing about the point of this battle. Because of this, I stress my ignorance, my incomprehension, and my unknowledgeability every time other people come at me with their certainty, their knowledge, and their global comprehension of all the events in this troubled drama. But all the same the occasional twitch of this or that cabinet minister's face, the slips of the tongue in statements by generals and lieutenant colonels, and the confusion in what gets said by ordinary people involved in the conflict all tell me that their knowledge doesn't exceed my ignorance: on the contrary.

The baron, Proust's, feels immense stress when, reading the newspaper, he perceives the chroniclers' victorious tone in depicting *a fallen Germany* every day, *"an exhausted animal, utterly worn out,"* when the opposite was the honest truth, and at that moment our hero *would go mad with fury at their cheerful and cruel stupidity.* Because stupidity makes itself known not only by way of clumsy and murderous threats but in the constant cheeriness with which the fool thinks he will solve all the world's problems. *And this thought of his displeased him all the more because he lived in France. In spite of everything, his recollections of Germany were* (already) *remote, while the French, who talked about the destruction of Germany with a joy he found distasteful, were the people whose shortcomings he knew and whose personalities he found unappealing.* Because it's impossible for individuals who betray stupidity as their basic and almost natural tone to come across as appealing people. The naïveté of the people among whom I have been living is a far cry from the troglodytic, murderous, steppe orientation of my distant compatriots, and yet I'm not much happier among the relatively polished individuals who blurt out nonsense day after day without any brake system, which also ought to be a component part of the human machine. Thus I call attention to my *baronage* not because I see baronage as some sort of advantage, an intellectual one, but to explain to anyone who is curious my hostility and my frequent unfriendliness in conversations that are wearing me out with their senselessness, of a hereditary sort. Because, of all the tortures man can be subjected to, one of the most unbearable is to be among senseless and hopeless individuals who will even try to draw you into their hopeless senselessness with their hopelessly senseless soliloquies. My war, in other words, isn't a war between different nations, or different concepts of morality or society; instead, my war is in defense of those few sensible—even suspect in their sensibleness—words and sentences that are struggling against a wave of nonsense, a high and dangerous one. A south wind is blowing here, and the sea is rising to our cliff, but how this cliff will extricate itself from that tepid southern Triestine air, from this periodically morbid climate, that I still don't know. Because *the desperate and painful fact is that every country says the same thing.* But this is entirely understandable and almost inevitable in order for countries to survive in their mutual sameness, counterposed as it is; what remains like some almost insuperable element is the circumstance that there are more and more individuals, or subjects, virtually incapable of justifying their own subjectivity, subjects who say the same thing, make themselves understood and converse on the basis of their deathly stupid and unalterable samenesses. Thus in Proust one patriotic conversation unfolds in a sacrilegious fashion, in a whorehouse. The men have been at the front but at the moment are in Paris; here they are once again among male homosexual partners, and in this inverted atmosphere they continue in passing to discuss their only true love, mother France. *What else can we do? We'll do as our comrades have,* even though *of course I don't think I'll be killed,* but all the same, I'm going back there again, and for as long as it takes to pay off the sonly debt, one way or another, that I feel toward my homeland. I listen to that graveside talk of the young French grenadiers from the beginning of the century, and I think I'm hearing our recent warriors with their same rapture and the same belief, and I see once again that in that sense I don't have any such mother of my own, and that I don't go anywhere for her, nonexistent as she is, in order to prove this nonexistence of my sonly state when I get there. At the age I am now Thomas Mann went into exile, and then he began to talk the same way about his apatridity and the pain of belonging to the nation he belonged to. In passing, I am reading his pieces "of no literary merit," but which reveal merit of an entirely different sort: how he was tormented by insomnia, how he wrote letters, to no avail, to this or that individual who, within the bounds of their shared German language, still believed in him, and how he drank tea, swam, and went for walks, tired and depressed. I sit here, on my hill of exile—because our region, Pulj, Pola, or Pula, fits etymologically with this meaning, of "banishment"—and everything I can say in this new homeland of mine *pietas iulia* is material from my constant reading, Proust, in which I am finding my own current situation, that of an *apatrid.* No Bruno Walter writes to me, because my contemporary of today, the great composer who came to Rovinj on a brief visit from Paris, I saw only in passing, when he waved to me, from his bicycle. Letters reach here rarely and with difficulty, so I don't know how many other people of my language ever give any thought whatsoever to my own language or whether they want to, but the only counterinsomniac event I can record is that without going anywhere I lost my homeland just as if somebody in a fakir's act had pulled a rug out from under me. I am standing where I am, but underneath me, if I take a good look, there's nothing—nothing exists. And standing on "nothing" is a ruinous and miserable situation, so therefore all that's left is to go on reading that book, because "miserable" situations have always been about the best ones for reading books in. That's why there are so many examples of nonreading among our masses and our people in general during the times everything is going fine and the very course of that existence is enough to take the place of any sort of reading matter. Reading, in other words, is a sign of despair, and I keep thinking, in those moments, of depression, that somebody who has been even more dejected will know more about this, because if he hadn't been more dejected than I myself am, he wouldn't have written that writing he wrote. Reading is a sign of dejection, and what has been written all the more so—there are always people even more dejected among the authors of reading matter. Cheerfulness in writing is just an illusion and a literary figure that writers make use of, gladly. The dejection comes through even among the happiest, though, and the person reading, if he has only come upon his own precious dejection, will understand that. Reading is thus an agreement, more or less attainable, between depressed people. Because if I myself "couldn't care less," let me see how a person feels who couldn't have cared less to an even greater degree, given that he did set about writing his material, lighthearted though it may appear to be. Hence that satisfaction, which is universal, that there are also other dejected people in this world, perhaps some even more deeply dejected than I am, and that this is the case is proven by this book, *his,* a dejected man's in many places, which I am reading.

A *French* friend of mine asks me why we *German* intellectuals (who obviously don't agree with *German* policy, since we live in *France* instead of *Germany*), why don't we at least speak out on behalf of *France,* which is under attack? An intellectual is one who has to speak out on every issue, and if he doesn't speak out on one issue or another, then what sort of intellectual is he anyhow? My view, though, is that that is a tyrannical form of conversation with intellectuals that was introduced by Sartre. To have to say, about every possible problem, what one thinks, how he thinks, and what he thinks that way for anyhow!? And the way what an intellectual thinks becomes a public matter, an article to be sold, merchandise—I see nothing intellectual about that. In that I see mercantile work, which is performed at a market, indoors or outdoors, or on the public square, where thoughts of this or that sort— intellectual and semi-intellectual—are applauded and clapped at. The intellectual's trade ought to establish the right of the tradesman in the domain of thought not to have to speak out at all, because what sort of thought is it that is suddenly completely thought through and immediately proclaimed on the public square? And what if immediately after that there appears in that same thought an antithought, counterthinking completely the reverse of what was just sold at the market? What should we do with such a totally contradictory thought that is nevertheless the property of that same brain and that same human and maybe intellectual head? Or is this head hoping that one of its thoughts, thought through and immediately proclaimed as a final afterthought, that that momentary brain product will be understood to be the endpoint of all thinking, both its own and all thinking in general? This is why I'm unable to express myself on *French-Ger-*

man questions, and it's not because I'm for the *French* or for the *Germans,* but because I'm for them both, or it would be more precise to say I'm against one side as much as the other. Everybody including my Rovinj friend Mr. Verdurin thinks that thinking intellectually means finding out exactly whom a thinking person is for and whom he is against, whereas I, who of course think in a totally counter-Verdurinal way, think that no such thing could exist in that intellectual head! That this same head tells itself that all in all it's hard being "for," no matter what the case, while being "against" is practically the only possible way for this head, as a head, to survive its headly life. I am reading one of our philosopher-poets who has come out against many things, especially the enemy nation, but when he comes to what he is "for," there you find the name of the president of the republic and leader of "our" people. Praising the leader of the people is coming back into style again, on the basis that if this leader didn't get such praise, especially from the intellectual profession, he would get very nervous, a lot more nervous even than he is anyway. I think a leader of the people ought to be as nervous as his leadership of the people prescribes him to be, because one leader of the people will lead his people with very little nervousness at all, while another finds this nervousness to be his surest indicator of success. A leader of the people will therefore be as nervous as his feeling that he is the leader dictates to him to be, and the support of our philosopher-poet won't help him here in the least! It could even be said that such philosophical-poetic support, if the leader managed to hear it at all, that such undisguised praise (as if it were some sort of concert review) would make him very suspicious: what's going on here when philosopher-poet so-and-so, who ought to be busy with his poetizing and his philosophy, when he has decided to praise me in front of a whole big audience?! I therefore will not make my views known, in an intellectual sense—

other than to say that I'm ready to make known the view that I don't think of making views known as being intellectual work or an intellectual gesture. Because, as we see, such making known of views can only pose a temptation and a really unpleasant dilemma for the one on whose behalf that intellectual type has made his views known! But it's something else entirely if this same type, in a moment of some incomprehensible courage, were to come out against one or another individual and one or another phenomenon whose phenomenalness comes directly from that individual. To be marked by such a poetic-philosophical creature could mean to even a totally negative person that he isn't quite so negative in his negativeness once he has become the object of an intellectual making known of views of the sort that is the custom in our day.

The people in the worst situation, therefore, are those nobody makes any views known about—neither for nor against—just nothing! However, I have been in this zero position a long time now, so I can say I find very little to object to even in this position—quite the contrary. In any case I am condemned to express myself and confess alone on this stage of ours, I am called upon to make my view known on one issue or another, when instead I have the simple idea that an alternative to formal statements and television appearances, which are often nervous, would be a meditation like this one, utterly intimate. But we are "onstage," the stage is a social institution, and *an institution,* as Lyotard says, *is always distinguishable from a discussion in that it requires additional prodding in order for statements to be permitted within its framework.* Let us, let's hear, let's say, and so on. But since there are always "things that shouldn't be said," the whole problem collapses, since even if I did have something to say, it would be something from this realm which one ought not to speak of "right now," for one reason or another, so let's remain silent then, and whatever conclusion someone draws from this silence, it is truly and utterly his own business. Because our social rules are adjusted in such a way that it's very well known *what a person needs to say to get people to listen to him, and what he needs to hear in order to be able to speak,* so let's just listen carefully to what they're telling us—and surely we'll be able to state the same thing "in our own words," however deformed they may be.

In order to comprehend "the development of one's own thinking," one simply cannot constantly put the texture of that developing thought on public display, because not only does it contradict itself daily as it develops, but it is "in progress," as they say, and in its production cycle, and whether the final product eventually satisfies its semi-intellectual purchaser or not is of absolutely no interest at all to this industrialist.

The philosopher Foucault not only poses the cardinal, anarchistic, dissident, and libertarian question of why it is necessary to put anyone in charge at all, but he ponders first and foremost why anyone gets the right to be in charge of my answers to questions that I would otherwise, given my personal intellectual makeup, ignore unless coerced. Nowadays *a subject is expected not only to tell the truth but to tell the truth about himself, about the state of his soul,* that which I, being that soul, am. But what my soulfulness actually consists of is that there is hardly anything about the state of my soul that I know completely, while what I can know about it in some hypothetical, and thus temporary, maybe improvised, possibly poetic way is precisely what I am not prepared to answer in an inquiry into my conscience by society or at the demand of the state. I therefore do not make known my views on the state of my soul, and I think I have a right to this, so long as plenty of esteemed and thinking heads are available whose owners will make their views known, go all out to make them known, and bend over backward going all out making them known in the greatest detail, so that this quota of public inquisitiveness about "what this or that person thinks" won't go unmet.

In any case the language I am writing in isn't the language of the nation that speaks that language, not in the sense that it is somehow two different languages, but because what is written here in my-and-their language isn't getting read by any of them. I don't speak that language of theirs either, because they themselves speak "their" language to each other while riding our trams there in the cities, while waiting in line for some necessity or other, a wartime one, and while conversing, later, with each other, about those tram rides and that waiting in line of theirs. Because in the condition we have been brought to by who knows what cosmic laws, who is going to turn around and read something when the language is already being expended quite enough in this daily linguistic madhouse, where the people talk the way you only hear in a madhouse—which is periodically lucid, but most often jumbled, at great speed, with neither speaker listening to the other, who is also speaking. A madhouse conversation is a collection of monologues, madmen's, of course, and as such becomes part of the fund of a nation's speech, as a jumble and as an inventory of individuals' ravings. And when I from my half-mad observation post attempt to record some of this mad talk, insofar as my own semimadness allows me to grasp and decipher it, naturally nobody is mad enough to take this mad retelling another time and probably in some mutilated form and check it all over again. Everyone who writes is checked as to whether he has written what he should have written, because "they"— the ones who do the checking—know what should and shouldn't be written, and in this situation we're in, naturally they don't feel like doing such checking, which is idiotic; indeed, they themselves are too busy with their nonidiotic and exceedingly smart talk to check something like this anyhow.

I am reading a little book by a psychologist, an American whose name is Milgram, who describes crazy experiments in that country, rather recent ones. A person is sought who, for purposes we'll call scientific, will give another person in a booth an electric shock. Of course there won't really be any electric current, but the person who thinks he's "turning it on" doesn't know that. He just has to push a lever down and watch the fake victim writhing there behind that glass, and then he gets four dollars and goes home. It all comes down to the question of who consents to turn on that electricity, which is fake, and why. And how the "electrician," no matter what the actor in the booth does—and he doesn't know it's an actor—how this electrician of ours will react to this picture. The book says that the results are astounding, in that the majority of people who are asked to participate in this as an experiment, a scientific one, have no emotions at all toward the person in the booth. What obedience is, our psychologist Milgram says, is that a person begins to perceive himself as a tool for carrying out someone else's wishes, and that as a result he doesn't consider himself responsible for what he is doing. A tyranny, the psychologist says, is maintained with the help of insecure people who are powerless to resist. There are some in the experiment who disapprove of what they are doing, and yet something prevents them from stopping their insane participation. He says that the participants are mainly postal clerks, high school teachers, engineers, and laborers—in short, that anybody is capable of doing what is being done to the person in the booth. It's odd, says one of the people who "turn on" the current, how you start to forget that there's a person inside there, even though you hear him. And that you pay more attention to your switches and the rules written there, on the board, than to the screaming — human — from the booth. That person, imprisoned and sentenced to be jolted by the current, really does have to answer some questions, absolutely accurately at that, and if he fails, then he gets his shock, just as he deserved to. So he pretends then that he doesn't know the right answers, and our man off the street who signed up to punish this fellow's "ignorance" and get four dollars is actually angry at him for not being able to answer right, or else not wanting to. He's tempted to go ahead and tell him what he's "supposed to" say, since he hasn't got all day to shake him with this electricity. So that the guilty one, of course, is the one who "doesn't know," rather than the one who punishes him by shocking him for not knowing. This is how he perceives it. Just as he perceives that in society a person always has to appear who will exert some sort of control over the events in this society. Even if it's just an usher in a movie theater, while he controls who will sit where, there in the dark. This is *why a state of freedom in a country always means universal and consistent skepticism toward the canons that the authorities insist on.* So says another American, Harold Laski, who is quoted by that American of ours, Milgram.

How do the authorities succeed, the philosopher Deleuze wonders, *in getting discipline to penetrate into every part of the social field, even the smallest part, attesting thereby to great independence vis-à-vis the course of justice and even the political apparatus; power has no substance — it is operative. It is not an arbiter, but rather a relationship.* Our recent rulers knew this well: "That's your problem — we don't interfere in that." Thus was a widely applicable doctrine created that reached from the philosophy of the concentration camp overseers to that of the editorial staffs of certain newspapers. We are nothing, we don't interfere, we're only an instrument, the operatives of history, you decide for yourselves how you're going to behave in your work camps and your editorial offices. We only provide a framework for your relationship with history; it, then, is the arbiter—we aren't, we only enable your paltry subjectivities to encounter its massive force. This is why *law is the management of illegalities; the new ordering of illegalities* Deleuze finds in Foucault's analysis of the seventeenth century is established thereby. Except that that century has lasted three hundred years already, nonstop.

It isn't too hard to imagine, says Heller, *how the new collective consciousness constricts receptivity to a message even when the issue is historiography.* History isn't what happened; it is what our collective consciousness maintains at the moment was history and the way it took place. Man thus not only *chooses his own past,* as in psychoanalysis, but it actually takes place over again before our eyes in a way that it never could have. But when an individual "realizes" what actually did happen, then these events come to bear primarily on the states of his soul, which is still salvageable later on; human society, however, considers its own neurosis as a history that amounts to a series of *criminal cases,* and here there is nothing left to salvage or in any way "cure."

How is one to make any sense out of this "historical" behavior, which is insane? *First and foremost,* Heller says, *it means assuming that neither the past nor the future justifies anything. The fact that a piece of land belonged to a country in the past doesn't justify the claim that this piece of land belongs to it in the present. The fact that some nation has violated our rights in the past doesn't justify our violating their rights in the present. No image of future freedom justifies today's oppression, no fear of the future justifies a Machiavellian policy here and now, no insecurity with regard to the future justifies today's indifference.* All this assuming that emotions will dry up and that science will get the right to be heard—that reason will start being put to use to a greater degree than our patriotic heart.

If there exists only one possible route to freedom, and all the others lead to nonfreedom, freedom is destroyed in the same measure, she says, because a person can't walk a one-way path freely, except for a certain period of time, which is to say part of the way. Sooner or later this free walker will start wondering why he should feel free on this path of freedom when it's the only one he has, so if this is really true, maybe in his tired brain he could find a totally crazy and counterbrained opportunity and pick a path of semifreedom, at least, just so the one he's walking down isn't the only one! Man's path cannot be one way, even if it's strewn with roses, and his brain system, even turning anti-roses, does all it can to find, in the change-ability of his route, a little piece of his own inventiveness and even, perhaps, a little hunk of happiness. *We are able to learn from history only because we are capable of not learning from it. We learn from history because we forget and because we remember.* But as it turns out, what we remember isn't what we had forgotten, but something else entirely, which is material from our reconstructed memory.

If an historian places the highest value on the concept of "the nation," says Agnes Heller, *he shouldn't ascribe that value to his nation alone, but to all of them. The historian ought not to criticize other nations' nationalism and admire that of his own. If the historian selects "culture" as the concept with the highest value, that value shouldn't be applied exclusively to the historian's own culture, but to all cultures. The selective use of values also takes an unconscious form. Values themselves can appear conscious. But their identification with our awareness of ourselves can develop unconsciously.* Unless we aren't historians at all, but rather lampooners and daytime craftsmen of the newspaper craft similar to the craftsmen who craft their craft the same way on that other side. Then an entire culture, Byzantine, let's say, will get abandoned in favor of ours that is non-Byzantine, but what we'll do about the places of worship in Parencium, and in Ravenna, and so on, our anti-Byzantine and anti-Hocke and anti-brain brotherhood is using no brains on, because they have a deficiency in that regard. Because in the book by Georges Duby about the era of the cathedrals one could read—if anyone at all still cared about reading—about how the West found and took its intellectual procedures *from cultural regions outside Latin Christianity, which were much richer than Rome ever was: from the science of the Moslem world and, through it, from the treasury of knowledge of ancient Greece.* And Byzantium synthesized this the most accurately.

Because it is the froth of stupidity and dazzle of glory, my Proust goes on to say, *that war has left behind when the loss of a finger, canceling out centuries of prejudice, enables one to become a member of some aristocratic family in a dazzling wedding, and a war decoration, even if it is earned in an office, is enough to get you triumphantly into the national parliament and practically into L'Académie Française.* And not just the French one. Because here, too, these people missing part of a leg and without their left ear will display their maimed parts in the years to come, and one sortie near Dalj that is described in our press will be worth as much as a decade of diligent work at some institute. We have seen all this before, and we'll be seeing it again—war heroes sitting in the cafés on postwar mornings, completely resigned and at times also dangerously upset that those golden occasions of confusion, disorder, and siege were over so fast. Because it is in dangerous situations that our manliness, our human violence, and our gift for murder come to the fore. We were nothing, then we became everything, and now after that we're again pretty much threatened with definitively and once more becoming nothing. The dead will have monuments of the homeland's gratitude newly erected to them, but the living who didn't seize the opportunity to become commissars, supervisors, cardinals, and chief assistants will be left sitting in that familiar postwar café, and now and then firing a bullet at the ceiling. We saw more of those bullets getting fired than we wanted to some half a century ago, and we will probably see them again in the period ahead. A batch of young poets will come along to sing the praises of these soldiers, who are innocent in their soldierly virtue, but a bit bewildered, stressed out, and somewhat dazed about what are we to do with ourselves?! Man as a rule doesn't know what to do with himself and how, but a man who comes out of a war doesn't know this to a much greater degree. Now the task is no longer to hit someone's human head in the other trench, but instead the issue is how to use your own for even one reasonable human thought, a postwar one or any other kind. Even a man who shoots at another man has some thought in his head, even if it pertains to nothing more than shooting at that somebody's certainly very hateful head, but after the shooting stops our head goes on producing thoughts of some sort; they come out of it even if we don't want anything to come out of there at all, except that those heads, those hateful *German* ones, suddenly aren't in the gunsights anymore, and that would be the highest level of frustration for a man who thinks but doesn't have anybody left to shoot at. Except that thoughts can crop up in that same head that are even more unpleasant and negative for that same head: for God's sake, what on earth did we shoot at that somebody's head for, and how on earth was it possible at the peak of our heroism, even if that head *was* the most hateful one, that we shot at it?! Such are the dreams and sleepless nights that await us now and the nervousness over already beginning to comprehend this a bit now, as the war is ending. Except that, I tell you, poets and writers and painters and theater people are going to appear who show in their works that our boys have no such thoughts, negative ones, nor can they, just as we used to hear, read, and see for a good many decades that only a very small percentage of those fellows had such thoughts back then. But nevertheless, here or there, one former soldier or other did strangle his wife, or put a shot through his own skull, or, at the very least, tip over a table in our very respectable, metropolitan café. We know how to do in peacetime what we knew to do in war, being that one tipped-over café table in peacetime echoes louder by far than that shot-through skull, the enemy one, that we put a hole in in that wartime hellhole near God's Lower Hellhole. Everyone has to fight near one lower hellhole or other, because war itself is a hellhole we have gone into without having any idea why we got into it or whether we'll find out why we got into it if we finally — perhaps by chance — get out. Because we are brave lads from Lower Hellhole and we won't be coming out onto any Upper Promenade — even if we survive the lower hellholes — not ever. The ones on the promenade will be those who were on the promenade before they sent us here, to the lower hellhole, and they'll be telling some telling tale of theirs then about how, unfortunately, we never came back.

These are postwar tales, not because the holy spirit has entered us so that we have had our own Catherine of Siena vision of such a situation, the postwar one, but because this has already happened, many times, before our eyes. It has all happened before — Lower Hellhole and the Promenade and the stressed-out soldier with one eye missing who fires his bullet at the café ceiling, except he was wearing something different then and he believed he was firing this bullet for different reasons than the time before.

My stopover in Rome, during the month of October, now reminds me of *those several days* Proust *spent in Paris before he left for another sanitarium,* seeking to be cured of his shortness of breath, and his nervous cough, unsuccessfully. But all of us cough even with no internal irritation of the lungs, because there are a great many elements in our body that hamper this same body precisely in its intracorporal anticorporality, built upon that assumption, a contradictory and almost insane one. A body system, the human one, hampered by that part of it that is described as the seat of thought—this is its initial defect and its leprosy of the spirit that, sooner or later, has to be treated at a sanitarium, of one sort or another. I, in fact, without even traveling, am receiving treatment here on my hill such that I don't think I need to leave this hill and go anywhere else, and because in the sanitarium atmosphere of this Gothic monastery of mine, the differences between the corporal and the spiritual in me are at their least, even under these conditions, of war. And the writer I'm reading, now, during the war, says there are diseases that are a little more closely tied to the nervous system, such that the progress of those diseases is characterized by a particular type of tendencies or exceptional anxieties, and that they endanger our organs, our joints, our strictly physical and material being, so that it turns out even one such anxiety or bad tendency is enough to destroy our entire physical and material life. I still take walks for fitness, while wondering whether there is any incontestable framework for this walking—human—and how it is possible, as one of my characters* wondered, that man as a creature, two-legged and able to walk, is able to keep himself in this upright and walking position?! Thus am I reflecting on the illnesses my writer had and the way he reflected on these illnesses between two sanitariums, in a war long ago. Because a war, in itself, is a stay in a sanitarium, mostly with a fatal outcome. The generals are our Zauberberg administrators, and the counselor who waged the battle for Hans Castorp's health was fiercer and more decisive than the colonel who is busy today leveling some Slavonian town to the ground. Man, the incurable animal,

*Dr. Krleža.

sits on his bed, whether it is in Proust's sanitarium or on my hill, in Rovinj, in a war. For that matter, reading is itself a disease, a morbid impulse that is anticorporal in many respects, including the attitude one has to adopt in order for a book to be read. So thus it turns out that an individual who is already sick as it is will, by reading, double the seriousness of his case history, which is sealed and unalterable anyhow. Thus one ought not to read anything, just as one ought not to be sick, but instead, healthy and vigorous, this individual I envision ought to stroll along the cliff between the Church of Saint Euphemia and the embankment, down below, then back, and nowhere else. That would be a simple sort of concept, maybe "more healthful" than all the other concepts being imposed on me in my reading and in the conversations I'm having these days with healthy citizens of our republic apropos of that morbid reading of mine. Indeed, why do I read when my eyes often hurt as it is, and when these eyes of mine get even redder from this reading? Indeed, eyes need to be saved for nonreading phenomena, except that I don't see so many of those phenomena around me, and whatever phenomena I do look at with my rabbit-red eye I no longer know how to see. Because every eye, even if it is still quite youthful and healthy, sees something it only thinks with its brain attachment (with which that slender cable of the sense of sight connects it) that it's seeing. Does the eye see what is there at all, the way it actually is, or does it see something that may not be at all what it, being the eye, tells its brain it has seen? I have been asking myself this question ever since my first look at the bay that has been the object of my observation for several decades, but as for how this bay "really" looks, I haven't had the nerve to claim that I have an entirely certain and exact answer to this simple question. Because the bay, the seascape, the forest above it, and those several white houses that poke up through that forest—all this is on one side of existence, while my eye, which would have to see this other side, is on its own separate—I would almost say "opposite"—side. So I am amazed at the clarity with which my evening friends watch the news reports, the war ones, seen through someone else's eye and that crazy self-confident "eye of the TV camera," and I am astonished at their certainty that they are seeing what others have seen for them and delivered to them to be their own view. I doubt my own subjective view across the bay, and I have cerebral reasons enough to doubt it, but those who see with the eye of the war cameraman have faith in that view of the war and believe that they are where—fortunately for them—they will never be. Such are my morbid meditations, on the eye, on looking, and the true view that is hard to come by even at a time that is without war and is entirely calm, much less now, when even in the falsifying lenses of our eyes this calm is gone. Somewhere an event is happening and I am supposed to be an integral part of that event, and lest I become part of that structure I resist with all my understanding that I am not an event I have thought up—I don't know how to accept that and I can't! I don't accept "wartime events" not because in my notorious solipsistic narrow-mindedness I don't care about others' suffering, but because I'm not even capable of joining a conversation I don't see as a part of my own life's events. So how then can the eventedness of the world at large try to obligate me to be in it on the basis of a single very lofty and inevitable principle? I marvel at my neighborhood, a friendly one that, since the very first moment "on the inside," has said "we" as soon as some regiment "of ours" is mentioned, just as Mme Verdurin would *say "we" when speaking of France. Well, here's the thing,* she says, *we are demanding of the Greek king that he withdraw from the Peloponnesus, and so on,* while those who would be ordering the Greek king to do this don't themselves believe to such a degree in these "we's" of theirs that they use for state purposes. All this is in very refined and almost provisional statements, because even among kings who, naturally, when saying "we," always have in mind the whole country they're the kings of, sometimes forget that country, behaving as if they were in some palace cricket match. Such are the conversations, on our *Magic Mountain,* where we are being treated for a disease, the "war" one, and in this monastery of ours where we await a *Decameron,* perhaps many years long, to drive the plague from our gate.

To be in the remote isolation of a shelter, in the night-time darkness of a city's underground passages and cellars, in various skillfully dug versions of wombs, really does bolster this metaphor: we are in a state of being hidden and comforted that only a mother's uterus incarnates. Those others can do what they please, because we are inside, in the depth and cavity of the mother who sooner or later will bring us out into the world and the light of day! Thus does the mythology of motherhood get created when it actually looks as if only the tactics and rules of war are being discussed. Because war, too, in itself, is other than it is and than *our boys* who are being killed by the dozens every day think it is. War is some sort of fundamentally symbolized condition in which peacetime phenomena and objects are arranged in an entirely different arrangement, as if in some codex. Everything is right where it is, and yet nothing is where it is, because where we think our really real reality is, there is a state of hypnosis, and maybe only a dream.

I had a dream, and in it my mother, still quite a young woman, left her husband, saying she would be gone all day, but I knew what my naive father didn't know—that she wouldn't be back the next day or ever again. In the dream my mother was young, a pretty dark-haired woman like she never was really, and in this dream she looked more like my own wife, so I anticipate various commentaries, psychoanalytic ones, of these dreams of mine. Anyhow, my mother-wife appeared in my dream on the day our homeland fell apart the way any family falls apart if the mother goes somewhere and never comes back, even though she has said she would be back. This is why I don't need any psychoanalytic commentary, because the intent of this dream was to reveal my idea, about the mother who left me even though she insisted that she never would. The mother, and likewise the wife, always abandons the one she has told she won't abandon, while the one she may not have promised that to she most often doesn't abandon at all. I, however, am that case in which the mother-wife does "abandon" me and leave even though she has assured me repeatedly that she would never go anywhere. Now my little book about a war and about reading a certain book during that war turns into a conversation, a psychoanalytical one, about the mother who abandons me and the wife who may also abandon me one day. This is a conversation on that topic with the ladies and gentlemen of Rovinj, in the course of one summer, who have no inkling that they are acting in a book, a novel, written long ago. Because that same book also has the basic idea that the writer's mother maybe doesn't love her son enough, but loves him only half as much as a writer who has a mom needs. That is why the writer worries whether his mother will come or not to kiss him good-night, and if she doesn't do this, maybe she'll abandon him one day, forever. In this way Proust, too, underscores the idea I myself have, according to which this mother of his is his homeland, which wages a war at the end of the book with its age-old enemy, the German one. And according to which, on the subject of this homeland, which is exhausted already, not every writer, even if at the outset he was exaggeratedly devoted to his mother, country, and the environs of his own childhood, not every writer has an obligation to write dithyrambs and odes in praise of that country until he faints dead away. Here this decadent and aesthete is very close to my dream about the mother who abandons me, and about the feeling of virtual indifference when this actually happens. This little book is meant to confirm the indifference, my own, about the fact that my mother country has abandoned me with no regrets, and that I in turn accept this departure of hers the same way, with no regrets. I have many colleagues who talk about our mother country as a mother and wife they can't live without, and, moreover, with whom they are going to share a bed in the future, incestuously and depravedly.

The majority of poems being written nowadays on this subject are poems of depravity on the part of these poetic children toward their mother whom they can't live without. We have murdered our own father (who was no father to us anyhow), and now we're going to climb into his bed, which no one will ever again be able to get us out of. Because our mother has no need for that man who fortunately is gone, but she does need this love from childpoets that is full of depravity and poetic indecency. In this steambath and house of love, Hamlet would have to occupy his mother's bed to the end, once he had murdered his father, and not halfway, as the British poet indicates. I am writing this little book with a sense of shame, because I'm not prepared for this incest and because I am letting my mother leave with no regrets. My mother country is abandoning me without kissing me goodnight, and oddly enough, I feel no bitterness about it. This is a testimony to the way a son of the mother land feels who had no obligations to that mother land. I will be satisfied if, on her departure, and in the fury characteristic of one who is abandoning someone (not of the one being abandoned), if in that anger she doesn't kill me for bearing witness that one really needn't love one's own mother. Many other interesting topics could be woven in here, but the unloved mother really is a very exciting topic, even the most exciting one, and every expert in psychology has a hard time grappling with it. It's easiest to take this love as the point of departure when one needs to deal with somebody's head that's confused and try to unconfuse it, which is much harder without the mother of this confused person. I myself am confused, and I admit that here without any hesitation at all, and besides that, I don't love my own mother land, just as she has never loved me.

This is a piece of writing about a sacrilege, because all of us are children of our mother country and to her we must profess our love, completely boundlessly. All of us are her children, and as such, as a consequence, we behave in a childlike, childish, child's way. *Lord, Virgin Mary*, says one of Proust's female characters who is a child of the people, a little part of the childhood of her people, *isn't it enough for them that they've occupied poor Belgium? Yes, Belgium, Françoise, but what they've done in Belgium is nothing compared to what they're going to do here. Moreover, because the war had thrown onto the common folk's conversation market a great many expressions that they were familiar with only by sight, through reading the newspaper, and that they didn't know how to pronounce, the manservant would add: I don't understand how the world is so crazy . . . You'll see, Françoise, they're preparing a new, bigger attack of greater "scop" than all those others. Because after that will come battles that will make these present ones look like pure child's play.* But along with the war being waged over there, simultaneously here and almost everywhere that people feel themselves a part of their homeland, games are going on—language ones, conversational, dialogue ones—all of them child's play. If someone says they *are going to have to give back more to us than we gave them in 1870,* then they aren't taking part in war conversations, but in the game of buying up and losing tiny little hotels and gasoline pumps, from the game of Monopoly. All too rarely does this nation of children realize that maybe everything is too childish and simple to be regarded as the world and life of adults. Proust's old servant woman who, when she calls Germans "Krauts," regards charges against the Germans as a fighter would — as being credible, suddenly stops short with all her servant and peasant brain, then says: *I used to believe all of it, but a while ago I began to wonder if we aren't as despicable as they are.* This blasphemous thought has been perfidiously planted in Françoise by the manservant, who, when he saw that she felt a certain partiality for Greek King Constantine, portrayed his situation to her as if we were depriving him of food until he gave in. Therefore the king's abdication greatly upset Françoise, who even declared: *We aren't a bit better than they are. If we were in Germany we'd do the same thing.*

The children of this country worry the way little Proust did about whether their mother land will kiss them goodnight, or not. Because if she does kiss them, that will be some sort of sign of her concern and love for her offspring, but that just isn't the case. This I tell them — I who was abandoned by my own mother land just as theirs will abandon them, sooner or later. The only method for a son, if he doesn't already figure on plunging incestuously into his mother's bed, is to leave her, this mother, who has no interest in her own offspring, and head for points unknown.

OCTOBER 1991

HAMSUN'S BAEDEKER

FOR SUADA

*AS SOON AS I OPENED MY EYES, I BEGAN STRAINING TO THINK:
do I have anything to feel happy about today?* That's a
hard one for me to answer, even though I am reading this
sentence, of Hamsun's, under the sky over Padua—the
same one that's over Venice. In pre-Christian times here
the Sea of Venice, Golfo di Venezia, used to rise to the
level of the streets, and later, during the Renaissance, there
used to be river channels here. This is now marked by
small inscriptions in the sidewalk: there once was water
up to here, but now it's gone, and the entire town that
once was has, like mighty Chioggia, been somehow turned
upside down; here I am walking around upside-down
Padua and I don't know which way is up! Everything
about my meandering here is topsy-turvy, because I am
sitting in the Caffè Pedrocchi, founded back in 1831, and
thinking about some hyperborean writer, from the North,
the same way some predecessor of mine wrote about the
North while here, in Italy. On the wall of our café, where
politicians from the Risorgimento period held court, along
with local poets and small-time provincial Venetian actresses, is a mural of our globe, only it, too, is upside down:
our southern regions are somewhere near the top, while
the countries of Europe's North hang down to the very

bottom, so that visitors lean their backs against the little Norwegian part—Hamsun's, in other words. For several weeks I had been thinking about the book that Knut Pedersen* wrote in his youth where he kept track of how he went hungry, and his anxiety, as a writer. A hundred years have gone by since this Norwegian youth sat on a bench in Christiania† and *wrote column after column for the newspapers, about all manner of things, amazing events, and the moods and perceptions of a restless brain, and out of despair took up even the strangest of topics;* because a writer even when he isn't hungry has to have some sort of sensation inside him, and there's hardly a topic around him that isn't a bit strange. Whatever isn't a bit strange ought not to be written about, because the unstrange problems will take care of themselves, while the ones we're dealing with nowadays we don't know about yet! *Since I was anxious and irascible* I wished I could reread this sonata, the northern one, about going hungry, only I had left the book in my attic in Belgrade, and there wasn't any Hamsun to be had in my neighborhood in Rovinj, or even in the fine bourgeois homes of Zagreb! Then a kind soul brought me my copy from there, from the East, along with my coat, the winter one, which I had also left behind. So now I am sitting in this Padua café, I even have something to throw around my shoulders, and I am following what was written about hunger in Europe's North, a century ago. I am finding that much less is said there about the discomforts of an empty stomach and much more about the nervous exhaustion that, more than hunger of a physical sort, is ensconcing itself in our heads. *My head was overloaded with thoughts,* only they needed to be put in some sort of order, like once long before. *By this evening my feuilleton about crimes of the future will be finished,*

*He eventually took the pen name Knut Hamsun.—Trans.
†Former name of Oslo.—Trans.

except that this work of Hamsun's from the end of the last century describes the very moment we are in today and the crime going on everywhere around us, now. So it isn't all that easy to explain what is happening to us right now if an article we knew nothing about was written about it, in Christiania, sometime long ago.

My friends here are asking me where I got the idea to read Hamsun's awfully old book right now, since it may have lost its relevance. I tell them it hasn't, and I also explain to them, rashly, that it portrays human hunger as a universal phenomenon. But my companions don't understand what I mean, so they take me to Padua's bountiful market, to which Friulian and Venetian sheep have been brought for centuries now, by boat. So I am just another sheep, a Schiavonian one,* to whom well-meaning people are attempting to explain that with sights like this one, the human race shouldn't have to go hungry. In other words, just like many times before, I can't explain my ideas to my closest contemporaries, and therefore they don't comprehend what I mean by my own hunger, at the moment. What the writer labors to explain he is incapable of explaining, try as he will, while something that doesn't occur to him as an explanation unexpectedly explains it all for everybody. Anyhow, once there was a writer who, in his youth, wandered the streets, up there in the North, and he was hungry, in body and soul, and he kept trying to write about that hunger, an all-encompassing one, in those several columns of his for the Christiania newspapers. So, too, do I wish to put on record my hunger for this book left on a shelf in my former home, and how I finally dispatched that hand, a precious one, to get it. But until this happened, I thought all I had left behind at the other edge of the country—as if it were some South Pole of my life—was gone forever. How is it, one of my traveling compan-

*Schiavoni—Slavs (Ital.).—Trans.

ions asks me, that a writer will read a book, and then jot down some things about it, but that in those jottings there's scarcely a mention of the book, but instead, these jottings jot down something else entirely? That, the writer says, is because there is always a lot more of that "something else" about a book than there is of what belongs to it per se, only the other content, that "something else," is very rarely noticed. Besides which, the writer wants to write, maybe he has a topic that could be that he still doesn't have any topic whatever, but then the ever so pleasant people around him inquire about this work of his and everything is back at dead center again the way it was before. But actually, this "dead center" may be a really good situation to write in, and a kind of salvation, because if you're not at dead center you're not wondering where to go next.

People can understand that a person with meager opportunities may be hungry, but as for the anxiety that suddenly comes over some individuals—this almost no one wants to understand! Maybe it comes from improper thoughts, and a person simply shouldn't have such thoughts, period! And even if this can happen to ordinary people, at least a writer's thoughts ought to be proper, every last one of them, or else he shouldn't have any at all! I am pondering this remark now and fancying what a writer without any thoughts would be before he set about some piece of work, and how this piece of work might be the best that a being without any thinking of his own could achieve. Thoughts make for confusion, even confused thinking, particularly confusion concerning life, and this really should be curtailed once and for all. So thus I am trying not to think about the hunger that has somehow turned out to be "my topic," but rather about the way a man who is starving but for some doggoned reason wants to write, how such a being's writing-and-starving system behaves.

I am always getting on my traveling companions' nerves for reading a book of some sort while I'm traveling, and all the more so because the book never has much to do with my travels. So what is there about writers, anyhow, that "things themselves" are never enough for them, but that they have to have something else besides? And of course this takes its worst form when that something else is a book. In the common view, people either don't read books at all, or else they make use of them in some completely neutral and peaceful situation, so that reading some doggoned book on a trip is a downright ill-bred and senseless thing to do. However, books always have more in them than we think they do, and that is why I am reading this Norwegian of mine, thinking that in him I will discover that still-unexplained kernel of his writing that will be of value to me personally, on this Italian trip. A writer is never sure whether his book will be of value to anyone or not, and what's more: what he believes will be of greatest value in his book—this people usually don't notice, while what he didn't give all that much weight to himself is what turns out to "be of value" and help somebody's nervous stress, in his life and travels. Because a person feels like traveling because of basic frayed nerves, which drive him to get away, anywhere, just so as not to remain where he was and where that original nervous stress of his appeared. Any person will develop nervous stress in his brain sooner or later, only this nervous exhaustion travelers have is something different. Because our European, except in fits of extreme misanthropy, doesn't travel alone, and as soon as he has somebody next to him, that is all it takes to start being plied with questions: how's it going, are you glad to be traveling, and do you like the places you're traveling through now? The human race is doomed not only to the nightmare of being compelled to answer questions, but also to the even greater nightmare of having to ply those around them with questions, constantly. Because those who do the plying don't have it easy, either—one could even say they have it much harder than the others. A person may or may not answer one question or another, but what choice is there for the one who has to formulate these questions one after another, for some reason he himself doesn't know?! So what am I finding in this book of mine that I am reading on my way around Italy, and that tells about a young writer's hunger a hundred years ago? I try to explain all over again that the hunger in his book isn't just that physical sensation, in his stomach, but also a much worse trouble that for many reasons occurs in his heart, and that I who am not going hungry am finding help there with a theme of my own. The only thing is that I can't explain this theme of mine all that easily and immediately. Because if I did clarify it, I would stop being engrossed by it, whereas now in its unclarified state it still interests and tantalizes me.

Anyhow, my narrator tells not only about his exhaustion, of a physical sort, in former Christiania, but also about the motives for his completely incomprehensible behavior. So how does he take it into his head to *drive* some lady of the street *into a panic,* trailing her and tormenting her any way he can? His *rattled mood followed* him and *kept whispering the wildest words* to him, and nicest of all, he *heeded them all, one after another.* Most of the ideas that come to a man's mind are wild and inhuman, but only a person more rattled than the rest can heed the wildest ones. Nor is that rattled state of the brain always something special: *I didn't get anything written, though.* After a few *lines nothing more came to my mind; my thoughts were elsewhere entirely, and I couldn't get myself collected to make any sort of effort.* Here is how it is with thoughts: they are always elsewhere, because where I myself am they have no business being, and for them to be my thoughts at all, they have to exist in some entirely different realm, miles from my restless body. Thus I am

thinking now about faraway Christiania at the end of the
last century, and the odd name Barabas Rosenknospe,
which is mentioned in that tale from long ago. Actually,
even there it doesn't mean anything; rather, the author
invented it so as not to raise doubts among his relatives by
using his own name. Likewise, I may be reading this book
on my trip through Italy to keep the people around me
from asking me about other things. Except they keep
wondering, if I really do have to read on this trip, why I'm
not reading Goethe's book on the subject instead of some
completely different one in which a young man who is
quite desperate roams and "travels" around his own city.
Because even there he experiences all sorts of interesting
things, meeting other vagrants, peddlers of this and that,
and from time to time some newspaper editor or other
that he will bring one of his articles to about these things.
Because this was the city where he was to go hungry, and
write the strangest pieces: indeed, it has sometimes happened that hours have come *when, with no effort, I could
have written other articles, too, even very successful ones.
But here I am now, sitting on a bench and writing the
same number for the hundredth time, writing that number back and forth and up and down, and waiting for a
good idea to come to me.* But my companions ask me if
traveling through their pretty country isn't good idea
enough, or do I have to keep on hunting for some other
doggoned thing to interest me?

But that globe at the Caffè Pedrocchi is turned on its
head, and the little Norwegian island, Norvege, hangs
down near the bottom; everything is upside down the
way it all is in the story I am reading. Its narrator had *on
his shoulders a head that had no equal in the entire country, and yet to his own disgrace* and to the disgrace of that
same country he went bitterly hungry in the middle of
glorious Christiania. There was a time when even the best
head a country had didn't fare as it should have, and now

this time has come once again and I am writing about it, as I read my old book. Books don't get written during that momentary time of writing, though, but during a time we still don't know the whereabouts of. Time isn't anywhere, in any case, but we just think it's where we are, and this is precisely where it is not. There's more of it where we already have been, or where we are going to be, maybe. In any case, time can only be told about from a philosophical point of view, which isn't the same as that other one, the point of view of life. Likewise, it is possible to hunger in a different way than having that unpleasant sensation in the stomach. And so I am reading the tale of my hero and his attempt to chew up a wood chip he found along his way. And later how he sticks a round pebble in his mouth, just to have something there, in his mouth. What is it I am chewing on these days instead of some ordinary thing intended for chewing? The main character in the book I'm reading picked up a splinter of wood on the street and started to suck on it, while I, who am traveling through Italy without thinking about it, am picking up every crumb and tiny impression along my way that can help me in my uneasy state.

In the region around Monselice, where I am heading to see the residence where Petrarch died, in an area with no byroads, and on main roads chewed up by silicon, mothers didn't used to teach their children to talk; it was unnecessary there. In a place with no traffic or outside visitors, the children learned what deaf-mutes were taught and in the very locale of Petrarch's poetic speech they lived growling like little beasts. The mothers of Monselice Province mastered the criticism of idle chatter—Heidegger's—very long ago. I, too, feel no obligation to answer every question from my traveling companions, who are interested in every last idea of mine and how I arrived at it anyhow. In a certain sense they are taking stock of me, watching how an idea of someone's who has arrived "from over there"

comes out of that foreign head anyhow, and what it's
worth as an idea anyhow. I keep thinking I am playing
Petrarch's cat, which is mummified, which we watch with
the same sort of attention, from behind a glass, there in
the poet's house. Maybe I'm not good for anything else
anymore than to be looked at, with fascination, like a little
old animal from long ago. Because how can one "be from
over there" and be able to think any better than a cat
mummified long ago—how is that possible anyhow? So
here I am in the role of some exhibit at a retrospective of
extinct specimens of human thought and the bizarre,
barely surviving vestiges of Valdemar's movement. I'll
just go on thinking these thoughts of mine, and they can
go ahead and see what a person who has such thoughts
looks like anyhow. So I keep swallowing that liquid in my
mouth that, like a little puddle of nothing, irritated a character of Sartre's, and Hamsun's hero found comes in
handy when a man hasn't a thing to his name but his own
bodily substance. How does a hero become one, anyhow,
if not by having nothing to begin with and hoping he'll
have everything later on? Hence the patience with which
the character in my book keeps trying to chew up the lining he yanked out of his pants pocket. Today we are nothing and have nothing, but later on, of course, it will be a
completely different story, times will change and we'll get
even more than we need! The human race lives on that
hope, which is an absurd one, and books about that absurd
feeling are even written by one segment of that race, the
absurdest one. So why, then, am I reading a book that
obviously upsets me, my traveling companions ask, since
I am undoubtedly grimacing as I turn the pages, which is
unpleasant for everyone. In pleasant society people most
likely read books without grimacing, but I, who come
from an unpleasant society, seem, unfortunately, and
with great apologies, unable to do without these grimaces.
And most interesting of all, they say, is that from time to

time as I read this same text that upsets me, something like laughter, nervous and malicious—as laughter often can be—comes out of me. Because laughter that's merry, naturally, the way it ought to be—that kind we can deal with, but what are we to do with this laughter of yours, which causes us great concern? If you need some sort of medicine that would calm you down while you're reading this dangerous book of yours, then say so and we'll stop at a pharmacy and solve the problem, but if not, then we don't have the slightest idea what to do. I tell them, though, that it's a completely normal thing for a person reading something desperately hopeless to suddenly get a hysterical urge to burst out laughing, to roar with laughter, in fact, over all the horror he is confronted with. Because the desperate people themselves create situations that are insanely comical, such as when our hero slapped one of his traveling companions, on the street, for no reason. His landlady kicks him out for not paying his rent, he hasn't eaten for three days, his coat is unbuttoned because he cut off the buttons and pawned them but spent the money, so then the only way off this street we're on is to walk up to some wretch without a thing to his name and slap him hard, for absolutely no reason. People give one reason or another for slapping each other, but the real fact of the matter is that at that moment the person doesn't know what to do with his hands, with himself or the people around him, so they fire off walloping slaps all over the place, and if laughing at this spectacle is forbidden, it's certainly news to me!

Obviously I am an especially evil-minded person who looks at everything in a very cockeyed way, and such people probably shouldn't undertake any sort of trip— better for them and everybody else if they stayed put at home! Except that I don't know where my home is and where I could do this staying put. So that is why I'm reading this book that shows how you can feel like an outsider and an utterly superfluous person even in your own hometown. Thus I am finding relief in the tale about the hunger, of all kinds, that this young man feels and how he tries to chew up the lining of his pocket he has pulled out. Previously he had tried this with a wood chip he found on the street, and a round pebble he put in his mouth to at least have something there. The human fluid that's in there, that eternal little puddle of Sartre's, can also serve in lieu of everything that exists everywhere in the way of earthly food, and as for a man biting into his own finger in hopes of assuaging his primary urge for a moment, that, too, is in my book—Hamsun's, I mean. What all is in that book, anyhow? my traveling companions wonder again; it's not all that thick, and yet I'm reading it constantly and raptly. That comes from the fact that, very familiar though it is, I keep discovering things in it that I myself hadn't noticed, on many occasions, earlier. A person on a trip, an evil-minded person especially, one who doesn't know at the moment where his home is, ought to reread all the books he read before he got so evil-minded and into such contorted positions. Then he would understand that all the familiar books he had read earlier have become unfamiliar, and that they can be read again with no apologies needed. Books don't change everything about themselves all that often or noticeably, but what does change is their reader, who is evil-minded one time, and then another time much less so. So I myself don't totally blame this writer who first loved his own people, then stopped loving them and took a liking to some other nation that had conquered his country.* Why an individual would do this remains unclear even after the courts of his own country have pronounced the harshest of verdicts, without appeal. Perhaps I am finding something of this treasonous urge today in this writer's book written in his early youth. Because this is a tale about wandering around his own

*Hamsun became a Nazi sympathizer.—Trans.

town, and about the rude hunger he endures there. He wasn't able to chew up his pocket, or the wood chip he picked up off the sidewalk, and he barely escaped death only by dint of his getting an article published in the newspaper, about crimes of the future. To go on writing, he needed only a bit of paper and a pencil, which he redeemed, then, from the pawnshop. His mind was always going full speed, just as, in my case, this urge of mine, to read, is going nonstop today. Thus the bewilderment I am provoking in my traveling companions as to how I can read at all when I come from "that" country, because if somebody comes from such a country, the last thing you expect from him is to sit calmly in some compartment, on a train, and read. But the very reason that I am reading this book is I am from over there, because if I weren't from there I might not open such a book at this point at all. A person will open a particular book on some impulse that is unclear on the face of it, and yet later on it will turn out that for various reasons this was absolutely the only book he could have opened. People get other people accustomed to expect that they are immediately and certainly going to show some motive for their actions, when in fact the majority of anybody's actions have no human motive of any sort.

They're asking me now whether I could retell this book of mine to them, and I say that anyone could. Except that one person would retell "one thing" and another "another," and what the right material for retelling would in fact be is something no reader of any book is able to fathom entirely. I am consoled only by the fact that even the hero who appears in this tale doesn't entirely fathom what he is doing, because a hero who did completely and totally fathom what he was doing in his tale probably wouldn't be a hero anyway. And so our hero decided to find a man in some house in Christiania, but how on earth this man could help him—that remains unclear. And does any such being who would be at a man's service exist in any city at all, if not Christiania, that hyperborean domain in Europe's North, then in some other? And do we perhaps only invent that "man" of ours we are going to see in order to get the patrolman, on the corner, to stop inquiring where we are going, who we are going to see, and why? Because there isn't a city, European or not, where you can loiter this way with no purpose without having some watchman ask you what your purpose is, and aren't you ashamed that what you call your purpose you dare consider a purpose at all?! Thus it turns out that the book I am reading isn't really a description of somebody's hunger a hundred years ago in a city that was then called Christiania. Rather, it is a tale about events that happen to people every day without their wanting to participate in them at all. Because the ones a person would like to join in take place without any contribution from him whatever, while these others, which are really repugnant to him or at the very least bore him— these events seem to be just waiting for him to join in apart from any will of his own.

Just now one of my traveling companions is again asking a question about the book I am reading, which is called *Hunger/Sult*. Once more I say that aside from the theme of being famished, there are all sorts of other things in it that aren't directly related to this theme. And I say that a woman friend who has arrived from Sarajevo, which is under siege, says hardly anything about the hunger there, but talks surprisingly, as Hamsun does, about all sorts of other things. About the way the people go from door to door as if they had business of some sort there, when in fact they have neither errands to do nor anyone they know there to go and see. This is why it looks as if this book I am holding tells about life in that besieged city that is constantly being shelled and is difficult to get out of. Every city has the problem that in it we don't know at any given moment what we ought to do, but then comes a situation, the quintessential one, when all these questions about the incomprehensibility of life become even more pronounced. Thus does my friend tell about activities in that city, the besieged one, that wouldn't occur to people in normal times, and yet there are very few insane people there. Which is to say, this is a tale about people who would ordinarily have every right to be insane but, in spite of it all, are not. How does one person manage not to go insane when he has all the preconditions for it, while others go insane for no good reason and with practically no justification? Insanity appears out of somewhere as the prerogative of relatively happy people who are living in normal circumstances, but when these circumstances themselves go insane, all a person has left is his normality. Perhaps now it might become clear even to my suspicious traveling companions how much I hungered for this book that itself is called *Hunger/Sult.* I am also hungry for many other books I left in my old house, and for the people there—altogether several of them. I am hungry for the table I sat at with them, even though I was going hungry with them at that table, like in some tale that tells about hunger. Each of us sometimes thinks he is living inside a story, because it is hardly conceivable that what he is inside of exists outside of a story. Thus are all things divided up into those that exist in a story and those not in such stories. And anything that's outside the text of a story turns out to be unbelievable and unfit for even the most fantastic tale in the world, while some things might be believable just because they are written down.

And as for how I knew what I would find in this book, which I read long ago, I say that in fact I didn't know. Some sort of hunch just drew me to the title of the book that, being entitled *Hunger/Sult,* stirs urges of that sort by its title alone. Now finally I am reading this tale about going hungry in the city of Christiania, at the end of the last century, and the fact is, I keep discovering incidents that my friend in besieged Sarajevo recently lived through.

And since I have already written several pages about this book and the circumstances I am reading it in, *following the old practice* of Hamsun's hero *I wanted to amuse myself by* reading the text I had written, *which seemed to my exhausted brain to be the best one I had written up to then.* This is a frequent occurrence with writers, who will enjoy the last couple of sentences they've written, while sometimes forgetting everything else that came before. Because I have forgotten an entire life that I left behind without even knowing where or how. The fact is, every life has to be left somewhere, and maybe it's best that this is what happens rather than our dragging it with us everywhere, for who knows what reasons. Everyone ought to worry a lot less about his own life and let it take its own course, and the individual whose life it is would be best off not to reflect on it at all. This is why I am thinking right now about the life of my friend who came out of the besieged city, and the life of the writer who described this life of hers, without intending to, a hundred years ago. Because being hungry in Christiania, at the end of the last century, and being in even worse straits today, in a city being destroyed unjustly day after day, turn out to be almost the same thing. The young hyperborean hero had in his pocket some kind of little knife and a bunch of keys, but not one red cent, and I know that the girl who told me about her experiences didn't have even that. In the city she came out of, nobody locks their apartment, and in many places they have chopped their very doors up for firewood to cook soup over. In other words, I am reading this tale about what happened to one writer long ago, and the farther I have read, the more anxious I have gotten, primarily because the anxiety the writer felt more than a century ago I, too, have felt. Now I want to compare these two anxieties, and am finding that a few of the things that could once have served as some sort of solace are no longer a solace today.

The young man in Christiania wanted to do his writing, but it turned out he didn't even have a pencil handy, and when he got one, the nights were too long and the days too short, so he needed a candle in order to write, besides which, in order to light this candle, he also needed some cursed little bit of space, a corner of a room or at least an eave over his head, but then everything fell apart anyway, so we can see now that about the best space for a European writer is still the one behind prison bars. *The bright cell looked so inviting,* our narrator felt *cozy* there *and enjoyed listening to the rain fall.* He *wanted nothing else than to* have *such a cozy little cell.* But how are you to find a cell for even your weirdest human idea if you live in a city that has turned itself completely into a prison, and where every house is but a cell—uncomfortable, ice cold, and with a roof that artillery has removed a goodly part of? As I try to explain this to my traveling companions on our trip, the Italian one, *I knew I was fantasizing, I knew this by what I was saying.* Whoever wants to explain something to somebody gets into a state of fantasy and fantasizing that seems to his listeners like raving. *My madness was delirium brought on by weakness and fatigue,* and that in turn came from having attempted to explain something inexplicable to individuals to whom the explanation itself, if explained fully, wouldn't have meant a darned thing. *And suddenly the thought rushed through my brain that I had gone mad.* Because a person sees he is going mad when he attempts to clarify something to somebody and sees that this clarification doesn't clarify anything and that the person listening to you is looking at you as if you were a madman. *Am I truly without a single friend, even just one acquaintance I could turn to* with my tale who would understand it at least in part? *And so I have been teaching myself to pretend.* I am just pretending to recount some sort of content of my own because I'm telling it in such a way that I am interpreting some old book by someone else in my own manner and for my own purpose. But I know that no storytelling has any purpose other than to make people yawn out of boredom. My whole life I have been telling stories of my own while the people around me yawned, and now at the end I see I could perhaps have kept them to myself. But inasmuch as I had started to think at that point that I had gone mad, I persisted with my tale, because only a madman can persist in doing something he doesn't see any grand purpose in. *Surely,* says one editor from Christiania back then, *surely you labor a great deal over your articles, but you are too bitter. If you were only a bit more guarded. Too much feverishness!* Just look, though, how this writing of mine today, with practically no fervor, and such feeble rage, comes across almost the same way, the same darned way! Maybe only this girl for the sake of whose soul I am reading that old book will find in it what she herself lived through a hundred years later. *And to punish myself I started to run. I ran down one street after another, driving myself on with stifled screams while inwardly screaming like crazy whenever I felt like stopping.* This is the only way I can explain this writing of mine that would make sense to put a stop to, yet for some reasons—crazy ones—I don't. *Please give me half a crown for my glasses!* And when the merchant in Christiania doesn't want to give him anything for them, the writer sits down and copies over what he can write only while wearing his glasses—which are completely worthless. *I am only joking, of course. But I have a blanket I don't need at all, and I thought you might at least take that.* Because a writer needs glasses to be a writer, whereas he may not need a blanket, not even a very thin one.

I haven't asked the girl who arrived from the besieged city how the people there keep themselves warm, and she herself hasn't said anything about it, either. I see that I am shaking because of some people I don't know at all, and because of blankets somebody yanked off their backs.

Surely some weakness has come over me or my conscience has been lulled. As soon as I got tangled in those nets I immediately felt a premonition that it would end badly, and that was precisely why I tried first with the glasses. I wanted to find out what happened to those little articles, the everyday ones, that my friend left in her house in Sarajevo, but then I realized that I was asking someone who had left everything she owned at some sort of pawnshop, forever. *The actor Magelsen has my watch,* says our old storyteller, *I was almost proud of that, the calendar my first attempts at poetry were printed in was bought by an acquaintance, my cloak made its way into the hands of some photographer, who loaned it out to various customers of his studio.* Nothing whatever has been lost, it has just changed hands, forever. I tell my friends in Italy about this, and they say that these things are awful, quite awful. Only why am I tormenting myself over this, they say, when I am here, in a safe place, and not lacking for life's necessities. And that I am a European gentleman, and that perhaps gentlemen weren't obliged to occupy themselves with these matters that didn't concern them directly. I tell them, however, that my fellow citizens in a certain besieged city, whether I know them or not, are also to a large extent European ladies and gentlemen, except that the articles and objects that could give Europe proof of their gentility they have had to pawn at a pawnshop—a planetary one. But that there is no city, European or otherwise, whose possessions, even the most precious ones, could be swallowed up forever by such a pawnshop. Let these people think about that now as they interrogate me, in Rome, about my gentility.

How, they ask me, can an old book tell us anything about the events of our day, and I say that the friend who arrived from besieged Sarajevo tells about life there as if she were reading passages from Hamsun's book. Because the hole in the wall she stayed in resembled the mysterious, gruesome coffin that the writer from Christiania took refuge in: *there's no decent lock on the door, there's no stove*, all that was missing there in that ice-cold Northern city was for outlaws to appear out of the mountains near-by. Life in Sarajevo, besieged Sarajevo, is life without a stove, without any key in the lock, and with a floor that creaks like a coffin unless the people living there have already set fire to it, board by board, warming themselves around the fire built in the middle of the room. How long such a situation can last no one knows: *many vague replies, half-promises, and an outright "No!", encouragement of illusory hope, and new attempts that always come to naught* — thus does our writer, of long ago, attempt to res-cue himself from hunger in his Christiania, while my friend who wanders around besieged Sarajevo tries to fig-ure out the reason behind this wandering and a way to put an end to it once and for all in some humane way. In Christiania a person ought to find a job, so let's go knock on somebody's door, but the people who answer are all very distrustful, *one clerk just shook his head and said he couldn't count on me because of my glasses.* Glasses are a sign of nearsightedness of the human eye, but they also brand a whole group of people who have looked at books a great deal and are now unable to see anything except those books. To be in a besieged city and be branded a book reader is an utterly insane situation; thus my friend tells how, when taking refuge for several months in the apartment of a specialist in American history, all she did was study the American Constitution and try to learn the Declaration of Independence by heart.

In Christiania, if you wore glasses you couldn't even become a firefighter, just as all of us glasses-wearers living under the circumstances of our European enmities are a suspicious breed, obscure to people, and an ethnic group that can't be trusted. We are neurotic people, limited by the work we do — reading, and perhaps it's right we aren't trusted, no matter where on our noses we display those glasses of ours. Because glasses say that something's wrong with the eyes, and when the eyes aren't functioning, how is the head that has those eyes in it going to function, and what could such a person, in bad times, when we are forced to live under siege, what would he know how to do anyhow? *And since I was anxious and irascible,* I am feeling angry at what I have written about these glasses and am counting up the injustices that people in glasses have suffered over the centuries. And once you get anxious and irascible, then you do a hundred things you might not otherwise do—you shout at some utterly innocent individual, you insult someone, you accuse somebody of something he isn't to blame for at all, until you suddenly realize: *the patience with which* these people *stood my harassment of them had completely disgraced me, and I lowered my eyes.* Thus am I lowering my own eyes now at my own anxiety as I write about it in a house, in Rome, when I realize that my friend in besieged Sarajevo lived through her war with no anxiety whatever. *Why* then *have I of all people been chosen by the whim of fate to be a touchstone,* for describing the events in other people's lives as though they were my own? *Is it an utter certainty that my feuilleton is a little masterpiece of inspired art,* just because it tells about other people's suffering in a relatively seemly fashion? Because I have the crazy notion that it is possible to write in a calm and seemly manner about even the most unseemly situations, because with regard to the unseemlinesses of history the most unseemly thing of all would be to tell about them in history's own unseemly way. *I kept having a premonition that this same history would address me, give me some reprimand, or play some sort of joke on me,* the only purpose being to make my prose, which otherwise is relatively calm, go berserk from being tested and addressed in this stern manner. I am telling my tale without bitterness about the girl who wanders through the besieged city, because she herself went about that city without bitterness, and came out of there the same way, without any mental illness, which is virtually inescapable. Which is to say, I would be unseemly if I were to take her stoic and simple life there with nothing to her name, and attempt to turn it into a tragedy, a genre she herself finds entirely unacceptable. History keeps telling me to be as violent in my writing as it itself is, but I just keep stressing the way the girl whose story I am recording walked among those ruins there, not knowing a soul she could turn to.

Where in this whole world can I find shelter for the night? Isn't there a single hole I could get down into and spend the night till morning comes? A tale about a solitary life in Christiania thus turns into the chronicle of my girl who in fact does find that hole in the historian's house, the one in ruins, where for many days after that she tries to learn the American Constitution by heart. Outside there's shooting, outside you can get killed just like that, while inside, behind some sort of wall, a totally precarious one, a creature continues her adventure in reading, and no mockery, of even biblical dimensions, is going to disturb her. *Instead of that I feel somehow pleasantly empty, untouched by everything that is around me, just happy that nobody can see me.* Because it isn't seemly to watch a person who, hungry, frostbitten, in someone else's apartment that is in ruins, is reading the American Constitution all day in all her serenity. And it is even less seemly to write about this case, which may be a special one, under the blue sky of Rome, furious on someone's behalf. All the more do I see my distant ancestor from the hyperborean North as a brother. He, too, was depressed at times and *without energy, mercilessly called back to life, to human misfortune.* Except that I, in the course of my whole long history, have resisted getting involved in life, so the largest share of the misfortune there, in life, has passed me by. *I wrote articles for the newspaper, and worked day and night and read like a madman,* but didn't come into any particular contact with any other kind of life. And even now, when I have already written and read everything there is to write and read, I am rereading what I've already read, and writing about it again in perhaps some even more bizarre way. *Here I am,* says my book, *living in some hole that God himself and the human beings escaped from last winter because snow was falling into it. It all makes absolutely no sense to me.* Because without a trace of malice or envy or bitterness in my thoughts, I keep having dreams about the apartments, from long ago, that my life went by in without my ever having uttered a word about them and how uncomfortable they were. Except that many times, finding myself in that city I left behind, I will think I can go to such and such a street, to such and such an address, and only later will I realize that my things and my dear ones aren't there anymore and that I have no reason ever to go back there again.

You keep asking me why I insist on this old Norwegian book, and I say that what prompted it was that a dear friend got out of besieged Sarajevo and her experiences there reminded me of Hamsun's text, which I read long ago. This book, I say, is called *Hunger/Sult,* and my recollection of it describes better than anything the anxiety I was feeling until I got hold of that book, which I had left at my old house in Belgrade. Now I am listening to what this girl is telling me about her life in Sarajevo and can thus confirm that much of it has already been written down in Hamsun's little book called *Hunger/Sult.* And I keep repeating that the little book I am writing here in Rome could also be called something similar, because in it I describe how I hungered for that little book until I finally got it, from my old house in Belgrade. The friend who managed to get out of Sarajevo doesn't talk about any yearlong *hunger* there, though, although she does talk about things that Hamsun already described in detail a

MY FAMILY'S ROLE IN THE WORLD REVOLUTION

hundred years before, writing about his own wanderings in Christiania.

My Italian acquaintance (who is completely unfamiliar with my books, as far as that goes) inquires whether I am intending to have this text of mine published here in Italy, too, and I ask him: why? *You know what our public is like,* it says in Hamsun's old book, too, as a matter of fact. *Can you write something simpler? Or bring in something else that people would find intelligible?* I am unintelligible in Italy, mainly because no one in Italy has read a single word of mine yet, and that is truly a really good reason that someone, being unread, would be unintelligible by that fact alone. But I came to terms with the issue of intelligibility a long time ago, when I stopped really finding myself fully intelligible, and once I had attained this self-unintelligibility, somehow things became much easier for me. Because I am my own blasted audience, of sorts, and since I keep envisioning hundreds of readers' expectations for me, I can also understand the person who, without having read me, doesn't understand me. But I tell my Italian friend that unintelligibility between people isn't any real obstacle to their living side by side at all; in fact, I would say that in some way they will live better next to each other if they do not fully attain that ultimate mutual intelligibility. Because in that ultimate mutual intelligibility the human being, using an inner mechanism he has, will begin to ask himself that fateful question: how have we come by this total and universal mutual intelligibility of ours? And where such a rosy arrangement between disparate beings would take us, you can picture that for yourselves. I am getting by, in any case, by reading an old book and copying a few words out of it instead of pulling various idiocies out of my own head.

As it was, my nerve-racked brain had immediately poked out its feelers back when I lived in Christiania a hundred years ago and was named Knut Hamsun. *For seven or eight months now I haven't had a single carefree hour,* he says, and I can only add that my own nervous strain has already lasted twice that long, because one or another friend of mine in besieged Sarajevo may well want to describe his life but, like young Petersen from hyperborean Christiania, doesn't have a pencil to do this writing with. *If only I had a candle, I would finish the article for the newspaper.* Because even though I have a pencil, I need a candle and a little piece of paper so I can finish the article by this candle in the darkness of the cellar, and then I just have to make that two-hundred-meter run to the print shop without getting hit en route by a shell that some criminal on the neighboring hill is preparing for me. Because why do I need to write and run across the street with my foolish scribbles when now isn't the time for such scribbling but instead is the time for someone to shoot at that fool and his scribbles from the neighboring hill? There is a time for scribbling and a time for shooting, and now is our time for shooting, and this idea that belongs to the bandit behind the rifle I am pondering intently today, in Rome. Because they say that a colleague of mine who arrived on this hill from Russia was treated to the chance to shoot at those people down below, in the city, whether they were writing something or not. I, however, still stand by the one who searches for a candle in Sarajevo's darkness so he can write any darned word he pleases, and not beside the one who takes potshots at that poor devil down below as if he were trying to win a prize. Except that the one down below doesn't realize he needn't write anything more, since I am reading his unwritten text here, in Hamsun's book. *For several weeks I had been wearing the same shirt; it was already completely hard from dried sweat and had rubbed against my body till the blood came. A little bloody water dripped from the wound, but it didn't hurt much.* For several months now many things that used to cause pain no longer do, my friend from besieged Sarajevo explained to me. She brought her own handbook out of there on how a person can survive in Sarajevo, *Survival Guide–Sarajevo,* and I later added my own nerve-racked commentary about how a person can die there, too. I leafed through her little book, which is put together like some *Michelin Guide* to hell, except that instructions on how a person can die there are missing entirely.

Everything there, in that little book, is arranged in an excellent sort of order, and thus it describes the Sarajevo climate, and a way in that climate, of war, to toast a piece of bread. You need how to run across the street if you write some darned thing and decide you want to take that thing over there to the print shop. My Italian companions are getting upset again because the Sarajevo guidebook doesn't mention *Hunger,* which in Norwegian is *Sult.* I, however, am reading a section of Hamsun's book that tells about something else, about a living species that just may belong to us more than any other. *Would you please give me a bone for my dog,* says the young man from Christiania, who doesn't have a dog. *Just one. There doesn't have to be anything on it. Just for something to chew on. I got a bone, a magnificent little bone that still had a bit of meat on it, and I stuck it inside my coat. I thanked the man so warmly that he looked at me amazed. There's nothing to thank me for, he said. But there is, I mumbled; that was very kind of you.* So, too, the little handbook from Sarajevo, *Survival Guide,* tells about everything in a kindly manner, a hyperborean one: how to be a dog, and how it doesn't matter that at the moment we are living like dogs. I also know many individuals who live entirely undoglike their whole lives without seeing it as any particular blessing. This is now turning out to be a piece of writing about how gnawing on a dog bone is all a man needs at certain times; in fact, maybe this same text is imperceptibly turning into the memoirs of some dog—an exiled one. And this is why I am once again listening to a big dog of our European literature, from the hyperborean North, tell about the dog's life he led. *You are undoubtedly convinced that I live and dress this way because I want to, right? But I can't do otherwise, I tell you, I am very, very poor.* To be poor, when you're a dog, is a very special, I would say noble, thing, even when it's your bone, your dog bone, you can't get hold of. *My brain (again) began to work kind of strangely,* not only because it had begun to think like a dog's. Humanity, which is in rags from time to time, longs—even when it is in rags—for some sort of better order and some structurally higher purpose. The human brain may have unraveled the impenetrable nets of its own mythological secrets as found among the Bororo Indians, only it doesn't know how to organize even those few odds and ends that encompass our life. *It occurred to me that those shacks by the market, and the warehouses and old wooden boxes with the worn-out clothing are a disgrace to the neighborhood! They spoil the appearance of the whole square and make the city ugly!* This shows me how our continent, which got used to thinking a long time ago now, predicted back in Hamsun's old book that without realizing it, that it would even have something to say about this Balkan city in which all human order has been destroyed. But you, my Italian friend protests, you are really linking the unlinkable, even what has no link at all with European thought. It looks that way, I say, because you don't understand that when the European dog-man thinks, he just keeps on thinking in that doglike-European way of his. Because the way European thought began, it was like dog thought, canine thought, cynical thought did. *I became insolent,* says my predecessor from long ago, who knew something about the doggish things in human life, and thus I keep trying to change the subject of our conversation, the Italian one. But since the dog subject, once it works its way into human conversation, has a hard time getting out, this acquaintance quotes a Hamsun sentence now without even

realizing it: *May I ask if you have something to spare me?*
I don't continue where Hamsun left off, though, but
instead I ask him a cynical question that surely ought not
to offend anyone: just what does a dog who has left his
own country need?

My friend who came out of the Sarajevo siege composed a guidebook to life there, just as the Michelin firm
puts together similar guidebooks to many of the world's
major cities. Because with the help of a little book like this
it's easier for a person to live in a major city, and I would
add in my anxious state that such a guidebook tells how a
person can die somewhere, too. Our girl tells in her little
book where in Sarajevo you can find a bucket of water,
and how to send even the teensiest letter out of this city
which is besieged by criminals' tanks. But she doesn't
explain in it what she told me privately—which intersec-
tion it is where you can get yourself killed from out of
concealed rifle barrels, when you finally get sick of it all.
So there's why I'm reading my book—Hamsun's, I mean—
here, in Rome, because I see it, too, as a sort of Baedeker
in which everything about life and slow death in the city
of Christiania is described. Maybe every book in our
European literature is composed in such a way that it has
in it how a person can live in a certain place and what all
the hazards to life in that place are. Life without such hazards would have no need for any sort of guidebook or any
sort of book at all, and this is why the books in our European literature are manuals that explain to us what bad
things will befall us and where, although for some strange
reason they don't explain anything at all about why this is
so. Many people think every book ought to explain this
basic problem—why, for some reason, something is the
way it is, but I who compose books of this sort from time
to time myself know that nothing is ever said there about
these questions of making sense. What people talk about—
whether it makes sense or not—stays in talk form, while

the books that somebody writes outside of these conversations are written practically in opposition to them. On the whole, books are always written in opposition to something, because writing a book "in favor of" would be a dumb and quite ill-mannered thing to do. It turns out that I am now writing a book in opposition to all possibility of explaining the phenomena outside such books, and that this is the result of some illness I have in my brain, and it just might be absolutely true. Because as I read this *Michelin* about life and death in one city, a European one, I see how I, too, ought to write a little handbook about my own behavior, here, in Rome, where I am occupied with various ideas, some of them possibly contrary to nature. *In short, every man will flounder once, over precisely the simplest questions.*

So here's how the book I am reading, Hamsun's, which interweaves the strangest happenings about life in the city of Christiania as if they were utterly normal, here's how it explains what I want to put together as a kind of report on my own life. The young man in Christiania tries hard to survive in spite of the total hunger he feels inside of himself, while I am attempting to clarify, also for myself, in as seemly a manner as I can, a reasonable order for my own movements, the everyday ones. Because I am constantly worried that I am going to do something unseemly in this pretty city, that I'm going to bump into a person I didn't want to touch at all, that I'll fall down on the street and cause a traffic problem, or that I won't know how to get back to my apartment on Via Nomentana, where I am staying, after spending so much time here. Because every man will flounder once, and for me this is the moment, that I am living in now, in Rome. Because even the girlfriend of that character in Hamsun's book *had laughed insolently at him several times in the last few days, when he had the misfortune to stumble on the steps or get his coat caught on a nail and rip it.* I as a rule don't stumble at all, nor do I rip my coat on nails, I just keep thinking about such a possibility, almost Mishkin-like. What if I stumble on the steps or rip my coat on a nonexistent nail, here in Rome, in front of people who aren't expecting this of me at all? My unfortunate hero, Hamsun's, got to pondering, and in his pondering was unable to remember a single place in the whole city where he could spend even an hour. My friends, the Italian ones, wonder in turn how I could have an idea like that at all in such a gracious setting that so generously opens up every door to me, but I repeat that it only has to do with my own inner experiences, and that I am not thereby calling the graciousness of the city of Rome into question. Along the way I say I want to go to some bookstore or other, and my friends wonder why I need still another book besides the one I am reading so nervously. But I tell them that that's the thing with me, that I am constantly thinking that along with what I have in my hands something exists in immediate proximity to me that keeps slipping away from me in spite of everything. This is why I say I spent the entire morning combing Feltrinelli's on Babuino Street, which is named for monkeys, and that there I was looking for and finally found two books, of Kafka's. Because since I can't see what Hamsun's book looks like in Norwegian, but only know what its title, *Hunger,* is in that language, I am now looking at a little notebook of dreams that Kafka dreamed, and at the other book, too, which may actually have something to do with ours, and is called *Hunger-künstler, A Hunger Artist.* Then later I find that a freak who goes from circus to circus showing how he is choosing to go hungry is pained most of all because audiences don't believe in his proficiency, but keep checking to see if someone isn't slipping him crumbs on the side. And worst of all, *Man gewohnte sich an die Sonderbarkeit, in*

den heutigen Zeiten Aufmerksamkeit für einen Hunger-
künstler beanspruchen zu wollen. People have gotten used
to the freaky idea that even these days someone is still
expecting them to take an interest in a hunger artist. Try
to explain the art of fasting to someone, even if it's just the
heading of a little book that's like the Michelin books.
The nicely written signs had gotten dirty and illegible, the
signboard with the number of days spent fasting hadn't
been changed in a long time, and the hunger artist really
did go on fasting, as he had dreamed of doing (and as a
Baedeker of people who fast would explain), *but nobody*
counted the days, nobody, even the starving artist himself,
knew how high the total was. Now I see what's missing in
Hamsun's book, and in that other one that my friend put
together as a travel guide to the life and death of Sarajevo.
Some idle man stopped in front of the cage, in Kafka's tale,
and started ridiculing the old number on the sign and talk-
ing about fraud, even though the hunger artist hadn't
cheated, he was working honestly; in fact the world was
cheating him by denying him his reward, denn nicht der
Hungerkünstler betrog, er arbeitete ehrlich, aber die Welt
betrog ihn um seinen Lohn.

My Italians are wondering now, as I travel through
their country, what I myself think of my current psychological state, and I tell them I'm a happy pessimist, *pes-*
simista allegro. And that this mental state of mine is not
influenced by the beauty of their country, which is indu-
bitable. Rather, that it is influenced by what this beauty
provokes in the form of very bad thoughts, which, as
always, I am arriving at very easily. Because there is no
country, however beautiful, that is exempt from the possibility of having the most unpleasant individual take its
helm, a person odious in every regard; and how such people, who are utterly odious, run their countries, this we
know. Now I ask my hosts, who want to oblige me in
every way, whether they have noticed an unusual thing,

that recently these odious people* have been coming to power in a completely free election match, which is to say the people's will is mercilessly casting its vote for these beings. This is why I am striving—with this tale of Hamsun's, which I am attempting to write again, adding some anxious ideas of my own—to steer this entire piece of writing, which was begun by one person and is getting finished by another, as only a ship can be steered. Because our hero who is fleeing Christiania and saying farewell to it for now boards a Russian ship, whereas boarding any ship that's Russian today would be total idiocy. This is proven also by my girl with her Baedeker, of Sarajevo, who left the city of her torment and flew here, to the West, and may go on farther. Now my friends are asking me whether Hamsun is the writer who was convicted by his own people of treason that he had committed against them, and I say that he is. But that in fact he hadn't committed any treason at all, but had spoken out, publicly, in favor of the power that had subjugated his country. Because anyone can have an idea of one sort or another in his head, and his was to speak out in favor of his enemies and against his own people. And because of this he endured having those people put him on trial and denounce him, and having his books—including the one I am holding—returned to him by his readers, in heaps. So, too, by the way, am I being scorned and ostracized by my own people, even though I haven't spoken out in favor of any foreign power, but only believe that my erstwhile tribe has subjugated its own self and is keeping itself under some sort of occupation.

The country that was mine has been occupied by its own people, piece by piece, down to the last intention that a still unconquered country could have in it before its

---

*Niente amici. Un difficile rapporto con le donne. Carattere tenebroso. Antisemita. Thus are the newspapers here, in Italy, writing about the newly elected Russian rightist Zhirinovsky.

conquest. Every country that is threatened with conquest hides away some knowledge and valuables to be found later. Except I don't know where such a country can hide its valuables, the spiritual ones, if its own people have decided to conquer it and keep it in that counterspiritual subjugation forevermore.

Well, if that's the case, my friends ask me, why not let such a people as this go ahead and keep itself self-occupied, and I say that that's what I'm doing. In other words, I am letting them go on being occupied by themselves, only I have removed myself from this self-occupation once and for all. Now it may be more understandable why I am reading my Hamsun here, and why I am secretly enjoying his treason. Before he was tried for treason, Hamsun was first put in an asylum for the mentally ill, in order to determine whether he could stand trial. And since he managed to hide his insanity as both author and intellectual, he was tried mercilessly, without appeal or the sympathy that the insane in Europe sometimes receive. Psychiatrist Langfeld did address several confused questions to him as only this science—in its desire to resolve a person's psychological problems—succeeds in confusing them and heaping them all into a single pile: *I presume that over the course of the years you have analyzed yourself thoroughly. Insofar as I can conclude, you have always been aggressive. In addition, one gets the impression that you are very sensitive and vulnerable. Is this correct? And what other traits do you have? Are you distrustful? Selfish, or generous? Do you love justice? Are you logical? Compassionate, or cold?* Here I will take the liberty of replacing Hamsun's answers, which were too polite and pertained largely to his case, with my own conclusion, in case it could be of interest to any Norwegian doctor I may happen to have. I never cared about my inner motives even when it seemed I was blotting them out in many of my manuscripts. My aggressiveness has been related to my hostility toward people who wanted to dig out of me what I wasn't prepared to give them. Hence my ungenerosity and my uncooperativeness toward the psychiatrist, the police, and literary critics. I did and still do consider every question of this sort to be an outrage that a decent person shouldn't have to put up with. Hence my cold compassion and my logic that, by any measure instituted on our continent, is illogical. To talk about a love for justice in a psychiatrist's office is also shameless, just as no decent individual would dare ask a close relative about his vulnerability, it being intrinsic to him. I am ashamed on behalf of anyone who is asked a question by somebody who himself is unwilling to give those around him an answer of his own.

PADUA—ROME, DECEMBER 1993

■ □ ■ □ ■

FINAL CONVERSATION WITH
MR. VERDURIN, OF ROVINJ

MY MR. VERDURIN IS TERRIBLY ANGRY. IT WAS THREE YEARS ago that he turned up as a character in a book of mine, but as for how he was presented there, this in fact he doesn't know because he didn't read the book. Actually, he hasn't read it even now, three years later, but his relatives have started telling him what he is like in it and that's the thing that has turned him utterly livid. My gentleman* Mr. Verdurin doesn't read books, and what's most interesting, he doesn't even read one—heaven knows what kind it is—that he hears he's a character in, although surprisingly enough in his closest circle there are two or three people who sooner or later, after a really long time, will read some book or other, and this then would be his truly most accurate source on what is in a certain book and why. And to actually get right down to it, this time not even these most closely related relatives of Mr. Verdurin's read this unfortunate book of mine that has him in the main role, because they don't have all that much time to waste reading a book like this either, but instead they found out what this book is about from some very good acquaintances of theirs who live abroad, because abroad is actually the only place

---

*Have you noticed: ever since the term "ladies and gentlemen" was introduced here, how few of them there are among us!?

a person from our land has time to read books from that same land. Maybe that's entirely normal: while a person is in his native land he can't and doesn't get time to read books about that land, but as soon as some evil wind carries him off this land and beyond this land to some utterly foreign land, then hey, what the heck, such an individual just may read some damned thing about this land here that he's left behind! And since Mr. Verdurin, mine, this one here, has a deep faith in his relatives, who have an even deeper faith in their acquaintances from faraway Switzerland there, thus has Mr. Verdurin finally grasped that he is a character appearing in a book of mine, and that as a character who appears in this book he is shown in a completely negative light and portrayed in some utterly unbecoming way. I'm actually not sure that any character portrayed up to now in any book of mine is portrayed "unbecomingly"; in fact, I even believe every one of them is portrayed not only becomingly but also with a certain amount of extra sympathy that such a person doesn't warrant at all. Maybe it is a failing of mine as a writer that I portray "my characters," the personnel of my possibly overwritten books, with a kind of masochistic sympathy, even though all in all as people, personalities, characters, and so forth they don't deserve this in the slightest. But then again I think it's almost more mocking to take a subject who "doesn't deserve any sympathy" and portray him with a little dose of sympathy than if I portray that same creature as an out-and-out idiot. Here, in fact, is the paradox: that the individuals I am closest to—the poets, the melancholics, the *apatrids,* the luckless, the banished souls, women abandoned by their lovers, and so forth—that all these come across in my writings as idiots, and that this idiocy of theirs I accept as my own and as something an individual, in his unidiotic sojourn here on earth, must somehow attain if he is to be a human being. In other words, my idiots don't get "sympathy" from me but, rather, sincere and unfettered love that flows straight from my veins into them, while the ones I do show "sympathy" for, because of their common everyday dull-wittedness, mindlessness, and so forth, well hey, maybe those folks could bristle a bit at a writer apparently so totally warped. So that's why Mr. Verdurin has gotten angry at me without discovering the reason why. Somebody told him all about the story he turned up in, while meanwhile for years now I've been dying to have somebody, well-intentioned or not, tell me all about some—any—piece I've written, because I think that no matter what way it is retold, it would be more interesting to me myself than in the form in which I myself, composing it who knows when, composed it. In any case, I haven't figured out which story my Verdurin is enraged over—the one I actually wrote, or the one that reached his nonreader's ear out of faraway Switzerland. Switzerland is a pretty bizarre country in its own right: various nations, individuals, expatriates, émigrés, Nobel Prize winners, hunters, cows, very hardworking peasants, yodelers, mountain climbers, mountain dogs, Alpinists, financiers, well-concealed international criminals, revealed and unrevealed spies all live in it, so that getting a story from that country retold in any form whatever is a circumstance of the greatest interest to me as a *litterateur*. Certainly Mr. Verdurin is angered because I, in describing him, allegedly also described his entire homeland (which also is mine), except that is same homeland is "his" in some rather different way, whereas for me that same homeland is mine in a really incomparably different way. A homeland can survive only if every citizen of it has his own personal homeland inside of him, which is much better for it as a homeland when it is in a position to bring such a large number of homelands together into a single one, while in the situation if everybody accepted that homeland in a completely identical way, in that pretty unfortunate case this same homeland could come to the realization that it doesn't exist as a homeland at all. All these, then, are some sort of preliminaries for us that naturally have nothing to do with Mr. Verdurin from my Rovinj hill nor with his possible informants, because such stuff wouldn't grab them even if they read this current material of mine in the tranquillity of a nice Swiss meadow, to the mooing of the nearest Swiss cow, which creates the most satisfactory and truly spiritual mood for reading any sort of material. Be perfectly clear, I'm not bringing this cow in for any satirical purposes, because the job of a cow that grazes on her Swiss grass, produces her Swiss milk, and then to top it all off benevolently allows world-renowned Swiss chocolate to be made from that milk—this I wouldn't dare compare to a person who neither produces anything nor is famous for anything except that he considers himself a worthy subject of our land, who loves this land more than he does himself, even if what he himself signifies as a part of that land or what that land signifies that tolerates him on itself as a part of the land, of that he unfortunately doesn't know a thing.

So here's what we'll do. I will once again do a brief description of the person who has lived near me for decades, and whether I make use of a classical text for this, this his faithful reader, Swiss or not, will be able to establish very readily. Verdurinity, then, is a colorful concept, one could almost say fantastic in the changeability of what it values—at one time it was actually most partial to music: the most ta-ta musicians of that time appeared in Verdurinal salons and the way they performed this music of theirs was well-nigh dangerous to the health of our lady of the day. *"Oh, no, no! I won't let them play my sonata!" shrieked Mme Verdurin. "I don't want to catch a cold and get neuralgia in my face from crying hard like the last time; thank you very kindly, but I don't feel like having that back again. It's nothing to you—obviously, you* won't have to spend a week in bed!" "But please, let's agree," says M. Verdurin, "they'll just play the andante." "Just the andante, as if that were nothing!" shouted Mme Verdurin. "That andante is the very thing that makes my arms and legs ache." So, too, do we see how our ladies today sometimes worry that our Maestro Nagorescu will reduce them to tears, but still they muster their courage and—come what may! "Admit that the poor little fellow can really play that sonata! You never dreamed so much could be done with a piano. I swear that can't possibly be just a piano!" It's a superpiano, you could say, a whole orchestra—maybe even more than an orchestra, because what is an orchestra, after all, when you take a closer look, but a bunch of neurotics of all sorts who play every man for himself, so that only by some miracle does it all finally come into any sort of harmony. And where there's music there are belles-lettres as well, because there's also a lady there with literary aspirations: "You'll be surprised," says M. Verdurin, "when I tell you she writes nicely. Have you ever heard her nephew? It's amazing, isn't it, doctor? Would you like me to ask him to play something, M. Swann?" "Why, yes, that would be great good fortune," Swann started to say, because with Mr. Verdurin it can't be any other way; with the Verdurins it's almost like hardly anything is possible, because supernatural happenings happen in that company that outside the Verdurinal world simply cannot happen: "How is it permissible at all for someone to play Wagner so well!" Because Mrs. Verdurin will get a migraine from good music, which is for some reason unbearable in Verdurinal circles, whereas music not quite so good—now that, I tell you, these Verdurins, ours and mine, might be able to cope with somehow without a migraine. Our Verdurins as a group are characterized by a permanent migraine—their head aches because somebody writes well, their head aches because they haven't had a chance to read this supposedly well-written thing, and most of all this head of theirs practically splits open if they hear from somebody very definitely well-informed that there's something in shall we call it "this well-written thing" that would concern their own Verdurinal character.

So maybe I am "that lady" who writes well about something of this sort, only we haven't ascertained yet what it is she "writes so well," but when with the help of some informant of ours we do ascertain what this person "has written," boy oh boy, it turns out not only that we will no longer think about her and her writing the way we used to up until recently, but also that this person had really better keep her trap shut in this pretty land of ours or else God knows she'll have a run-in with the police. Here's the way we are: we don't read books, but if somebody else whose mind we really do, um, trust implicitly tells what's in those books, we will truly act as if we had read that thing ourselves, and actually it will turn out that we know better about that writing than if we had read it ourselves. Sometimes a person has the rare opportunity of being in the company of somebody smarter than he is who will take some book we unfortunately haven't had a chance to read and read it in such an expert way that this will be a real gain for us who, even when we don't read a bit, profit more than if we were to read every last thing. This is that really clever plan of ours that is worth more to us than if instead of that cleverness we had something in our heads maybe a lot less important than cleverness itself is.

Mme Verdurin herself was honest and came from a good bourgeois family, as rich as Croesus but completely without renown, because the way we are here it's possible to be rich as Croesus and yet not be well known, and this is that holdover from relatively proper bourgeois life when the newspapers didn't report the wealth of an individual family, nor were even the children in those families permitted to talk about money, ever, under any circumstances. Verdurinity has gone downhill a bit here, however, now that even our most refined ladies spar with each other over where it's cheaper to buy a pair of panties—in Graz or in the wonderful town of Palmanova. Palmanova is that unusual architectural creation, multiangular in form, that was conceived not only as a *fortezza* impregnable at that time but also as a *città ideale,* and thus a delight to a heavenly eye. G. Savorgnan began this stellar walled city sometime about 1593, and Scamozzi added some more to it between 1603 and 1605, but all that remains of it in our Verdurinal story unfolding today is that the department store there has the cheapest and best deal on underpants for our needs of the day.

Such are the wonders of our modern civilization and of us whose duty it is to live in it as one lives in a civilized civilization, in a more or less civilized manner. We are civilized even when we don't act all that civilized every moment, and we aren't acting that way when we believe we are the only civilized ones and absolutely nobody else is or could be. Being civilized is a truly special state that encompasses the imperative of tolerating quite different and perhaps even antagonistic civilizations, and the moment that different ways, that we lose account of there being different ways of being civilized, then I tell you we owe an accounting to somebody as to this mistaken definition of what civilization and being civilized in some rudimentarily civilized meaning of the word means. Because civilness, and that could perhaps be the first characteristic of a citizenry, civilness as the opposite of anticivilian, or as it would be termed uniformness, civilness as nonmilitary be it in even the most cowardly and most unheroic sense, civilness requires a few facts in your noggin that go beyond the very successful but I'd say rather limited notions of left, right, forward march! Because *"Who is that gentleman?" Forcheville asks Mme Verdurin. "He seems to be a real first-rank fellow." "You mean you don't know the celebrated Brichot? He's famous all over Europe." "Ah, that's Bréchot," shouts Forcheville, who hasn't heard it right, "his name alone is enough for me. It's always interesting to have dinner with somebody prominent. I must admit, you always invite us in choice company. It's never boring at your house." "And nicest of all," says Mme Verdurin modestly, "the guests feel completely at home here. They talk about anything they want to, and the conversation sparkles like fireworks."* Thus, unfortunately, has my Verdurinal file expanded ever so slightly, revealing Verdurinity as a comical, nonsensical, and yet somehow diverting thing, which I hadn't expected in the least to show.

For Mr. and Mrs. Verdurin things are always as they are at this very moment, which is to say two and two are still four, there are nine planets in our solar system, and Alfred Dreyfus is surely guilty. Dreyfus is guilty according to the positive laws of the moment in which he was pronounced guilty and in that sense we subjects of that same law have to hang on like a drunk hangs onto a raft, and if it happens that some improbable turn of events happens in our hapless solar system which brings a totally unexpected planet into that system which in turn proves Dreyfus's innocence, then, um, that is, I mean, of course that would be an entirely different matter and then it really would be brutal to go on keeping an innocent man in chains and on Devil's Island. The thing is, though, that the new planets, new systems of thought, new theorems, and fine points in grimy and criminally compiled court documents aren't being discovered by some sort of terroristic individuals, rebels, or no-goods from the street who've gotten hold of some "truth" or other that they themselves don't know what to make of; rather, it is very polished gentlemen by the names of Edmund Husserl, Niels Bohr, and the contemporary Richard Rorty who are establishing the above-mentioned. This universe is being turned upside down in their heads, but the one in whom this same universe got turned upside down in the first place and in the extreme was named Nietzsche. He may have been crazy, just as Freud had somewhat of an obsession, and Popper now, he, from the standpoint of our illustrious left wing, was a reactionary. But all the same they all had that same neatly fastened stud on their shirt, although, now that we've brought up this crazy item of haberdashery, even Proust himself notes that on Parisiennes' clothing there was *that row of little silk buttons that didn't button anything up and that couldn't be unbuttoned.* We are people who keep all sorts of things buttoned up that we aren't duty-bound to unbutton, because if we once got started unbuttoning, our nervous exhaustion would only increase to unheard-of proportions.

Maybe the bourgeoisie got its start through numerous financial bank transactions, the establishment of compound interest and growth in surplus value that suddenly reached an unheard-of limit. Maybe the bourgeoisie absorbed all the victorious rallying cries of a revolution, cries that pleased the ear of the ordinary nonbourgeois, only to reduce that same nonbourgeois as well as many members of the bourgeoisie themselves—through the opiate of those slogans—to the status of slave and beggar. But this same bourgeoisie also built structures never seen before—in metal, in concrete, and in the cells of philosophers' brains. Except that for me personally it began when Thonet designed his chair, Hofmann his "Besteck," and Kolo Moser his bizarre big lamp. When Olbrich built the house for the Stöhr family, and Adolf Loos in the year 1903 constructed the Café Capua in the city of Vienna. This is how that arrangement came about, very beautiful, appealing, and cozy in every facet of its coziness, in which only a human brain could wonder whether it as such deserved this and whether it wasn't time, right in such a setting of continental settled comfort, to start a battle with one's own conscience and, more importantly, with what lay unconscious in that same head. Now Grimmelshausen's hero was an idiot, and Diogenes of Sinop was pretty nutty, but insanity as a philosophical movement was invented in the bosom of our bourgeois class, and given this, I'll have a hard time allowing my exaggeratedly normal, exaggeratedly conscientious, and utterly conventionally proper Mr. Verdurin into this class. Because even if through some cosmic error he went mad in some shall I say mild form, he wouldn't have a clue about that. Above and beyond Freud's famous Judge Schreber, who communicated through nonexistent wires coming out of his head, there are a large number of inventors of widespread idiocies: the one who measured the width of hats, from the year 1879; the creator of sidewalk scales, from 1886; the designer of the machine that dispenses chocolate candies, from 1887; the inventor of stereoramas and panoramas in which one can see everything that has already happened or is going to happen, and that jolly railroad worker who ran little tracks into Gaston Menier's house that deliver the food from the kitchen right to the guests at the table. The bourgeois got themselves caught in a trap of their own making in that they created their own evening dress, their multiroom dwelling place, and finally, their conversation. They became a world apart, building this world with a combination of intelligence, foolheadedness, and often very funny scenes. They showed enough imagination to invent tens of thousands of unnecessary necessities that inundated their rooms but that at the same time became weird objects, something halfway between an objet d'art and a magic weapon. Finally, they thought up their newspapers in which everything enumerated became visible even to those who didn't have *gadgets* of their own. Indeed the bourgeoisie became a zoological species that can't just be measured by the measures of political economy and surplus value. Because to describe this entire unwieldy population as just a rabble that gets deliriously rich at the expense of the pauper lying on the sidewalk dying of hunger is also a form of fiction and may someday come to be read that way with no bad blood. The bourgeoisie is one of the wackiest bunches because never before had such a countless quantity of sharp cookies, poets, cruel egocentrics, and polite neurotics turned up in one place. They decked themselves out in their own outfit of trousers, jacket, and hat; to this they added their high-button shoes, their collar stays, their gaiters, their shirt studs, their neckties, their lorgnettes, and finally that quaint little buttonhook, so dear to Krleža, with which the multitude of buttons on the high-topped shoes, both men's and women's, were buttoned up and unbuttoned. I myself have kept one such little item as a relic and a memento of an era in which it was practically impossible for a person to have all of this on him and at the same moment not get some sort of idea—anxious, suicidal, poetic, maybe even philosophical.

All of us are prisoners in a suit of clothes in which the trousers, coat, and shoes make up the uniform of an elite guard that doesn't march, that doesn't serve any particular army, but that fabricates itself a garrison of epochal nonsense in its conversation and an occasional brilliant piece of sense that originates out of the very foolheadedness of that conversation. Thousands of photographs that Sander, Cartier-Bresson, and Diane Arbus left behind them attest to this. We are a class choked tight by our own collars, and being such, all we've been able to do is write a poem about human anxiety or else hang ourselves. The man in the stiff collar, even the poor peasant who came into town on business and while there got choked by that top stud on his shirt that he couldn't stand—that whole crowd characterized a certain era more accurately than all the historians of the first, second, and who knows what other world war have described it. We are a nation of collars that choke, and I swear with shoes we aren't any better, I tell you, because as a rule the first two or three weeks they pinch and later they get so horribly ruined we just want to throw them out. What could become of the soul of an individual who even under our modest conditions is Verdurinal, which is to say semieducated, that is, conceited, ergo moderately well-off, relatively carefree, all in all and forevermore superfluous and meaningless? The human individual may be meaningless for many other reasons and in a cosmic sense be an incident, a mistake and nothing more. But this specially organized unit of the bourgeois class, that likable Mr. Verdurin of mine, he really has no idea what to do with his Verdurinity.

When did the life of the bourgeois class begin? Was it when the first textile manufacturer hired twelve underage girls to spin wool for him in Manchester or when Baudelaire, well-stoked with hashish, went to see the spring Salon in Paris? Was it when Otto Wagner, over whose shoulder the tender young Josef Plečnik was standing, sketched the royal park in Vienna, or when Proust, constantly present here, met his fateful counterpart, Count Montesquiou-Fezensac? In any case, didn't something have to have happened in that crazy region for the entire universe as it had been up to then to be turned on its head, if only by Nietzsche's pen while his head was aching unbearably in that Alpine hideaway? The bourgeoisie as our illustrious social historians customarily view it is equated with order, almost exaggerated order—in industry, the schools, morality, and café-hopping. Our social science has made a study of every hair of that unusual assemblage of people that decided to behave identically among themselves, insanely identically—and only two major things could result from this: inventiveness and neurosis. Even so, this is all in all a fun-loving crowd and within its own limits it invents not only what has been uninvented up to then (such as the Eiffel Tower, Bakelite, or cellular discoveries in genetic engineering), but—something a lot nicer and more interesting—it invents what is already invented, but just in some much more fun-filled way. The bourgeoisie, therefore, if we leave aside *The Origin of the Family, Private Property and the State,* isn't characterized alone by Mr. Krupp or Mr. Agnelli, or who knows what Japanese financier I can't pronounce; rather, the bourgeoisie in its unpredictable history is represented by Bouvard and Pécuchet, who wanted to restore everything in existence and have this restoration of the familiar amuse them and give them endless intellectual titillation. Their attack on an already existing civilization by using that same civilization parallels the act by Musil that had the intention of proclaiming an entire empire an empire all over again, and of recognizing everything that had happened in it, whether sensible or crazy, as being legal, even though it had all been legally recognized long before. Only under the aegis of the bourgeoisie as a not entirely "normal" phenomenon did it happen that many members of that fun-loving community got the idea it might be good if what was happening right then were to happen one more time, just in case. Thence the great quantity of spoken sentences that had already been spoken before and the great number of happenings people entered upon knowing that something of the sort had happened a thousand times before. The bourgeoisie discovered the modus according to which repeating the same thing might not be exactly the same, but rather, this time, if "we" are the ones repeating it, something at least a tad more surprising and unusual might happen, which unfortunately in the majority of instances hasn't happened, though. Psychoanalysis originated in part on the basis of an archetype, even when it didn't adhere to Jung's idea with its similarity to the Tarzan comic strip. The archetypal situation was born inside that nicely buttoned-up gentleman who lay on the couch of the even more nicely buttoned-up professor man, and the talking that was later engaged in between these two gentlemen concerned an often similar fate with regard to a great many tiny details. Modern man has gotten anxious because he has come to realize that he can't get out of his buttoned-up attire, and that all he as an individual is capable of doing in this buttoned-up state of his is to start boiling like a pressure cooker, and whether this apparatus, also constructed in the early prebourgeois era, will explode here in front of everyone or not, that would have to depend on the professor man and his skill at handling the vent. Bourgeois life is some sort of carnival, of uninterrupted celebration at which infinitely many predictable things happen, and a few completely unexpected and crazy ones as well. Thus these gentlemen of ours go like orderly bureaucrats to their orderly administrative bureaus (though sometimes it's not entirely clear what is administered in those bureaus and why), the ladies go shopping (even when they really haven't any need for any of the things they're shopping for), they dine punctually on time, they snooze a bit after dinner, some of them will read the paper, and then comes supper, the quiet pleasures of dusk, the little whisperings of adolescents in bathrooms, school homework, nighttime, and various, one might think, orderly dreams. But here, as Hamlet already foresaw, here's the rub, here the entire day's schedule gets turned upside down in an impossibly wrong side up and topsy-turvy way and nothing is the way it was anymore: order is gone from our glorious bourgeois homeland, and the jovial Viennese professor sits at his desk and writes his own history of the twentieth century such as not even the best-established annalist or chronicler is capable of recording.

We are, as they would say, an orderly bunch, everything here is as it should be, but when sleep overtakes us then this isn't quite exactly just as it should be in every respect, and then what we've got is an utterly different kind of story and another sort of report on the universe entirely.

FINAL CONVERSATION WITH MR. VERDURIN, OF ROVINJ

Disorder originates from order, from excessively thoroughly agreed-upon order, in fact, and the more we insist on our orderly agenda, the crazier, the more topsy-turvy, and the more indecent our dreams become. How is it that a group absorbed in such decent thought who for its own purposes has invented hundreds of thousands of helps, grips, holders, banisters, and handles, how is it that in its dreams this very race of people commits monstrous deeds not even a Sacher-Masoch would have been capable of inventing? What is this, dear people, about our dreams anyhow, and thus also about our wakefulness, during which even the most levelheaded individual will be reminded of what he did in that bad dream he had and who he did it all with?! The human race is a cursed race not by dint of what it does, but by dint of what it dreams about—indeed, dreams about almost unerringly and relatively interpretably. All the more so because dreams are not what they are at all; rather, they are only a road sign for what, if there were any cosmic justice, we would dream about openly even without any visible trickery. The Glembay complex has created here among us a baroquely luxuriant yet still partially visible picture of Verdurinity as a phenomenon: our Verdurins are the newly rich petty shopkeepers, the thieves, perjurers, and outright murderers for whom running over an old woman on the street is no big thing, and after all these evil deeds that in more orderly societies are punished by law, we have a migraine. We have a headache, our head is desperately racked with pain, and along with it all we have in this Verdurinal family of ours a positive idiot, a Hamlet who à la Kropotkin is plotting to knock our head off, and before it's over I swear somebody really will lose his head. For seventy years now the left and right members of our society have been taking part in this Ibsenesque tragedy (which really does take place in Helsingør) and one should say each is satisfied: the proletarians have lived to see old Rupert's woman's corpse duly avenged, the leftist intellectuals are aghast at our cream, while that part of our cream, even if it isn't all that creamy, thinks this has nothing to do with "us" for goodness sake, but only with two or three thieves of the sort that—big deal!—any better-grade society has. At the same time the Glembay picture ought to be taken as a fictional marker and a kind of philosophical dispute—and the fortunate thing about great undertakings in fiction and thought is that they seize upon real reality as their inspiration and that in a collective historical and social sense they remain on the sidelines. Glembay reality is the theater, a dream that lasts two or three hours, and after that the actors, whether they're in a good mood or not, go home as if nothing had happened. The Glembay farce is a literary flourish and a work of brilliant fantasy that is saved by its own feverish fantasizing from time to time—that same time that apart from this fantasy may not exist at all.

The bourgeois class really has fostered some sort of amazing hybrid of a person, a cross between Wittgenstein and Bouvard-Pécuchet. He has amassed in his brain all the spiritual energy that this race (the human one) is still able to muster in spite of all the forces to the contrary, yet at the same time he is capable of such a heap of monstrous deeds that only the pen of a satirist can begin to write them all down. Bouvardism and Pécuchetness have demonstrated what a lot of mental tricks can come forth out of the heads of a pair of perfectly decent copyists of something that somebody in some office had already written down before they did, and what that predecessor wrote was doubtlessly a copy of some even earlier copy of some utterly improbable European nonsense. Bouvardism-Pécuchetness only negated a model in which everything is "as it should be" by their wearing themselves out trying to show that it could be even more "as it should be" than that, and this led them straight into insanity and to Freud's as yet unestablished medical practice. Freud really did set about trying to fathom the surplus that the bourgeoisie obtained in their orderly sojourn on earth, but in a different way than Marx conceived it. Freud tried to gather up the profusion of fantasy that jostled in the heads of these top achievers every night and that periodically ended in vitriol, in a leap from the fourth floor, or in infanticide. The totally "normal" hero of Fassbinder's first film goes to the office, does household chores with his family, listens to his wife banging on the piano, having the neighbor woman over for coffee, etc., and then all of a sudden he kills his wife and children and the neighbor woman and himself— "for no reason," to use the police's terminology. *The style of a monument does not always correspond to the time to which it is attributed. Life might perhaps be able to improve its outlook by means of gymnastics. But since the existence of the world is only one uninterrupted transition from life to death and from death to life, instead of everything existing, nothing exists. Perhaps it is an excellent habit to regard all things as symbols. On the other hand, anyone who wants to make everything deeper is slipping down a dangerous slope. Let's admire without understanding! But if one sees metaphors everywhere, what will become of the facts? A single instinct always splits in two: one side bad, the other good. A fearless child instead of becoming a robber will become a general. A drawing, for its part, consists of three things: a line, details and crisscrossed strokes, and overtop of this the shading. Things that offend you at first become acceptable once they are delved into.* No, *Bouvard and Pécuchet* is no breviary of nonsense, no encyclopedia of juvenile foolishness—it is the distillation of a class that has studied too much, that has read too much, and out of it all has managed to draw the fatal conclusion that there's no point in reading whatsoever. Hence my Mr. Verdurin doesn't read anything, even if what's been written might have to do with him, but instead he settles for having a very smart and nice veterinarian who lives in

Switzerland recount this material—which she herself hasn't read. Because the most interesting books are still the ones nobody reads but that someone just retells in a very engaging way without having read them. *Bouvard and Pécuchet* is a book that was actually never written— its author just eavesdropped on certain people discussing certain things without ever getting into the meaning of them. The bourgeoisie is a truly amazing phenomenon that lives in such a way that it doesn't even notice that its own life is merely being recounted by somebody, some outsider, whether bad or not. The bourgeoisie is that nonexistent species that can be filled up with all sorts of stuff without their even noticing it. For this reason every millionth bourgeois whose name is Wittgenstein withdraws to some Austrian village to note down a few of his notes about this truly peculiar phenomenon. That is the story of the life of Verdurin, a respectable gentleman, at times a bit glazed over, by now somewhat elderly as well, and of his life which has gone by without his so much as noticing it. His biography is now being written by somebody else, with affection and sympathy, because no life has to go by so meaninglessly if it is looked at from the outside and with a little indulging. Along his long way he got the idea that he should take everything for granted, and also that everything happening around him was good, after the manner described in *Candide.* He is aware that the various constellations and social systems, that the numerous governments and structures are changeable and mortal, but until they become such, and until they land in the junk heap of history, for our Mr. Verdurin they are an inviolable fact and untouchable till kingdom come.

How is it possible, though, that our miserable political and social upheavals every twenty, thirty, or fifty years always get one and the same reaction from this eternal Mr. Verdurin—that is, a positive one? How is it possible that every banner (always new) that he has hung from his balcony is valid, but the one he hung half a century ago was not? The fact is honest to Pete he isn't as monstrously immoral as that unfortunate banner or Krleža's flag might indicate, but rather, if we want to be honest, to tell the truth I swear to God that flag frightens him. Because in his Verdurinal cabbage head he has some illusion that on the basis of that hung or unhung banner he himself with all his Verdurinal reputation could be hanging from that balcony as well. Because the bourgeoisie doesn't take to the streets to welcome every government turnover, but only rather quietly hangs out a new flag on its balcony. Out on the street there are lunatics, homeless people, frustrated losers, abandoned wives, apprentices, soldiers, the unemployed, sluggards, outcasts, maniacal depressives, thieves, pick-pockets wishing for a crowd, "reporters on the scene," wit-nesses to history, lovers of their country, lovers of their homeland, lovers of power, paralytics, crazed people whose names are in various medical files, firemen, Esperan-to buffs, foreigners, tourists, and children. The bourgeois, meanwhile, stay home, listen to the radio, and a banner, newly changed, hangs from their balcony, of course. Our bourgeoisie, inasmuch as it doesn't rush to join the masses on the square, has nothing to worry about because nobody is going to run them down in their stampede, and yet these Verdurins of ours, the Verdurinal bourgeoisie, are frightened of some damned thing. Our bourgeoisie was frightened for fifty long years lest some incorrect word fly out of their mouth at the office, where nothing but the correct words were to be spoken, and surprisingly they are frightened again now as before because now, too, some newly coined incorrect word might escape their lips in a public place. It's as if the entire life of our bourgeois class consists of fearfulness lest something fly out of them somewhere in front of somebody that later will turn out very nasty both for us out of whom this something flies and really also for the one who hears this monstrosity, to his own misfortune. Our bourgeoisie's teeth are chattering in their fearfulness, and they don't know the simple truth that their teeth needn't chatter nor is there anything to be frightened of. The bourgeois class has fostered within itself an uncounted quantity of neurotics, madmen, psychopaths, and lovable melancholics, but that still doesn't mean it is utterly and totally mad and that it can be crammed whole into some planetary madhouse. After all, the bourgeois class along with the huge number of its own monstrous deeds and everything else did dig that cursed Suez Canal, construct the possibly senseless Eiffel Tower, and manufacture Bakelite, the telephone receiver, and the bicycle, which is to say that in its neurotic thinking it has arrived at a huge number of peculiar inventions, it has gone through a fair number of wars and revolutions — and here it is now sitting in a corner of our society and being frightened of something. Mr. Verdurin may be the last fool who doesn't read anything, who doesn't know anything about anything, and who is truly a totally comic figure in our theater, but along with all that he himself has no obligation to be frightened of the little book I have written about him — written with a fair amount of sympathy, I must say. He mustn't be frightened that he used to know me, that I used to sit at his table, and that already then, while sitting there, I was writing this little book of mine. Nor will anything happen to him even if by making a superhuman effort with his brain he reads this little book and convinces himself that what his friend from Switzerland reported to him about that little book was an outright lie, pure and simple. He shouldn't be frightened even, having convinced himself of this, of admitting — at least to himself, in the corneriest corner of his cornerdom — that it is so.

My Mr. Verdurin has got it into his head, in any case, that an integral part of the bourgeoisie, the bourgeois class, and bourgeoisdom as perhaps the most interesting socially psychological phenomenon of any sort in history, that an integral part of that peculiar and fantastic development in history is fear, not a Kierkegaard philosophical fear, but a fear that fills your pants, that befouls such a nice finely envisioned suit that was created not for people to relieve themselves in, but rather, in all one's distinguishment, to stroll through the park and sit in the café in. My Mr. Verdurin has not only forgotten everything that human beings of his class have invented, both on the plane of mental arrangement and on that no less important plane of subjective and so highly prized mental derangement, but our gentleman has disregarded Husserl (whom he hasn't read) and also Mishkin (whom he thinks is a character of Le Carré's), and Sloterdejk (whose name reminds him of the name of some astronaut). Finally, in addition to all this, Mr. Verdurin, of Rovinj and now unfortunately of Europe, has forgotten the individual whose name was Thomas Mann and who in all his Lübeck patrician buttoned-upness ascertained that the order that the bourgeoisie introduced includes disorder that that same bourgeoisie, when it needs to, can establish, and that the obedience that is the only distinguishing feature of the Verdurinal mouse ear has, in the gentleman from Zauberberg, been transformed into disobedience, into dissent, and into resistance of transcontinental proportions. So I say good-bye to my elderly fellow townsman without imagining that I have taught him anything, since in order for somebody to orient someone to something he has to show him that something in black and white, and this case is such that I am dealing with a nonreader so there's no hope for me there! And I no longer have the desire for a personal conversation. Then in fact *Mme d'Arpajon asks me in a barely audible voice: "Did a M. Verdurin ever actually exist?"*

■ □ ■ □ ■

WRITINGS FROM AN UNBOUND EUROPE